ALONG CAME JENNY

HARLAN HAGUE

Along Came Jenny
Paperback Edition
Copyright © 2021 Harlan Hague
All rights reserved.

Along Came Jenny is a work of fiction. Any references to historical events, real people or real places are used fictitiously. Other names, characters, places and events are products of the author's imagination, and any resemblance to actual events, places or persons, living or dead, is entirely coincidental.

Published in the United States by Wolfpack Publishing, Las Vegas.

Wolfpack Publishing
5130 S. Fort Apache Road, 215-380
Las Vegas, NV 89148

wolfpackpublishing.com

Paperback ISBN 978-1-63977-412-8
Ebook ISBN 978-1-63977-411-1
LCCN 2021950984

ALONG CAME JENNY

Chapter One

THEY CAN'T DIGNIFY what happened by giving the carnage names. They weren't just battles, they were massacres, every one of them. Doesn't matter if only one man died in one action. It was still a massacre. In one charge, the men on each side of me, not a foot from me, were shot down at the same time. Why not me? That night, I wished it had been me.

Josh rode bareback on an old gray horse. He still wore his uniform. It was all he owned now that he had left everything else behind. Everything but the partially filled canvas bag tied by a rope around his waist, substituting for saddle bags. The bag held a wad of greybacks. In the early years of the war, the Confederate currency was accepted all over Texas, but it became virtually worthless in the waning months of the war. He assumed it would have no value at all in Texas now but packed it out of habit. The bag also held his revolver, a Dance .44 caliber six-shooter he took off the corpse of a lieutenant two weeks before the ranks were notified that the war was over.

He'd rescued the horse last week from a wagon

that had been obliterated by a bouncing cannon ball in the very last hour of the battle, the last battle. Both horses were still in harness but had been spared. A trio of soldiers rushed to the horses, eager to eat meat that evening. Josh had to pull his pistol on the men, his comrades, to save the gray for himself.

He shook his head violently, side to side, looked up at the heavens. *Why am I here and not among the corpses of those good boys that lay along the road like so many fallen fence posts?* He shook his head again and cried out. The horse shied and settled.

Josh felt older than his twenty-three years. The past four years were lost to him. He would never recover them. He had joined up because his boyhood friends joined up, and it was a glorious cause they supported, the glorious South that stood against Yankee tyranny. He understood nothing when he joined and little more now. He only knew that leaders who sent young men to war did not understand what it meant to face death each day, each hour. He wondered how many wars there would be if each leader who initiated war were required to be the first casualty.

The war ended in early April when Lee surrendered to Grant, but armies in the field did not receive the news for some time. Two weeks after the war officially ended, Josh's best friend, one of the few men in the ranks he could talk with and the only one he could confide in, was shot at his side and died in his arms. He was devastated and wondered whether he would survive, mentally as well as physically.

For days now, he had been riding on narrow dusty wagon roads through country that was strange to him. He must have passed this way riding eastward that summer of '61 with his three friends. They had served in the same company, but none of the three survived. Now he rode alone, and that ride eastward a lifetime ago was a blur. He just knew he was heading west now, and home was somewhere out there.

He rode through country that looked like a battleground, though it had seen no battles. Fences were sagging or fallen, gates hanging. Fields that had produced crops were overgrown with weeds. Houses and farm buildings were neglected or empty. At one house, in need of serious repair, a gaunt woman stood in a doorway, staring at him. Two small children stood beside her, holding handfuls of her dress and leaning against her. A single cow, tied to a post with a rope, grazed in a patch of grass beside the house.

During the war, the infrequent letter from his mother had assured him all was well at home, that nothing had changed since he left, that she and his daddy and sister Nellie were doing fine. All sent their love and hoped he was well and would come home soon. The postal service had fallen on hard times this past year, and letters that had been regular were reduced to a trickle. He had received nothing for the past eight months.

He broke camp this morning at first light, waking with a premonition that home was near and setting out without any delay for a fire or breakfast. He still did not recognize the country, but he had a feeling.

After an hour's ride, he saw an old man just off the road, chopping dry tree limbs into short fireplace lengths. Josh pulled the gray up and called to the man.

The oldster straightened, flexed his back, and responded to his question. "You crossed into Texas 'bout ten miles back. Paris? You got another couple days or so to go, depending on how fast that nag moves." He pointed ahead. "You follow the road you're on for 'bout twenty miles. You'll come to a crossroads. You'll see a sign pointing north to Paris. Then you got another ride of a day or so."

Josh thanked him and set out at a steady walk, the fastest pace he could coax from the old gray. He rode through a mostly empty country, brown and overgrown with tall weeds and bushes. Scattered patches of green grass lay in the meadows, nourished by recent rains. A few longhorn cattle grazed in pastures along the road. On sighting him, their heads came up. They stood rigid and watched him a moment, then bolted and ran like frightened deer.

Josh sat on his horse at a crossroads where two dusty lanes intersected. The sun ball rested on the western horizon in a break in the oak forest. The sky, clear silver blue overhead, was a riot of colored layers of thin, wispy clouds above the sun. A road sign at the intersection pointed ahead, westward, to Dallas and Fort Worth. A slat on the post pointed to Paris on the right.

Paris. His eyes watered at the memory of attending church in Paris, talking idly with friendly shopkeepers, and passing time with good friends at the combination grocery saloon. A warm feeling coursed through his body. The family farm was on this road three miles south of the town, so he'll reach home without going into town.

He turned the gray onto the road north. He wondered how many miles to home. He could not remember ever being on this road. He had ridden only a few miles south of the farm to hunt occasionally.

Mostly he had ridden to Paris and north and west of Paris on cattle roundups and hunting, north a few times to Red River for fishing. He and some friends had even crossed the Red once so they could say they had been to Indian Territory.

He wondered about the state of affairs in Indian Territory now. He had heard that tribes were divided during the war on what side to support. Indians that owned black slaves supported the South, while those opposed to slavery supported the North. *Seems they had their own civil war.*

Growing up, he had never given much thought to the question of slavery. A few people in and around Paris owned a few slaves, but his daddy never owned any and believed that owning a person like owning a horse, was just plain wrong. Josh had never had to deal with the issue, and even when he was fighting for the right of southerners to own slaves, he still thought little about it.

Then what in the hell was I fighting for if not for the right of southerners to own slaves? The right of southerners to form a new nation? What do I care about that? He looked aside at the grassy meadow bordered by a thick stand of pecan and pine trees. *I was in the wrong place at the wrong time for the wrong reasons.*

JOSH DECIDED that he wanted to arrive home in the morning hours rather than late in the day, so he stopped for the night when he reckoned he was only a few miles from the farm. He made his saddle blanket bed at twilight as if reclining early would speed the night.

He broke the cold camp at first light. Josh was so

nervous, he hardly slept. He was on the road at first light. It wasn't long before he began to recognize the lay of the land. The forests, the plowed lands, a creek bordered by cypress and pecan trees, ferns and rushes thick on the banks. The break in the rushes where he would enter the water from the bank to cool off on a hot day was still there.

The gray approached a turning in the road that Josh recognized. The house was just beyond. He wiped the single bead of perspiration that rolled down his cheek. Rounding the turning, he pulled up abruptly. He stared, frowning. *Something's wrong here.* Lengths of the picket fence in front of the house had fallen, and the walkway leading to the front porch was overgrown with weeds. The front door was open. Dry leaves lay in piles on the porch and inside in the front hall. The garden at the side of the house was bone dry, with only a few desiccated stalks. No animals were in sight. No mules, no cows, no chickens. *Where are the dogs? They should be barking at the horse, tails wagging, tongues hanging.*

He looked at the barn. The doors were wide open, revealing a bare interior, no hay, no tack, nothing. The corral gate had lost a hinge and lay on the ground, corral poles sagging and fallen. No horses or mules were in sight, not in the corral or the pastures beyond.

He dismounted slowly, tied the reins to a fence post, stared at the house.

"That you, Josh?"

He turned to see a wagon. He had been so stupefied at what he was seeing that he didn't hear the wagon pull up behind him. The driver stared intently at Josh, frowning.

"Yes. That you, Pete?"

The man relaxed. He wrapped the reins around

the brake handle and climbed down. He walked over to stand beside Josh.

"Not much of a homecoming," Pete said, looking at the house.

They remained silent, both staring at the house.

"What happened?" asked Josh, without looking at him.

Pete took Josh's arm, walked him to the right, and stopped. He gestured with his head, and Josh saw the three graves in the backyard. The mounds were covered with tall weeds. Fresh flowers in vases rested at the base of rude crosses. Josh walked to the graves, Pete following.

Josh rocked back and forth slowly, wiped the tears from his cheek. "Who did this?"

"Happened 'bout a year ago, last spring, it was. We figure it was Comanches. Not sure since the Comanche don't usually come this far east, but a couple of hunters from Paris saw a bunch that they are sure was Comanche up near the Red, and they was headed this way."

"Why would they do this to my family?"

Pete shook his head. "Dunno. But there is a story that it might've been a revenge raid. Seems some Comanche hunters was wiped out up north of the Red by a bunch of our people who don't like Indians. Killed 'em just because they was Indians. If that's so, then your place could have been raided just by chance. Least, that's what folks are sayin'." He put a hand on Josh's shoulder. "Sorry, old man. Not a good homecoming." Josh nodded, staring at the graves.

Pete backed away, walked to the wagon, and climbed up to the seat. "You let me know if I can help, hear?" He shook the lines, and the mules pulled away. Josh did not see him go. He still stared at the graves.

Josh suddenly felt weak. He stumbled to the side of the house, leaned against it, and slid down to sit on the ground. His hands went to his face, and he sobbed, rocking back and forth. He cleared his throat, wiped his face with both hands, and raised his head, his eyes closed tightly.

Opening his eyes, he looked at the graves. He slumped. *What do I do now? Do I pray to God, or do I curse God? I was always taught at church to believe that everything that happens is God's will, part of His plan. How does the killing of my whole family fit into God's plan?* He remembered a verse that always bothered him. When Job lost his children and wealth in a single day and contracted painful sores over his entire body, his wife said: Curse God and die! *Is that for me as well?*

Josh inhaled deeply, wiped his face again with a hand. He struggled to stand, pushing against the wall. *No, I will not curse God, and I will not die. But I will not pray, and I will live in hell.*

IT REQUIRED but two weeks to put his affairs in order. He rode to Paris and took a room at a guest house, promising to pay the landlady after the sale of the farm. He visited with old friends who had buried his family and laid flowers at the graves. He especially thanked two of his father's friends who had ridden out regularly to ensure that the property was not damaged or occupied by vagrants. They knew Josh was in the war and hoped they would turn the place over to him on his return.

The sale was concluded quickly since he set a low

price. The lawyer was aghast and advised against the price, but Josh was unmoving. He wanted to sell quickly and was not interested in the usual practice of bargaining with potential buyers. The buyer, a local who had been friends with the family, promised to tend to the graves.

Josh insisted that he be paid as much of the sale price in coin as possible. The lawyer at first said that this was impossible, but when Josh offered to increase the lawyer's fee, he said he would do what he could.

After a week of scrounging and bartering, the lawyer came up with gold and silver coins amounting to something over half the sale price. The coins had been struck by a variety of sources, some in Texas and some elsewhere, notably the New Orleans Mint. The balance of the payment was in paper currency of dubious value outside Texas. Or in Texas, for that matter. He would ask his landlady at the guest house to sew the coins and paper money into horse blankets, concealed saddle bag pouches, and jackets. He expected to travel in country he did not know.

So, it was finished. He bought a good horse, and saddle, and saddlebags, and other tack at the Paris livery, and some necessities at the general store, including a supply of powder, shot, and caps for the pistol. He bought new clothes so he would look like a cowboy instead of a worn-out soldier. Josh paid for the goods and nodded his thanks.

The store owner, an old family friend, extended his hand, and Josh took it. "Hate to see you leave like this. I haven't seen you smile since you got back." Josh nodded again. "What's the plan?" the grocer said.

Josh shrugged. "Moving on."

"Take care of yourself. You've had a shock. Don't do nothin' foolish, son."

Josh hefted his bag of purchases. He raised a hand in salute, or goodbye, and walked through the front door.

THE FOLLOWING two years would always be a blur. He rode south to the crossroads, looked down each of the lanes, and turned east. He rode in country he had seen only a few days ago, but he remembered nothing. His mind was blank. A few days later, he was in New Orleans where he wandered the streets, frequented saloons where he drank, played cards, and learned to cheat.

He lived on riverboats for months thereafter, over winter, sailing north and south, going nowhere, playing cards in an alcoholic haze. He was pulled into gunfights over cards and women and because it was Tuesday. He was hit once in an upper arm and in a leg, both flesh wounds that healed with no professional care. He would be haunted the rest of his life that he killed two men in gunfights over nothing more important than card hands.

He stood at the rail on an upper deck one evening, sobbing, waving off strangers who offered to help.

He left the riverboat in spring and returned to New Orleans where he lived the rest of the year, gambling, wandering, living in hovels and on the streets. He worked at menial tasks, never stayed in a job or a place for long since he proved unmotivated and unreliable. He wondered more than once whether there was anything worthwhile left for him in this life.

Then for some reason that he was never able to

explain to himself or others, he sold all he owned, bought a horse and saddle, and rode to Texas. He had no plan, only a magnetic pull to the only place that had ever had a hold on him. If asked, he could not have described that pull. He had no home, no family. No life.

IN EARLY SPRING, he fell in with four men while drinking at a saloon in Waco. They were about his age with similar tastes in liquor and cards. They had heard a rumor that cattle could be driven north and sold at outrageously high prices. Having little experience with cattle they nevertheless hatched a plan, fueled by alcohol, to ride to Mexico to buy longhorn cattle to drive north to markets. They figured it made more sense to buy half-domesticated cattle in Mexico than to try to round up the local Texas longhorns that were as thick as fleas, but wilder than jackrabbits. It also made sense because none had any experience in rounding up wild Texas longhorns.

The group had not made much progress southward before Josh, in a rare moment of sobriety, decided he was on a fool's mission with a bunch of fools and left them, ignoring their drunken hoots and laughter when he told them his decision. He wished them good luck and watched them ride away.

He sat his horse in the middle of the trail that day, head hanging. His mind was blank. He stared in all directions. The road was empty, the land empty but for a stand of pecan trees beyond a meadow where a dozen longhorns grazed.

He slumped, and the tears came.

. . .

Josh sat on his horse on a sunny spring morning on the outskirts of a town, the largest Texas town he had seen. He hailed an old-timer who had overtaken him.

"What town is this?" Josh said.

The oldster pulled up. "Fort Worth. You never been to Fort Worth?" Josh shook his head. "Fine town with fine prospects. It's got more cows than people. Just keep your six-shooter handy. Cows are pretty tame, but not the cowboys." He snorted and rode off, waving over his shoulder.

Josh began riding around the fringes, planning to bypass the town, but had second thoughts, deciding that this place was as good as any other. He turned and rode toward the cluster of large pens that were filled with longhorn cattle. A considerable number of cowboys lounged about, joking, laughing, smoking, eyeing this stranger.

He rode down a dusty street past the pens and pulled up at a hotel that boasted clean beds and hot baths. He dismounted, tied the reins to the rail, and opened his saddlebags. He retrieved the thin money pouch. He figured he had enough to pay for a new change of clothes, a bath, and one night at the hotel. He pulled his pistol from the holster, checked the cylinder, and found three cartridges. Pushing the pistol into the holster, he walked toward the haberdashery two stores down.

Chapter Two

THE WOMAN who stood behind the counter at the hotel said good morning, smiled, and told him that he smelled a lot better than he had when he checked in yesterday. He returned the smile and responded that she could give his old clothes to a beggar if she could find one who was that hard up.

At his question, she told him that the best café in town was Andy's Eats down the street. "If you can find a table," she said. "It's pretty popular with the fellas. You cain't miss it." He touched his hat to her and walked outside.

He immediately saw why he couldn't miss it. A half dozen men stood on the walk, in front of the café. They moved aside when he approached, suggesting they had already eaten. He opened the door and walked in. And stopped. The café was small, only ten tables, and everyone was occupied. He turned to leave, but a cowboy stood at his table, waved him to come over.

"Just finished," the cowboy said.

"Many thanks. What do you recommend?"

"Anything you like, as long as it's steak, even for breakfast." He smiled, slapped Josh on the shoulder, and went out.

Josh had no sooner sat than a buxom, middle-aged woman, wearing a clean white apron, walked to his table. "What'll you have today? There's the menu on the wall there." She pointed.

"I've been told the steak is good, and whatever comes with it."

"You got it. Good choice." She smiled, turned, and walked toward the kitchen door.

He looked around. The patrons were all male, seemingly cowboys, probably employed at the cattle pens or buying and selling at the pens.

"Dammit, boys, how am I goin' to deal with this!"

Josh blinked at the outburst from the adjacent table. He had nodded to the four cowboys there when he came in, and they had nodded in return without interrupting their conversation. One of the men had become increasingly agitated, and a companion held up a hand to calm him down. Josh was too close to avoid overhearing.

"How am I gonna fill those two spots? Drives are gettin' underway, and there's no loose hands around. How am I gonna find a good hand to fill Jody's spot?" He drooped, shaking his head. "Hope he's all right. Leastways, he got the broken bone fixed up right away by the doc."

He leaned back. "Now this new problem I just learned about yesterday. How am I gonna find a cook on such short notice? Cookie decided that his rheumatism, or whatever, was too bad to risk going on the trail. Well, I feel sorry for him, but it sure puts me in a hard place."

"Boss," said Harley, a grizzled old-timer, "the outfit that's driving our cattle from the Rio Grande surely has a cook. Why not use him for the drive to Abilene?"

"Yeah. I asked him the same question when they left Fort Worth for the Rio Grande. He said that he ain't goin' into Indian Territory again. Couple of years ago, he was with two men hunting buffalo up there, and it didn't turn out well. They shot buffalo all right, and the Indians shot the two boys. One of 'em died. He decided right then and there he would never cross the Red again. So that's that."

The waitress delivered Josh's plate with a smile and withdrew. Josh ate slowly while something rocketed around in his head, and he hardly tasted the steak.

The man who had done most of the talking, the one they called 'boss,' slumped. He stared out the window, then casually around the room. He noticed Josh, sitting alone and eating slowly. He saw a fit young man, nicely dressed. He stared until Josh looked up.

"Howdy, hadn't seen you around before," said the boss.

"Just rode in yesterday."

"You buying cows or delivering cows? Anybody in this part of Fort Worth seems to have something to do with cows."

Josh leaned back, frowning at this inquisitive stranger. "Well, I had something to do with cows a few years ago, nothing lately."

"What are you doing now?

"Nothing beyond having breakfast."

"Sorry, I'm interrupting your breakfast." The boss stared.

This fella is just about to become annoying.

"Would you be interested in working with cows again?"

Josh leaned back, frowned. "I didn't mean to eavesdrop, but I heard your conversation."

"Bring your plate over and pull up a chair."

Josh pondered a moment. *Do I want to do this?* He picked up his plate and coffee cup and pulled the chair over while the boss moved his own chair aside to make room. Josh sat and nodded to the others.

"I'm Andy Miller, boss of this outfit." He paused. "Why aren't you working?"

"I've, uh, been on the road, originally from Paris."

"Paris?" said another man at the table. "Is that—"

"Texas," Josh said.

"Oh, yeah, course."

"Josh Nesbitt," he said. The others at the table nodded.

"You see, Josh, I need a hand," said Andy. "You look like a fit young man. I'd like to tell you about what we're about to do and see if you would be interested. Since I don't know you, I would take you on for a one-month trial. At the end of that month, if I'm not satisfied with you, or if you're not satisfied with us, we'll part company. How's that sound?"

Josh frowned, pondering.

"Here's what we're all about. We have two thousand head coming up from the Rio Grande that should arrive here in four or five weeks. In the meantime, my Fort Worth outfit will leave here in a couple of days to ride west of here and collect a bunch of wild longhorns to add to the Mexican herd. I'm thinking we should be able to round up five hundred or so. This is all on speculation, of course. We never looked for wild longhorns before, so we'll be learning as we go.

"We'll drive this combined herd north to the railhead in Kansas. Now, we're not sure where that will be by the time we get there. Last word I had was that the railroad reached Junction City last year and has been building west since then. I expect by the time we get there; it should be in Abilene. There's a rumor that the railroad is going to send agents south to meet cattle outfits and tell them where the railhead is, but I'm not counting on that. We'll probably send a rider ahead to see where it is.

"There's also a rumor that the farmers in that part of Kansas are real unhappy that the railroads are encouraging Texans to drive cattle up, and they say they won't let it happen. I don't put much stock in that, even if it is true. We'll have to be ready for that. A bunch of dirt farmers ain't gonna hold back progress. Anyway, those farmers like beef just like other people. Seems they were happy in the last couple of years of the war to buy cattle from Union-leaning Indians who had stolen the cows from the south-leaning Indians.

"The point is, we'll be one of the first herds this year to the Abilene railhead, maybe the first, and we should get top dollar. If we can find a buyer. Hell, I'm not worried if we arrive in Abilene before the railroad. I wager there will be buyers there who will be happy to buy a herd and put it on grass, and the cows will be one or two hundred pounds heavier by the time they go into a railroad car.

"Yeah. It's a risk, but what th' hell, it's worth the risk. If everything was a sure thing, it'd be boring, wouldn't it?" He smiled, slapped Josh on the back.

"Anyway, Josh, that's where you'd be paid off. If you're still with us."

Andy pulled out the makings and rolled a cigarette. He leaned over and lit it from another hand's cigarette. Eyes shut, he inhaled and exhaled a stream of smoke. "I'll tell you boys, this drive is going to be somethin,' if I say so myself. We're breakin' new trail. Texas cattle were trailed to Missouri in the '50s, but that just about ended when they said Texas cows carried a fever that infected their own cattle. During the late war, Texans sold cattle to both sides, but that didn't last long, as you can imagine, soon as the North got control.

"All that's changed. We're in on the beginning of a new trail and a new way of sending Texas cattle north and east. The railroad has reached Kansas, and we're gonna fill those rail cars with cows and fill our pockets with cash."

Andy grinned. "What do you say, Josh. Will you join us? If you give me the word, Paul here will tell you all about us and make all the arrangements for you joining the bunch."

Paul nodded and leaned toward Josh. "If you decide to sign on, soon's we get our apple pie and leave here, we'll . . ." He stopped when he was aware that no one was listening, rather staring across the room.

"Here she comes," said one of the cowboys softly, almost a whisper. Everyone looked across the room at the table near the kitchen door.

A young, pretty woman stood beside a table at the far wall. She talked with the cowboys at the table, smiling, laughing lightly. The loose dress did not disguise a shapely body. Her hand was on a patron's shoulder as she talked with the three men at the table. They looked at her intently, mouths open and eyes wide, listening, grinning. She patted the man's shoulder, walked away, hungry eyes following.

She stopped at Miller's table. "What're you boys up to? You been huddling like you got secrets. Or troubles." She smiled.

"How could we have any troubles when we got you to talk to, Jenny?" said Andy. "Troubles and worries disappear when you enter the room."

She grimaced, turned to Josh. "Don't listen to this guy," gesturing toward Andy. "He's the biggest bullshitter this side of the Mississippi. Haven't seen you around. You with this bunch?"

"That question is just about to be settled," said Andy. "And since you're complimenting me, I'll return the favor." He turned to Josh. "Josh, this is Jenny, the best cook this side of the Mississippi. She's why this café is always full. There's not a single man in Fort Worth who wouldn't like to get hitched to this gal for that reason." He smiled. "Well, maybe for some other reasons as well." He pulled a face.

She pulled a face in return. "It's gettin' pretty deep over here, and I need to get back to work." She turned to Josh. "Watch yourself with this bunch." She smiled and made to leave.

"Jenny, wait a minute," said Andy. "I got a problem you might can help me with." She stopped, turned back.

"You know we're leaving in a little while to drive a herd north." She nodded. "I thought I had my outfit all put together, but now my cook tells me he's not goin' with us. Rheumatism or somethin.' I'm in a bind. Actually, I'm desperate. I've asked around town, and I can't find a cook that's not already signed on other outfits. Do you know some experienced cook who can satisfy ten or twelve hungry cowboys three times a day who's looking for work?"

"No, sorry, Andy. Don't know anybody. Good luck. I'd hate to be in the same county if this bunch goes hungry."

She turned to walk toward the kitchen, then stopped, stared at the kitchen door, hands on hips. The cowboys watched her, looked at each other. After a long moment, she turned and walked back to the table.

She frowned, staring at Andy. Looking up, she stared at the window so long that Andy began to fidget. She finally looked back at him, still frowning.

"Well? Do you know somebody?"

She frowned again, then: "Yeah. Me."

The four cowboys laughed. Josh did not laugh, just stared at Jenny.

"Naw, really, Jenny, do you know somebody?" said Andy.

She grimaced. "Am I speaking Chinese, Andy? I said 'me.'"

"You . . . you would hire on to a cattle drive?" He started to laugh, then sobered when he saw she was not smiling. He spoke softly. "Jenny, women don't go on cattle drives. I couldn't hire you."

She put hands on hips. By now, everyone in the café, in hearing distance watched and listened.

"Why? Tell me something a man could do on a chuck wagon that I couldn't do."

He fidgeted. "Well, you sure can cook better than anybody I've ever known but cooking out of the back of a wagon ain't the same as cooking in a town kitchen."

"So? It would take me the better part of one day to learn."

"The cook has to hitch mules and drive the chuck wagon and—"

"Andy, why do you think I'm called 'Jenny'? I been hitching and driving mules since I was ten. I can handle mules better'n any man in your outfit." She was warming up to the conversation. "I wouldn't let any man hitch my mules or drive my wagon since I'm better at it than any man you got."

Andy looked around the table. The others looked down or aside, stifling grins.

"Andy," she said, "you said you had looked around Fort Worth, and no cook is available. You said you're desperate. Where else you gonna go? What have you got to lose by hiring me?

"Damn it, Jenny," he said softly. "It just ain't done, a woman on a cattle drive."

"Why?"

Petey, the youngest in the group at the table, who hadn't said a word, looked pointedly at Andy. "Yeah, boss, why?"

Andy clenched his eyes shut, opened them, looked aside blankly, then back to Jenny. "Are you serious?"

She glared at him, hands on hips.

Andy raised his hands, palms outward. "Okay."

The room erupted in cheers and shouts and laughter and back-slapping.

Jenny relaxed. She smiled. "You don't have to tell me my duties. I've talked to a lot of cowboys and a few cookies, so I figure I know what needs to be done. I'll handle my own mules and wagon. I'll expect every cowboy in the outfit to collect firewood every morning and every evening. I'll buy provisions, but I'll need somebody to hunt for wild meat since I don't 'spect you want to kill cows every day for meat."

"Hmm. Didn't take you long to fit in. I expect we can work all this out. I expect other outfits to get a few laughs about this arrangement."

"Just ask them people over for supper, and we'll see if they keep laughing," said Paul. The others murmured agreement.

Andy turned back to Josh. "If you sign on, Josh, you'll help Jenny at the chuckwagon at the beginning. You'll also be responsible for hunting. Jenny will let you know what she needs. You have done some hunting, I suppose." Josh nodded. "Jenny, anything else you need, talk to Josh. If he decides to join us."

"If you need somethin' Josh ain't interested in, Jenny, talk to me," said Tim, a young cowboy who had listened to all this, stifling a grin. Now he pulled a face.

Jenny glared at Tim. "That's one more thing," said Jenny to the table. "No funny business! I cook, sit at the campfire after supper, maybe drink a beer when we can get it, and watch sunsets. I don't pleasure any man in this outfit with anything but my cooking. If anybody doesn't understand this, I gotta say I can also take care of myself."

Andy smiled. "Yeah, I bet you can." He leaned back, "Okay, that's settled. Jenny, Paul will get in touch with you about arrangements." Paul nodded. Andy leaned back. "Now, Jenny, how about that hot apple pie?" She smiled, turned, and walked toward the kitchen door.

Josh watched her go. He had not said a single word since she first walked into the room. Since then, he had not taken his eyes from her.

Andy had not missed anything. "Well, Josh, what about it? You joining us?"

"Yeah." He looked toward the window. *What's happening here?*

MID-MORNING. Josh sat with Jenny at a window table in the cafe, holding coffee cups.

She sipped from her cup. "You don't talk much."

"Only when I have something to say."

"That's somethin' new. Most of these yahoos spout out anything that pops in their head. Sometimes takes a lot of siftin' to know what they're trying to say."

They sat quiet, sipping coffee, staring through the window at the occasional cowboy walking by.

She leaned toward him as if she spoke in confidence. "You want to know really why I decided to sign on with this outfit?"

"Yeah, I wondered about that."

"It sure ain't because I have a great interest in cows or cowboys. I've seen plenty of both. I want to see a train. Never seen one. I bet you haven't either." He shook his head. She smiled, sipped her coffee. They studied the window, watching passersby and a boy driving four milk cows with a switch.

"Jenny?" he said. "I don't suppose that's the name you were given at birth."

She smiled. "Nope. Barbara. As for Jenny, my daddy found me one evening at the corral with the mules. I was about twelve, I think. I was leaning on the top pole, and a half dozen mules stood there inside the corral, right up at the fence in my face, staring at me, all still and ears up. When my daddy asked me later what was going on, I said I was just talking to 'em. I told him that sometimes I sing to 'em, and they like it.

"He just shook his head and said he believed I

thought I was a mule. He called me 'Jenny' after that, and it stuck. I didn't mind it at all. I liked it, better'n Bar-bruh. He also said I was stubborn as a mule. I liked that too. I still like mules. They're smarter than most people I know."

"The name suits you. I like 'Jenny.'" He tried to smile without success.

They sat quiet, staring into their cups. He looked at the window as she watched him.

"Why'd you leave Paris?" she said.

He glanced at her, then into his cup. "I . . . I . . ." His eyes clouded.

She put a hand on his. "Later. We got a long time to talk." She stood and collected the cups. He jumped up. "Both of us need to get to work," she said. "I've given my boss notice, and he's still stewing with a lot of what-am-I-going to-do-nows. I promised I'd come back, and he can tell our customers that. Actually, he's got another woman in the kitchen who does a lot of the cooking I get credit for. That's because she refuses to come out front and talk to people. He'll do okay."

She walked toward the kitchen door. "We'll see a lot of each other on this drive," Jenny threw over her shoulder.

He almost smiled at how he might have replied had they met under different circumstances.

JOSH STOOD beside the chuck wagon, watching Jenny make friends with the three mules hobbled nearby, two for the team and one extra. She rubbed and patted their backs, offered the back of her hand to their nostrils, stroked their necks. And talked to them as they moved closer to her. Josh watched all this and shook his head.

Jenny then went to the rear of the wagon and fussed about. She lowered the hinged lid of the chuck box and examined the boxes, shelves, and drawers, all of which would be covered by the lid when traveling. Stationary, the lid was lowered to serve as a worktable. A rolled canvas awning above the chuck box could be unrolled and stretched above the worktable in case of rain. She bent and examined the boot under the chuck box which held the larger cooking items, including a Dutch oven. She checked the fittings on the coffee mill and water barrel attached to the side of the wagon.

She called Josh over. "Look at this." He looked under the wagon where she pointed to a cowhide that was attached to the underside. A few dry cow chips and bits of kindling lay in the hide, suggesting its use. "Never saw that before. Good idea. I've heard about using cow shit for burning, but never even seen it done."

"Some old hands call it prairie coal. I expect you'll burn lots of cow chips and buffalo chips before this drive is finished."

She described the small changes she wanted made, and goods and provisions they needed to buy. She gave him a list that began with the basics: beans, coffee, cornmeal, salted meats, bacon or sowbelly, onions, potatoes, lard, sacks of flour for biscuits, and finished with more items she needed before setting out.

Harley, the oldster who knew more about cattle driving than anyone else in the outfit, including Andy and Paul, hovered about the wagon and overheard these instructions. "Josh, I hope you can keep Jenny in the stores she needs. Cookies I've traveled with who run out of store-bought supplies sometimes had to rely on the country, and that ain't good. One cookie even served us rabbit. Anybody who eats rabbit tends to talk to hisself, and anybody who talks to hisself is gonna tell lies." He nodded, grinning at his own wisdom.

Jenny shook her head. "Thanks for that, Harley. I'll remember not to listen to you if I have to serve you rabbit."

Harley grinned again, touched his forehead to her, and started to walk away. He turned back. "Jenny, we had a cookie one time who didn't just call us to breakfast. He did a sort of sing-song call:

Bacon in the pan,
Coffee in the pot!
Git up an' get it—
Git it while it's hot!

Jenny frowned. "I'm not likely to be in the mood for singing before breakfast. But I'll yell loud enough that even you will hear." He smiled, touched his forehead again to her, and walked away.

Jenny turned back to Josh. She emphasized that she needed everything done and everything bought today. Josh said he would take care of everything, assuming that she would do most of it herself. He did not suppose that she would trust him or anyone else to mess with the wagon that she already referred to as "my wheely kitchen."

He listened to her babble and bubble, smiling inwardly, wondering what was happening.

"Josh!" He turned to see Andy striding up. "Didn't get a chance to talk to you earlier. I did say you are to help Jenny when she needs it, but your main occupation is trail hand. I suppose you know that. I don't suppose Paul has talked with you yet. We'll get you checked out at each position on the herd, from drag to point. You're the newest in the outfit, so you'll ride drag first and eat a lot of dust. We'll move you up as quick as you show us you're ready to move. I expect it won't take long.

"Since you'll be getting up before daybreak to help Jenny, you won't be riding night guard at first. Later, when Jenny's got everything in order, I'll likely call on you for some night guard. Any questions for me?" Josh shook his head.

"But I'm getting' ahead of myself. I mentioned in the café that we're going to go cow hunting to add to our herd coming up from the Rio Grande. We'll ride a few days west of here where we'll collect wild range cattle and teach 'em what it means to be part of a herd.

"If you don't have chaps, you'll need to get some. We're gonna be hunting cattle in heavy brush, lot of mesquite and cactus, and some of this stuff has wicked thorns. Get yourself a thick leather jacket if you can find one. I'm told leather stirrup coverings to protect your feet are helpful, but I doubt you'll find them in Fort Worth. Get some leather gauntlets to protect your hands and forearms if you can find any.

"Jenny, see if you can pack enough provisions in that wagon for a month. We may find a store reasonably close to where we're going, but we may not. Josh, be sure your pistol and rifle are in good order. From the time we leave Fort Worth, we'll be prey." He started to walk away, stopped, and turned back. "Jenny, I've told the boys that there's to be no alcohol in camp.

Some diehard may yet ask you to stash a bottle in the wagon."

"Right. Not in my wagon," she said.

"Thanks." Andy smiled, turned, and waved over his shoulder.

"Cow hunting," said Josh. "Never even heard of huntin' cows. And chaps? Never owned chaps. Never had any use for them."

Jenny rubbed the back of a mule. "Cowboys who actually work cows have told me they couldn't do without them. Saves their legs from being ripped up by thorny stuff. Then there's other fellas who never been west of Fort Worth who wear 'em because they think the chaps make them look dressed up and handsome." She looked him up and down, smiled. "I expect they would make you look dressed up and handsome."

He frowned. "I don't know about that. I plan to look for somebody's castoffs."

Chapter Three

THE RIM of the sun had just cleared the horizon when Jenny called the cowboys to breakfast. Most were up, but a couple quickly threw back their covers and ran for the bushes. The outfit had camped on the western fringes of Fort Worth last evening so they could start early this day. Now they crowded around the cooking fire, plates in hand.

The eight cowboys in Andy's outfit were joined by Silas, who Andy recruited in Fort Worth. Andy and Silas were drinking buddies in Fort Worth. Silas had often talked about cow hunts he had been a part of in the brush country west of his home, so Andy was quick to recruit him for this venture.

"Let's see what the new cookie has for us," said Harley, the grizzled old-timer whose wild gray hair appeared not to have seen a comb for years. His eyes opened wide as Jenny served him slices of beef, fried eggs, potatoes, and steaming sourdough biscuits with butter. "Oh, my, my." He stared at the brimming plate.

"Move on, pard," said Jenny. "You're holding up

the serving line. Josh has your coffee." Josh poured coffee into a tin cup and handed it to Harley." Harley took the coffee and walked toward the campfire.

"Oh, my, my," said Harley, still examining his plate.

Andy was the last to be served. "You probably shoulda served 'em cold beans and half a biscuit for this first offering. Now they'll expect a banquet every meal."

"Nothing special about this meal," said Jenny. "It's breakfast. As long as Josh keeps me in supplies, I'll keep serving meals. On that point, I don't suppose we're gonna be near any town for replenishing, so we might need to be gone a day or so buying stuff."

"We'll see. If you run short, the boys could probably survive a while on wild meat, biscuits, coffee, and cigarettes." He walked toward the fire.

Jenny filled two plates and handed one to Josh. He poured coffee into two cups on the hinged gate. "What do you think?" she said.

"I think you have found a place in this bunch."

THE OUTFIT RODE through Weatherford at sunset. The town was a single street of small shops, a combination livery, and blacksmith, and two saloons where the considerable number of horses crowded at the rail in front suggested that locals began their carousing early. A small steepled church at the edge of town was enclosed by a picket fence, both fence and church were a faded white.

When Harley suggested a short stop for refreshments, Andy said nothing, finally signaling a stop when they had ridden a sufficient distance to hear no laughter or shouts from revelers in the town.

After supper, the hands lounged at the campfire, smoking, and chatting. Andy straightened, frowned, and cleared his throat.

"Uh oh," said Harley, "here comes something serious." A few chuckles followed.

"Okay," said Andy. "We'll get on this cow hunt tomorrow. I saw a few range cows in the brush this afternoon. Now, this cow hunting is gonna be hard, and it's gonna be a lot of fun. Brush poppin' where we're going is not as hard or as productive as down south between the Nueces and the Rio Grande, so Silas says, but we should find enough range cattle to make it worthwhile. The hard part is convincing these critters to go with us. That won't be easy since they're as wild and quick as jackrabbits.

"Since I know nothing about collecting wild cattle, and I suspect all of you yahoos know even less, I have enlisted Silas here, who you met in Fort Worth, to educate us." Silas nodded, raised a hand in acknowledgement. "Silas has contacted two local boys to help as well. They'll join us tomorrow. We'll follow the lead and advice of these three fellas."

The range cattle weren't naturally wild. During the Civil War, a great number of young men from ranching families enlisted, leaving ranches undermanned. Many ranches were abandoned. After the war, both state and Confederate forces withdrew from frontier regions, leaving the inhabitants defenseless against marauding Comanche and Kiowa raiders. More ranches were abandoned as the embattled families moved to more settled areas in central and east Texas. Crops withered, and cows wandered.

"I hope everbody took me at my word and got chaps and leather jackets," said Andy, "because we're gonna be ridin' in some prickly brush. Most of the stock we see will be range cattle, but some will be branded. Leave the branded stuff alone. We don't want to be charged with rustling. If a calf is following a branded cow, leave it be. We're just collecting cows that don't belong to nobody. We brand what we collect, and they're ours.

"We'll probably see some fellas in the brush doing the same as us, collecting cows. Some of 'em will be from families that closed up the ranch when all the young help went off to war. Ask these boys to describe their brand and tell them we'll collect any of their cows we see and try to get the animals to 'em. Don't know how we'll do that, but we'll try. Silas and his two boys will help with this." He turned to Silas. "Would you give us greenhorns some ideas of how we go about collecting these wild devils?"

Silas nodded to Andy, turned to the group. "Well, first thang, you ain't leaving camp at all tomorrow. First thang we gotta do is build a pen to hold the wild critters when you bring 'em from the brush. They'll stay in there a few days, learnin' that they ain't wild anymore. Soon as they calm down, you'll brand 'em. Then you'll take 'em out and close herd them on good grass till you're ready to take them to Fort Worth."

"As for collectin' the mavericks, you cain't just round 'em up. They don't round up. You're capturing them, one by one sometimes, a small bunch sometimes. You'll often find them gathered in small bands of a half dozen or so. They hide in heavy brush by day and come out at night to graze. So when we take them in daylight, we're interrupting their bedtime."

"Silas," said Petey, "what's a 'maverick'?"

"A maverick, my green young friend, is an

unbranded stray that we will consider ownerless. They are also as hard to catch as jackrabbits. These cows ain't like any cows you know. These are wild animals. You can hunt and shoot a deer easier than you can hunt and shoot a range longhorn. And mean? The longhorn bull is the meanest creature you'll ever come across. And they'll fight each other. If you see them fighting each other, back off. The bull that's getting the worse of it will usually give it up, but sometimes nobody gives up, and they will fight till one has been gored and killed.

"Now, to ease the taking of the wild critters, we bring a decoy herd of tame cows into the brush. You saw the twenty tame cows the two boys brought in yesterday." The two local cowboys, Monty and Tom, smiled, waved. "When we find a wild critter or two or three, we push them in among the decoys, so they'll settle down. Then we move the lot outta the brush toward the pen.

"Be careful here. Sing or whistle to the wild cows to sooth them. The farther the mossy horns move from the brush, the more nervous they get, and the fiercer they'll try to break away. Put the wild critters in the pen and take the decoys back into the brush for another hunt.

"Some punchers collecting wild cattle cut off a good piece of the horn, so they won't hurt each other or a careless cowboy. But I don't hold to that. The longhorn is a beautiful creature, and I won't maim 'em. Some of my pards have told me I'm daft to think of cattle as anything other than meat, but that don't bother me." He sniffed and wiped his nose with a sleeve.

"Anyway, collecting mavericks is a slow process.

Andy said we got a month to do all this. I assured him we ain't goin' to collect the five hundred head he said he wanted. Now, any questions for me?"

"Why do you call 'em 'mavericks'?" said Petey.

Silas turned to Petey, frowned, and Petey cringed, looking about. "Well, I'm told that a man named Maverick sold a herd to another man who let the herd scatter. Now, Maverick had neglected to brand the calves in the herd. When the new owner finally decided to collect his cattle, he brought in the calves for branding. Now, when he was collecting his cows and their unbranded calves, 'mavericks,' he called 'em, he saw lots of wild unbranded cows and calves. He decided that he would collect these as well and brand them. From this, a wild unbranded cow came to be called a 'maverick.' Make sense?"

"No," said Petey.

Silas grimaced, shook his head. He pointed to Andy, smiled. "What do you think, Andy? Are we ready to lock horns with a bunch of mavericks?"

"We'll do what we can," said Andy. "At least, we'll have some fun and earn a few dollars in the process. Eh, Silas?" Silas nodded.

NEXT MORNING, Josh rolled out of bed before dawn to help Jenny but found her already standing at a fire working on breakfast. He puttered around trying to find something to do until she shooed him away. "Go get dressed. You're not even buttoned up." He felt his trousers and was mortified that he had not buttoned them after going behind a bush outside camp.

He turned and worked on the buttons. "Sorry, not used to getting up in the dark. Still a little groggy."

He asked how he could help, and she said to check the level in the water barrel, encourage cowboys as they approached the wagon to pick up any kindling or dry chips to toss in the stretched cowhide under the wagon, take the plates and utensils from the chuck box, get ready to pour coffee. He wondered how long it would be before she would tell him gently to just stay out of her way. He smiled to himself.

After breakfast, he helped her with cleanup until she told him that she had everything under control. He asked if he could help with the mules. She straightened up from the dishes she was washing, hands on hips, looked at him and smiled, said nothing.

He raised a hand, palm outward, as if to say, I hear you. He walked to the remuda where several hands were saddling up. He found his mount, threw the saddle on, stopped, and stared at the horn. I could get used to seeing that girl, that woman, each morning. He looked down, solemn, and his dark mood returned.

Josh rode to the campfire where six mounted cowboys were gathered. Three other hands stood beside the fire that had died to embers. Josh looked back at Jenny who worked at the rear of the wagon, putting dishes and pans and skillet away. She looked up, waved to him.

Tim stared at Harley's foot. "What's that on your foot?" asked Tim, staring at the heavy leather cover over the front of Harley's stirrup. Other riders turned to look.

"That's tapaderos, my green young friend," said Harley. "They protect your feet from prickly brush and prevent the stickers from poking through the stirrup. All you boys are goin' to wish you had some before this cow hunt is finished."

"Yep, they're useful. Got 'em myself," said Silas. He raised a foot, displaying his tapadero.

"Okay," Andy said, "Silas will lead us to the spot he has picked out for the pen. We should get that up today and begin the cow hunt tomorrow. I know you don't like any work that can't be done from the saddle. You keep telling me this by words and scowls, but this won't hold us up long. Let's get on it."

They set off, Silas leading. Josh looked back and waved to Jenny, sitting on the wagon seat, waiting. She waved, shook the lines, and the mules moved off, following the passel of cowboys.

AFTER BREAKFAST, under Silas's supervision, the cowboys began building the pen. The work was accompanied by an undercurrent of grumbling since cowboys indeed abhorred any work that could not be performed on horseback. They dug a circular trench three feet deep and planted six-foot posts behind the trench. Strips of rawhide were stretched between the posts and tied. Just before the sun touched the tops of the line of mesquite in the west, the pen was finished.

The small decoy herd grazed on a patch of grass nearby.

Chatting about how happy they were to finish the onerous task of building the pen, most cowboys went to the campfire where they sat down heavily to rest and gab while waiting for supper. Two or three instead walked toward the chuck wagon, collecting dry sticks and buffalo and cow patties, and tossed the tinder into the stretched cowhide under the wagon. Most paused a moment to watch Jenny at her chores. Some paused too long, and she playfully brandished a heavy ladle, only sometimes smiling.

Harwood waited until the others had walked back to the campfire. After dumping his load of dry sticks, he smiled and reached for her arm or a breast. She whacked him hard on the hand.

"Get lost, little boy, or no supper for you!" She glared at him; ladle upraised.

"Damn, Jenny, that hurt." He rubbed the hand.

"Not as much as your head's gonna hurt if I bang you on an ear." He grimaced and walked away, rubbing the injured hand.

"I was about to ask if you needed any help," said Josh. He stood in shadow at the back of the chuck wagon. He stepped to the cook fire. "I see you don't."

She smiled. "No. But I 'preciate you keeping an eye out. Sometimes a little urge or a little alcohol makes even good boys act dumb." She smiled, bent over the bubbling pot of peeled potatoes, and stirred.

"I promise to never act dumb, Jenny."

She stopped stirring, paused a moment, and looked up. "Well." After another moment, she bent and stirred. "You could get a load of wood and chips from the hide and bring 'em over by the fire here."

He bent and scooped up an armful of sticks and chips from the hide and dropped them at the fire. He stood there, watching her.

She continued to stir, seemingly ignoring him. Minutes passed. Then, without looking up, "you got me undressed yet?"

He blinked. "Jenny, uh . . ."

She straightened, set the spoon on one of the stones of the fire circle. "Oh, come on, help me get this pot off the fire." She gave him a rag to use on the hot handle, and they lifted together, bent to set the pot on a flat stone beside the fire. Standing at her side, their shoulders touching, he looked down the front of her loose shirt. She turned her head, and they were nose to nose.

He kissed her lightly, then again, lightly. She put her hand behind his head and pulled him to her. They kissed again, lingering. Both straightened. He put his hands on her cheeks, bent and kissed her nose, her lips.

She cocked her head. "Took you long enough."

"Okay, boys, here we go." Silas led the cowboys into an opening in the line of mesquite. Monty and Tom followed, driving the decoy herd. They rode into a maze of scattered mesquite, avoiding clumps of prickly pear cactus and other thorned bushes. An occasional expletive from a cowboy who had ridden too close to a mesquite branch cautioned the others to be careful.

After fifteen minutes of riding at a walk into the green maze, Silas pulled up. "See that bunch up ahead? Five or six, I'd say."

"Where," said Tim. "I don' see nothin' but trees."

"Look straight ahead. See the tallest tree, the one with the dead branch at the top? Look to the left of the trunk, behind the large cactus?"

"Oh, yeah. I see 'em!" Said Tim.

"Okay," said Silas. "Monty and Tom will push the decoy herd toward the wild bunch, and we hope they don't bolt. While that's goin' on, we move up, two riding on the left, two on the right, and two going straight in." He looked aside. "Josh?" Josh nodded. "Josh, you and I go straight for 'em. If the wild critters try to bolt, we have them surrounded, sort of, and we try to keep them together. Okay?" The others muttered their understanding. "If we have a reasonably calm bunch at this point, we drive the combined bunch to the pen. Remember to sing to 'em. Even range cows seem to be soothed by music, even cowboy music."

Silas stood in his stirrups, turned, and waved to Monty and Tom. They returned his wave and began moving the decoy herd of twenty cows.

The six cowboys watched the decoy herd pass and move slowly into the dense brush where the range cattle stood.

"Okay," said Silas. "Slowly. A little soft singing or whistling is okay." They moved out, left, right, and straight ahead.

They had hardly begun to move when a loud rustling and stomping sounded from the thicket, followed by an eruption of longhorns crashing through the thicket and into the open, scattering the decoy herd and galloping past the cowboys who sat dumbfounded, watching the mossy horns disappear in all directions.

Cowboys, wide-eyed and open-mouthed, looked at each other.

"Well, that was no fun," said Josh.

"Happens," Silas said. "You don't collect 'em every time." He rode toward the thicket and stopped, shouted. "Come on out. We'll start over."

BY THE END of the day, the hands were exhausted and discouraged. They rode toward camp, drooping. Adding to their mood, they sensed an unwelcome change in the weather.

Heavy skies had darkened and lowered during the

day. By the time Jenny called the outfit to supper, a few large drops had fallen. The meal was served quicker than usual. Afterwards, hands hurriedly dropped plates in the wash bucket and pulled bedrolls and tents from the front of the chuck wagon. There would be no cards and storytelling around a campfire this evening, the usual prelude to retiring. Josh stayed at the chuck wagon to see if he could help Jenny.

Suddenly, the skies opened. "Josh! Get my tent outta the front." She ran to the back of the wagon and pulled out a bedroll. "No time to put it up. Under the wagon. Hurry up, hurry up!"

Josh hurried to the wagon seat, reached under, and pulled out Jenny's tent. He jumped down, threw the tent under the wagon, and crawled under. Jenny was already there on her knees. They spread the tent on the ground and then the bedroll on top. Sitting on the bedroll, they gasped, catching their breath.

The heavy rain pelted the wagon canvas, streaming off the sides. "Whew," Josh said. "Now what do we do?"

She laughed, lunged on top of him, and began unbuttoning his shirt. He pulled the bedroll over them and fumbled with her clothing, pulling off her trousers as she wriggled out of her shirt. They were soon naked in the folds of the bedroll, and the wind and lightning and furious deluge blended with their passion, and all was spent and finished and calm and serenity restored.

They lay on their backs, breathing deeply, his arms crossed on his chest. She rolled on her side to face him. "When I first saw you at the café, I knew you were mine."

He smiled in the darkness. "You probably didn't notice that I didn't say a word in the café. I couldn't."

"Oh, I noticed. It didn't take ten minutes before I felt naked. Were you working on that?"

He laughed. "Well. I did see the mole above your left tit."

She raised on an elbow. "You didn't! You couldn't! Oh, you felt it just now." He chuckled. She patted his cheek, the last pat a soft slap.

After a moment, "never knew a Josh," she said. "Where did your mama get the name?"

"Joshua, from the Bible. Josh-uh-way, Mama called it. She said that Josh-uh-way was a good man, lived to a hundred ten years old. She said I should try to live a long life, doing good. She said the preacher was happy she had chosen a name from the Bible and urged her to remind me as I grew up to remember my name was from the Bible.

"He was still the preacher as I grew up. He told us in Sunday School that everything that happens is part of God's plan. Nothing happens unless God wills it. I never forgot that. I believed it as a church-going kid. During the war, I thought about it and wondered how the killing of all those good boys fit into God's plan. If God loves us like the preacher always said, why would he decide to have all those good boys killed?"

They lay still, quiet. She touched his cheek. "Sure don't know about that. We weren't church-going. I think Daddy had some problems with the church. Every time Mama said something about going to church, he replied angrily that he wasn't going, and she shouldn't go. He would say that it's a waste of time."

After a long moment, she rolled over and kissed his cheek. "Tell me about Paris."

He took a deep breath. And told her. About his

leaving home to fight for the glorious cause of the South, the end of battles, and loss of friends. The emptiness, the guilt. The ride home, the expectation that he would be restored at the sight of his family and return to a semblance of a normal life after enduring everything that was not normal.

And he told her about the loss of his family and then lay still, silent. She wiped the tears from his cheek and held him as he sobbed.

Then he was still. He rolled over to face her. "Jenny?"

"Josh?"

"You saved my life."

She waited.

"Before I came to Fort Worth, I decided that there was nothing left for me. Soon as I got there, I bought new clothes and took a bath, the first I had in months. I decided I would have a good meal, walk out of town and end it. There was nothing left for me, and it was becoming too hard. Then I met you."

She leaned over and kissed him. He rolled over to face her, touched her cheek.

"Tell me about your family," he said. "I don't even know where you lived."

She lay back. "That's hard. I haven't talked about my family with anybody for years."

He waited.

"We lived on a farm outside Waco. My daddy and big brother got the gold fever 'bout ten years ago and decided that they had had enough dirt farming and would go to California and get rich. My mother wanted none of it but decided that she would have to go with them.

"I was a strong-willed kid, old enough to think for

myself and said I would stay with my Aunt Bertha. Daddy was okay with that, but Mama was shocked I would think of such a thing. But she liked her sister and trusted her and finally was okay with it, seeing that I was determined.

"So they went, and I stayed, and I never heard from them again. They never wrote to me, and I had no way of getting in touch. I told anybody who I learned was going to California to look for them, but never heard anything. I don't know whether they are alive or dead. I think Mama at least would have written to me. I cried for years. I've got no tears left."

She rolled over and rested her head on his shoulder. "You and I have this in common. We have nobody."

"You're wrong there. I've got you and, like it or not, you've got me."

So, it went with the outfit's introduction to cow hunting. The days that followed included failures, but some surprising successes as wild range cattle were soothed by mixing with the decoy herd and the singing of cowboys. Silas showed the hands how to handle a particularly cantankerous longhorn when he roped a steer and tied its head to a tree. The decoy herd was brought over, and the steer released into the center of it. It calmed immediately. On another occasion, following the same routine, when the mossy horn was released in the center of the decoy herd, it spun around right and left, charged the tame cows, and the decoy herd burst apart in all directions.

They sometimes hunted at night when the mossy horns emerged from the brush to graze. The range cattle were easier to approach at night when there was sufficient moonlight. The singing cowboy moved close to a cow and roped it. Roping was the slowest way to collect the wild bovines, but sometimes it was the only way.

Between hunts, hands munched on jerky and biscuits, or chunks of bread Jenny passed out after breakfast each day and they had pushed into saddlebags. Canteens filled from the water barrel on the side of the chuck wagon slaked their thirst.

Throughout the day, two or three cowboys pushed the combined bunch of captured mossy horns and decoy cows into the pen. The decoy herd was cut out and moved from the pen immediately. After a few days calming down in the pen, the range cattle would be branded and released to the growing herd that was closely watched on a nearby meadow.

At the end of every day, before turning mounts into the remuda, cowboys pulled thorns from their sides and legs and treated punctures with prickly pear juice. Evenings, they sat around the campfire, pulling thorns from clothing and skin, treating scratches and punctures with prickly pear juice and poultices of prickly pear leaves.

Hands were discouraged at first with the small numbers of cattle collected. On the first day, they took only twelve. Silas assured the hands that the day's work was not at all unusual, particularly for an outfit that had never hunted wild cattle. It's the first day, not the last day, he said more than once. Succeeding days were more successful as the cowboys became old hands at brush-popping.

They learned more from Silas about taking wild cattle than they wanted to know. On one occasion,

Silas roped a maverick that turned on him and charged him. The cow bumped his horse and almost unseated him.

"Somebody! Git over here, and git a rope on this beast!"

Toby, nearby, rode over and dropped a loop over the cow's horns, pulling him away from Silas. Harwood rode over, and Silas handed him his rope.

"Hold 'im. Pull 'im over to that tree," pointing to a large mesquite. Toby and Harwood with tight lariats walked the longhorn to the tree as Silas dismounted, taking a short rope from his saddle. With the rope, he tied the cow's head to the mesquite trunk. "We'll leave him be for a while to cool down."

An hour later, Silas and Harwood returned with a few head from the decoy herd and brought them to the tied longhorn, now still. Silas dismounted, untied the maverick, and moved it to the center of the decoys. The cowboys had no difficulty moving the bunch to the pen.

EXHAUSTED COWBOYS RECUPERATED SOMEWHAT each evening with Jenny's welcome supper. The only thing they had eaten since breakfast was boring everyday jerky and bread and canteen water. At supper, they consumed potatoes, beans, biscuits, and coffee. The meal usually included steaks sliced from a particularly uncooperative mossy horn that had to be killed or the occasional deer that had wandered too close to camp.

On this evening, sitting around the campfire after supper, smoking, and jawing, cowboys watched Silas who stood outside camp, staring at the ground. Josh and Petey stood and walked to him.

"What's goin' on, Silas?" They looked at the stack of clothes on the ground. Ants swarmed over the garments.

Silas looked up. "Maybe you boys ain't bothered by lice, but I am. If you look close, you'll see that the ants are removing the lice. I don't know whether they eat 'em or just carry 'em off. But they get rid of 'em. Then I wash the clothes and myself." He looked back at the anthill and the pile of clothes.

"Where did you learn this?" said Petey.

"Some Comanche showed me."

Josh and Petey watched a bit longer, then turned and walked back toward the campfire. "Wouldn't just washing the clothes get rid of the lice?" said Petey.

"Washing seems to work for me," said Josh.

Josh walked to the remuda where he tended to lacerations on his horse and himself, then went to the chuck wagon. He sat and leaned against a wheel, watched Jenny. He was exhausted.

"Good day? Bad day?" she said, bent over the cooking fire, stirring beans in a pot.

"Yeah. Bad day since we found more range cattle than usual and worked harder; good day since we caught a bunch of them, twenty-six, I think, and got them all to the pen."

She went to him and knelt, leaning against his crossed legs. Taking his face in her hands, she kissed him. "I been waitin' for you all day, you know. You gonna be too tired for playtime tonight?"

He smiled. "I'm never too tired for playtime, sweetheart. After your good supper and a couple of cups of strong coffee, I'll be as wild as a mossy horn."

. . .

One day that began like any other proved quite different. After moving the decoy bunch from the pen, half a dozen cowboys stood beside the enclosure, resting, smoking, jawing. They watched a dozen riders' approach who reined up on the other side of the pen. They were not smiling.

"Who are you? What are you doing here?" asked one of the riders.

Andy frowned. "Pleased to meet you, too. I'm Andy Bishop, boss of this outfit, and we're improving the neighborhood by removing some fierce animals." He smiled.

"Not funny. Never seen you before, and I don't think you're from the neighborhood. You're taking cattle that belong to ranches hereabouts. That's called rustling."

"Oh? We're taking no branded cattle and no calf that's following a mother cow. The cows we're taking appear to be mostly three or four years old or older."

"They're all from cattle that come from ranches hereabouts. They were left to wander when most of the young men volunteered and went off to war. Soldiers also came around and as much as forced 'em to go off to war. Then the army pretty much withdrew from frontier posts. After the army was gone, the Indians and Mexicans came in and scattered and stole our cattle. Now we're back and picking up where we left off. All these cattle belong to local ranchers, and we're takin' 'em."

Josh strolled slowly alongside the pen fencing till he came to the gate. He stopped, then walked a bit more till he had a clear view of the riders.

Andy pondered. "Tell you what. I don't agree that you own the cows that we're collecting, but I understand what you're sayin.' I'll pay you one dollar for each head we take. I don't agree that we have to, but I will. How 'bout that?"

"That don't cut it, mister. You're stealing what belongs to me and my neighbors! Now back away, all of you! We're taking these cows!"

Andy replied softly. "Now that would be called theft. You'd be stealing my property, and I won't have it."

"By god, move away, you damn rustler, or I'll put a bullet in you and be done with it." He pulled his pistol and aimed toward Andy.

"Put it down!" The riders looked aside at Josh whose pistol was leveled on the speaker. The man didn't move, his gun still pointing at Andy. Then suddenly he whipped around, leveled on Josh. In that instant, he was blown backward by Josh's shot and slid from the saddle to the ground. The other riders went for their revolvers.

"Don't!" shouted Andy. He and all of his men held pistols pointing at the riders. "Don't do this! It's finished!" The riders looked at each other and slowly pushed pistols back into holsters. "Tend to your man," Andy said.

Andy and Josh walked around the pen to the riders who dismounted and bent over their fallen leader who was gasping, his eyes tightly closed, a hand grasping his shirt at the shoulder.

"He's alive," said one who bent over him.

"Take care of him," said Andy. "Somebody give us an address, and I'll send the payment I promised. Sad business."

Chapter Four

"Well, boys, and Jenny, that ends our cow hunt," said Andy. "We can't risk the local yokels coming back in force." He sat with the others at the evening fire circle. Supper had been hurried and limited. Jenny had apologized and said she would make up for it tomorrow. The hands had smiled and said they would count on it.

As soon as the ranchers had disappeared around a dense stand of mesquite that afternoon, Andy gave the order to pack up and leave at once. Josh had helped Jenny put the mules in harness and on her way. The remuda was soon in motion, and the combined herd of decoys and range cattle followed. Cowboys were hard pressed to control the sometimes-unruly bunch, but each mile was easier than the previous mile.

"We were a week short of what we had intended," said Andy, "but we did okay, I think. How many did we get, Silas?"

"We collected about three hundred twenty-five. Not bad, considering that it was greenhorns collecting 'em." He smiled and slapped Paul's leg.

. . .

THE DRIVE to Fort Worth was punctuated by uncooperative range cattle wandering from the column or suddenly bursting from the herd and running all out for timber or brush. The wanderer usually was controlled easily enough, though if the cow continued to resist, it was tied by the neck to a member of the decoy herd until she could be trusted to stay in the column.

On a few occasions, a wayward mossy horn proved more difficult. After trying repeatedly to push a sturdy wanderer back to the herd, the cow turned on Silas and charged, crashed into his mount, almost unseating him, then raced away, bound for a thicket. Silas cursed the beast loudly and kicked his mount after him. Drawing alongside the cow, Silas seized her tail and wrapped it around his saddle horn. He drummed his mount's side with his heels, and the horse pulled ahead sharply and slightly aside. The mossy horn was pulled sideways, stumbled, and tumbled end over end. Silas reined up and walked his mount back to the prostrate cow. He dismounted and dropped a loop over the cow's horns. Mounting, he waited as the cow, considerably subdued, struggled to its feet and submitted to being led back to the herd.

The hands to a man watched all this, open-mouthed, as Silas released the cow to the herd. The chastised bovine moved into the center of the column as if this were its proper place.

"What th' hell, Silas!" said Tim.

"It's called tailing," Silas said, coiling his rope. "Don't like to do it 'cause it can break a cow's horns, or it can kill her. But sometimes you got no choice when a beast refuses to cooperate. You have to do it."

"I think I'll pass on tailing," said Toby. "I'll just shoot it instead and cut him into steaks for Jenny." He grinned, and the other hands mumbled agreement.

THE EASTERN SKY at the horizon was still streaked with pastel yellow and magenta layers above the sun ball that had just cleared the horizon.

"What do you think, boys?" said Andy. He spoke to the eight cowboys who stood with him at the pasture just outside Fort Worth. Some of the cows grazed; others lay on the green grass, chewing cuds. "They look in pretty good shape. Johnny said two thousand, and we'll confirm that with our own count. Paul, see to that."

Approaching Fort Worth yesterday, Andy sent Paul ahead to look for a good place outside town to put the herd while waiting for the Rio Grande contingent. Paul learned that the herd arrived two days ago, earlier than expected, and was being held on good grass on the western outskirts of town.

"They're ours right now," said Andy. "Three boys in the outfit that brought them up from the Rio Grande are joining us for the drive to Kansas. You'll meet them at supper. We're eating at the café. It'll be a nice homecoming for Jenny.

"We have less than three thousand head, so we're not gonna have a hoodlum, and you'll—"

"What's a hoodlum?" interrupted Tim.

Andy turned to him, frowned. "I forgot that you ain't never been on a long drive. When a herd numbers three thousand or so, the outfit usually has a second wagon that carries bedrolls, tents, and personal stuff. That's the hoodlum. Jenny carries that sort of stuff in the chuck wagon, and it's pretty tight."

"Oh," said Tim, "sorry."

"It's okay, son, you know lots more about handling cows than I did at your age. By the time we reach the railhead, you'll be ready to boss a drive." He smiled. "If you work hard, do your job, and don't get into trouble."

Andy turned to the group. "Be on your toes, boys. We leave at first light in two days' time. We want to be clear of Fort Worth on that morning before the locals throw back their bed covers. Each of you has eight good horses of your own choice, so you'll have nothing to complain about if they don't perform. We expect to make fifteen or twenty miles every day, and we'll get to the railhead in Kansas in good time.

"You need to be well-armed. You'll want a reliable revolver and rifle. If you don't have what you need, I'll advance the cost. I recommend the Colt six-shooter and the Henry rifle. You shouldn't have any problem finding them.

"Hate to tell you this right at the start, but if we get to Abilene without trouble of one sort or another, it'll be an unusual drive. If trouble hits before we reach Red River, the Texas Rangers will help us deal with it. In Kansas, we might be able to get help from a town lawman or a local posse. But in Indian Territory, we're mostly on our own. A few soldiers are stationed at scattered posts, but I'm not counting on much help from them. Friends who have been up this way say payment in tobacco and a cow or two are more help than the army.

"This don't mean that tobacco and a cow or two

will always get us clear passage. Some Indians in the Territory are still mad at the government about a treaty a few years ago between Washington and a bunch of tribes. The treaty was supposed to compensate tribes for a massacre by the army at a place called Sand Creek in Colorado. Reservations in the Territory were supposed to be set up, and tribes were going to be paid money. Didn't come to anything, and the Indians are still mad. I don't blame 'em. The point is, Indians in the Territory don't like the way they've been treated by white people in general. So we'll be on our toes."

The cowboys turned to leave. Andy caught Josh's sleeve. "Stay, need to talk to you." Andy waited till the others were out of hearing. He turned back to Josh and spoke softly. "Need you to do something for me. Something ain't right with this delivery. When I met the Mexico herd yesterday, Johnny gave me a quick report of picking up the cows at the Rio Grande and driving 'em here. I noticed that while he was telling me, the two fellas with him had the strangest looks like they had swallowed a frog that was tickling their insides. They finally had to leave, grinning from ear to ear, looking back at us over their shoulders. Something's going on here, Josh, and I want you to find out what it is.

"So here's what we're about. Johnny said his boys need to loosen up a little before starting off on the Kansas drive, and I recommended the Glass Slipper a few storefronts down from the café. I want you to mosey into the Slipper and drink some with 'em. They don't know you, and I've already told my hands here that they don't know you, in case any of Johnny's men ask. See if you can find out if there's something going on I don't know. Stay sober, hear, so you can tell me what you learn."

"You hit the nail on the head, boss." Josh and Andy stood on the boardwalk near the café. They waved to some of Andy's hands that were going into breakfast. "Johnny's boys thought I was just another drifter. I told them a story about what I been doing lately, and after a few drinks, they told me what they had been doing lately. In between fits of laughter, they told me that the money you gave Johnny to buy two thousand head actually bought two thousand four hundred head."

Andy recoiled. "Uh-oh."

"Yeah. One of the boys said he told Johnny that Andy was going to be real pleased with the transaction. Johnny didn't say anything at the time, but later told the boys that Andy expected only two thousand, and he considered the extra four hundred head a bonus for doing such a good job with this purchase. So Johnny decided to keep the four hundred head for himself."

"Well, well, well. I guess Johnny wasn't at the saloon last night?" Josh shook his head. "Where are the four hundred now?"

"Seems he dropped them off at his brother's farm, about ten miles south of Fort Worth."

"Hmm." Andy lowered his head, staring at the boardwalk. He raised his head, staring blankly across the street. He turned to Josh. "Too bad. Johnny's always been a good man. Now. . . here he comes."

Johnny and two of his men walked in the dusty road toward the café. They saw Andy and waved their arms in welcome. The two men walking with Johnny stopped, staring at Josh.

"Need to talk to you, Johnny," said Andy.

Johnny stopped, frowned, looked at his two hands who had stepped back, still staring at Josh.

"You stole from me," said Andy. "That won't do."

Johnny looked at his men who had stepped back again. They now moved sideways and stepped up on the boardwalk, staring at Andy and Josh.

"Four hundred head," Andy said.

Johnny winced. "Aw, boss, you gave me money to buy two thousand head, and I delivered two thousand head to you."

"My money also bought the four hundred head you stole. Why did you do it, Johnny? You've been a good man."

Johnny grimaced, shuddering. "Aw, boss, I just wanted my own place. I never had my own place. This was gonna be a start. I just kinda thought the four hundred head was a bonus for doing a good job."

Andy shook his head. "Send me one of your boys to take a few of my hands to pick up the cows. I'll decide what to do with you later."

Johnny straightened, frowning, his face contorted. "No! Those cows are a bonus for my good job. They're mine!" His hand hovered above his holster.

Andy shook his head slowly. "Don't do anything foolish, Johnny. I'm not giving you to the sheriff, though I could."

"By God, those are my cows, and you'll not git 'em!" He drew the pistol and was bringing it up when he was blown backward by a shot to the chest.

Andy jerked aside to see Josh lowering his pistol. They went to Johnny who lay on his back, the six-shooter still in his hand. Andy bent on his knee beside him. "Johnny, Johnny, Johnny, it didn't need to come to this."

Johnny blinked rapidly. He whispered, "I never had my own place. I only wanted . . ." His eyes fluttered and closed. His head rolled slowly to the side.

"Dammit, it didn't need to come to this," Andy muttered. "Dammit." He looked up to see Johnny's two hands and spoke to them. "Take him to the sheriff's office, down there." He pointed across the road, a few storefronts away. "Tell the sheriff or the deputy I'll be down later."

Johnny's men picked up the body and stumbled across the street as Andy and Josh watched. "We'll send some men to pick up the four hundred tomorrow. Josh, you go with 'em." He shook his head. "Sad business. If he had brought the whole herd and told me that story about wanting to have his own place, I might have given him a couple hundred head. He's been a good hand for years. I can understand a man wanting his own place." He shook his head again. "Sad business."

Josh was both excited and apprehensive as his first long drive got underway. He looked eastward to see the rim of the sun peeking above the horizon, turning the underside of the filmy cloud layers from gray to pastel shades of yellow, pink, and magenta. The sky overhead was still dark, gradually turning to a cloudless silver blue near the eastern horizon.

The herd now numbered something over 2,600. The Rio Grande two thousand, augmented by the 325 from cow hunting west of Fort Worth and 300 retrieved from Johnny's brother's place. Andy gave a hundred head to the brother, much to his surprise. Josh assumed it was not so much a generous gesture as the guilt he felt at Johnny's death.

Three of the hands from the bunch that drove the herd from the Rio Grande joined Andy's outfit, bringing the number of cowboys to twelve. Andy had rather sternly told them that he was still upset at the theft of the 400 head and at their silence when they arrived in Fort Worth. They would ride drag until he was sure of their loyalty.

The dozen cowboys that made now up the outfit were old hands for the most part. Though some were young in years, they were experienced in tending cattle. Most were bowlegged from hours every day in the saddle. They were confident and accomplished horsemen, handy with the lariat and six-shooter. Their wide-brimmed felt hats protected them from rain and sun, and their red bandannas, usually worn around the neck, could be pulled up over the nose and mouth to protect against dust and wind. Boots had two-inch heels to prevent the foot from slipping through stirrups. Some wore spurs, usually nickel-plated, but some with a bent for class chose spurs of silver.

Josh twisted in the saddle to look back. Fort Worth was a dark line on the horizon. He turned to the front and pulled the bandanna up to cover his nose. He was one of four at the back of the herd, charged with keeping the laggards at the rear moving. The dust at the drag position was not as bad as he had been told to expect. He guessed there was less dust because the grass on the trail had not yet been pulverized to dry dust by herds of cattle.

The herd moved over a landscape that was not yet marked by a recognizable trail. The tall spring grass was green and lush. Patches of bluebonnets and the scarlet Indian paintbrush colored the landscape along with yellow blossoms of wild mustard and white prickly poppy.

Since there was no identifiable trail, an experienced hand or two would be detailed each day to ride ahead to search out the route. They also looked for water, but at this early stage in the drive, their primary task was to find the best route. One of the hands would signal to the herd from a high point, employing a set of signals that Andy had coached them on. Most of the signals were simply motions with a hat. A man on horseback, on top of a rolling hill, could be seen for miles.

ON THE THIRD day after departure from Fort Worth, cowboys were bunched up at the chuck wagon, handing empty breakfast dishes to Jenny, jawing about the coming day, laughing, pulling out cigarette makings.

"That was a fine breakfast, Jenny," said Toby. "Even better than you served up in the brush country."

"Thanks, Toby," she said. She turned to the knot of cowboys that stood at the wagon, some beginning to walk away. She called loudly, above the mixed chatter and laughter. "Boys, before you go." They stopped walking and talking, turned back to Jenny.

"Just a few things," she said, "now that we're on our way and I'm moving every day, just so we understand each other. The routine will be a bit different from the brush country. Don't hang around the chuckwagon before a meal. Don't come till I call. When you're heading for the wagon, pick up dry wood and chips and toss them in the fly under the wagon.

"Andy tells me that from now on, the outfit eats dinner in shifts. Half comes to the chuck wagon while the other half stays with the herd. When the first shift is done eating, I understand they'll saddle up and ride to the herd, and the bunch there heads for the chuck wagon. We'll do the same at supper. Any problem with this, take it up with Andy, not me.

"During a meal, if you want more coffee, the pot is on the cooking fire. If I'm busy, pour it yourself. I hear that if you're pouring yourself coffee and somebody yells 'man at the pot,' you gotta pour for anybody who holds out a cup. Sounds like a good custom.

"When you're done eating, bring your plate to the wagon and scrape the leavins' in the slop bucket before putting it in the washing bucket."

Harley raised a hand. "Uh, Jenny, it's properly called the 'wreck pan.' I mention this only because this is your first experience with a chuck wagon."

A number of cowboys leaned back and glared at Harley.

Jenny frowned. "Since you been on a number of drives and have more experience than me in what to expect on a drive, Harley, maybe you'd like to take over the cooking. I bet I can handle cows better than you can handle fixing breakfast."

Harley smiled. "You got me there, Jenny. If the boys don't mind, I won't trade places with you." This was followed by snickers and forget-that-trade comments.

Jenny turned back to the group. "By the way, if there's anything left on your plate, I may ask you why." She smiled. "Before I go to bed, I'll put some chips on the fire, and the coffee pot stays on the embers all night in case some night herder needs a cup. Put the pot back on the embers when you finish."

"Uh, Jenny," said Toby, "if th' pot's empty when I come by in the middle of th' night, do I call you? Or Josh?" He pulled a face and looked at his pards for approval. Some smiled, looked at Jenny. She glared at Toby, pointed at him, her lips twitching to avoid a smile.

"Before you head for the remuda in the morning, be sure your blankets and tarp are rolled and tied and put in the wagon. I'm not doin' it for you."

Harley raised a hand. "That reminds me of what happened on a drive last year." Paul and Charley rolled eyes, and Harwood bent over, feigning collapse.

"All of the hands had dumped their dishes and were heading for the remuda," Harley said. "Cookie finished putting the wagon in order and the mules in harness and was ready to pull out. Then he saw some crumpled blankets and tarp near the wagon, not tied up neatly like they were supposed to be. Cookie had not had a good morning anyway, and now he was furious.

"So he wrapped the tarp and blankets around a wagon wheel and tied 'em on. When hands came to the wagon for dinner at noon stop, cookie showed everbody the results of the day's drive. The tarp and blankets were torn to shreds. Then he looked closely at the torn stuff and realized that they were his own." This resulted in a few guffaws.

"Thanks for that, Harley," said Jenny. "I'll keep that in mind."

Cowboys paid little attention to Harley's stories, but they had listened attentively to all of Jenny's comments, looking at each other occasionally, hiding a frown or a smile. Paul leaned over to Charley, whispered. "Never had a cookie give me instructions before."

"If you're headin' out early on a water search and don't have a particularly good sense of direction," said Jenny, "look at the wagon tongue. It's pointing north."

"If we don't know which way's north," said Tim. "how do you know, Jenny?"

"Good question, Tim. Before I go to bed, I find the North Star and point the tongue at it. The sky at night can be real interesting. Sometimes I find talking to the stars a lot more satisfying than talking to this bunch here."

"You talk to the stars?" said Tim.

"Sure. After supper sometime, walk with me outside the firelight, and we'll talk to the stars, you and me."

"I'll walk out to the dark and talk to the stars with you, Jenny," said Toby. Hands sitting nearby snorted.

Jenny stared at Toby and couldn't hide the hint of a smile. She turned back to the group. "When we're on the trail, I'll eat dust like everbody else. But when I'm fixing a meal, and the wind is blowing, and you're anywhere near the chuck wagon, be sure to come in downwind. The hands don't want your dust in their stew. Don't stop at the chuck wagon. Don't tie your reins to a wagon wheel. I don't want to be bothered by your mount, and I don't want to step in horse shit when I'm doin' my work.

"Okay, boys? You do your work, and I'll do mine. How's that?" She smiled. Some hands nodded, some smiled, joked, and commented. You said it, cookie; sure enough, Jenny; I'll mind as long as you feed me good. They chattered as they walked away, a couple looking back over shoulders.

Petey walked with Harley. "She's pretty sure of herself, ain't she?" said Petey.

Harley frowned, looked aside at his young companion. "Yep. Most cookies know where they stand in an outfit, and most of 'em let the cowboys know pretty quick where they stand. A hand I rode with once put it this way: 'Only a fool argues with a skunk, a mule, or a cookie.' A feisty cook on a drive I was on a couple of years ago said it like this: 'The space for fifty foot around my chuckwagon is holy ground, and I am the Almighty. If things go wrong, I will raise hell, and you will feel the heat.' Don't mess with cookies, young Petey." He clapped Petey on the back.

After all of the cowboys had gone about their business, Josh walked to Jenny. She looked at him, her face blank. She cocked her head. "Well?" she said.

"The boys like your cooking real well. Now they know the rules. But you must have noticed that not all of the boys like to be instructed by a woman."

"Doesn't bother me." She stepped up and raised her face to his, nose to nose. "What about you? Do you mind being instructed by a woman?"

He smiled. "This woman can tell me what to do all she likes. Then she can show me how to do it, and that's okay too."

PAUL SPENT SPARE MOMENTS, during nooning or at the end of the day, telling Josh about trail drive routine. "I wake Jenny up before sunrise so she can get busy with breakfast. Sometimes I get the night herder to wake me up, but it's usually the meadowlarks that wake me.

"Jenny leaves right after breakfast to get a head start so she can have dinner ready at the noon stop. You keep in touch with Jenny and help out any time she needs it.

"We always want to be sure the herd gets grass and water before bedding down so they will be ready to move the next morning. A thirsty or hungry cow ain't gonna be in no hurry to move in the morning. They can be just plain ornery. We bed the herd on high ground if we can find any. That way, we may get some breeze and the cows like that. Right after breakfast, we get the herd up and on the trail. Questions?"

"I saw a new calf this morning. What about the calves?"

Paul looked up. "Ah, Josh, that's a tough one that I hate to think about. Most mornings, we're gonna find calves on the bed ground. Sometimes it's the wolves sittin' near the herd that notifies us that we got a new calf or two. The little 'uns won't be able to keep up with the mothers once we get moving. The mother cow usually wants to stay with the calf, and we can't have that. We'd like to give the calves to somebody, Indians or, if we're in settled country, to farmers. This usually is not possible, so usually, we have to shoot 'em, much as we hate to."

"That's too bad. I'm not telling Jenny, and I hope she doesn't see any calves."

"Yeah. On drives when we have a hoodlum, sometimes we can carry a couple of calves in the wagon, but even that's not always an option. The hoodlum is usually packed."

Paul went on to describe the night herd routine. "I swear the cows know that the whistle of the whippoorwill that comes from the woods or the meadow about sundown means it's time to bed down. And they do. You watch and see if I'm not right.

"Then the cowboys take over," said Paul. He explained the routine. "Three watches are assigned to night guard, two cowboys in each watch. Night guards ride in opposite directions to cut off any wandering bovine. They sing or whistle to give the cows notice they are there and that all is peaceful."

Each night guard pair sleep beside each other so they could be awakened without disturbing the whole camp. For bedding, each person was allocated two blankets and a tarp. Like their yellow slickers, tents, and wagon canvas, the tarps were soaked heavily with linseed oil to turn rain. They used coats and boots for pillows and slept in their day clothes. Everyone in the outfit was assigned night guard, except Andy, the boss, Paul, second in command, Charley, the wrangler, and Jenny, the cook.

The wrangler was usually considered the bottom hand. In most outfits, the wrangler, sometimes called the rustler, was an oldster, past his prime, who couldn't handle the tough demands of a cowhand. Or he might be a young hand without much experience with cows or horses, still learning to be a cowboy.

Not so with Andy's wrangler. He wanted a top hand with horses who also knew something about herding cows. He had employed Charley for years and was satisfied he had the best.

Paul warned Josh that night herding often did not go as smoothly as his description suggested. During storms or stampedes, when the herd was milling or running, all hands were called out to help. "The biggest complaint of hands on a drive is loss of sleep.

If you intend to take part in long drives, learn to do your sleeping in the winter."

Josh learned something about horses and night riding on his first night. Andy had paired him with Harley so he could learn from an old hand. When they went to the remuda to saddle their night horses, Josh roped the horse he had selected as his night horse and was busy saddling it when Harley stopped what he was doing, holding his loose cinch.

"That your night horse?" said Harley.

"Yeah, she's a nice, quiet little girl. She even seems to like my singing."

"You ain't ridin' that horse with me."

Josh looked up, frowning. "Why do you say that? She's my night horse."

"Not if you're ridin' with me. She's white."

Josh cocked his head. "That's an accurate observation, Harley. She is indeed white. What is it with you and white horses?"

"You obviously don't know that white horses attract lightning."

Josh was becoming a bit annoyed with the tenor of the conversation. "Harley, that's pure nonsense. Horse color has nothing to do with anything."

Harley squared his shoulders, also seemingly annoyed at his night pard. "And you been ridin' night herd and doing long drives how long?"

Josh slumped. "Well, it's all bullshit, but if it means so much to you, I'll pick another horse. Does roan qualify for night riding? My roan has a few white hairs, but not enough to get hit by lightning, I think."

Harley worked on his horse's cinch. "The roan'll do." He leaned against his horse, his head resting on his saddle as he stifled a snort.

Saddling finished, they mounted and walked their horses toward the herd. After a minute, Harley turned toward Josh, frowned. "You don't smoke, do you?"

"No."

"Okay, just checkin.' Don't ever strike a lucifer on night herd. Cows might ignore it, or they might go plumb loco. I've seen cows jump up and run in all directions when they see a lucifer flame up on a dark night.

"Night herd on the usual night is real quiet and still. You should be singing or whistling most of the time, but it can still get pretty sleepy. You have to fight it. If you drop off, and your horse wanders, that can mean trouble. I've never had much trouble, but I've known fellas to try all sorts of ways to keep awake. One fella I rode with, put tobacco in his eyes to stay awake. I tried that just once and felt my eyes was on fire."

They rode in silence as they approached the herd. Harley looked up at the sky, blue black, and filled with bright stars. "I'll sure enough get you checked out on night herding, and if you're nice to me, I might teach you the names of some stars and constellations." He looked at Josh who ignored the comment.

"There's the Big Dipper, straight up." He pointed, and Josh looked up. "Now follow the curve in the dipper's handle, and you see a real bright star. That's Arcturus. You won't forget the name, Arcturus, because you followed the arc, the curve, of the Big Dipper's handle to get to it. If you learn certain stars and planets, you can actually tell time by them stars when they come up or go away."

"Are you making this up?" said Josh.

"Nope, I'll show you my book when we get back to

Fort Worth." They rode at a walk, Harley still searching the heavens. "Somewhere up there, my young friend is the Sweet Bye and Bye. We cain't see it, but it's there."

"What is it, this Sweet Bye and Bye?"

Harley didn't answer immediately. He sniffed and turned aside, looked back into the heavens. "It's where the good folks go when they cross over. It's where I hope I'll be goin' when the time comes."

They rode quietly. Josh looked aside at his pard. The bright moonlight highlighted his lined face, the square jaw and wild hair flowing from under his hat brim.

"What does it look like, this Sweet Bye and Bye?" said Josh.

"Hell, I don't know. Never been there and never talked to anybody who's been there. But I know it's a place where there's no troubles. No stampedes, no river drownings, no lightning storms, no rustlers, no gun-happy drunks, no Indians except them that are satisfied enough with some tobacco, and a beef or two." He cleared his throat. "And it's where you'll meet the good old boys who have already crossed over." He wiped his face with a sleeve. "It's where I want to go at the final roll call. Soon."

Josh reached over and slapped Harley's shoulder. "You're not goin' anywhere but that herd up ahead, pard. We better get up there, or the night herd is going to be upset if we're tardy."

Harley glanced aside at Josh, then to the heavens. "There's one more star you need to know about, though you can't see it right now. When we get changed to the last night guard, you'll sure want to be able to find the Morning Star. When you see the

Morning Star, it means that Cookie is starting breakfast." He leaned over and clapped Josh on the back.

Josh smiled. "Harley, you're the biggest bullshitter I ever knew, and I love yuh."

Harley smiled, a hint of a smile, a sad smile. "You're on to me, young friend. But it ain't all bullshit." He looked up into the void. "I have seen the elephant, and I have heard the owl. Sometimes I'm scared to even think about tomorrow."

EVERYBODY, except the same cowboys who were exempt from night herding, rode in the various positions around the herd during the day. The trail boss, Andy or Paul, rode at the front. A point man rode on each side of the herd near the front. About halfway back, a swing rode on each side. About halfway between swing, and the back of the herd were the flank riders on each side. Two or three cowboys' rode drag at the back, eating everybody's dust. Cowboys were moved around the positions after completing an initiation at drag. A hand who had displeased the boss might find himself returned to drag for a spell.

Charley rode behind the remuda, keeping the horses in a bunch with little trouble. On very dry or stormy days, he might ask some hands to help. Horses had been added in Fort Worth, increasing the number to about a hundred horses, a figure that gave each cowhand eight mounts.

ANDY AND PAUL emphasized to the hands, some who were on their first drive, that they should identify each horse's strong points early. Which one is the best night horse, the best swimmer, the best cutting horse, the one that would bear up best on a long, dry ride?

On most nights, horses were loose. At first light, Charley was out rounding up the remuda and pushing the horses into a rope corral, made up of several lariats tied together and attached to trees or stakes. Charley impressed on the hands, especially those new to the long drive, that horses in a remuda were not pets, and no one could walk up to them and throw on a saddle. It was already well known that Harley and Toby were the best ropers, so cowboys customarily asked them to rope their mounts so they could saddle and bridle them. Harley expected to be repaid with smokes. Toby was content with a smile and a thank-you.

To some hands on their first drive, the rope corral was ridiculous. "Charley, that wouldn't keep a little kitty from walking away," said Petey on first seeing the corral.

"Well, my big horses are smarter'n your little kitties," said Charley. "They do break out sometimes, like in a thunderstorm, or an Indian raid, or a buffalo stampede, or the like. When that happens, you'll be helpin' me to round 'em up."

As EXPECTED, Josh rode drag at the beginning. He wore his bandana tied around his face, covering mouth and nose, but the dust wasn't as bad as he had been told to expect. He had leisure even to enjoy the ride. He only had to keep the laggards moving and in line and had more time to study the cattle.

All he had seen before was a cow or a mossy horn; now he saw a distinctive bovine. He concluded that longhorns were magnificent creatures. They had wide-spreading horns, as long as six feet. They were big-boned, stout, with long legs and hard hooves. He had never really taken note of the great variety of colors. White, roan, red, black, brindled, yellow, most often a combination of patches and splashes of color. A magnificent creature.

Even the routine of the drive, new to him, took on poetic nuances, though he would not likely have described it as such. From the drag position, when a breeze kept the dust from obscuring the view, the sun sparkling on the wide horns and the herd strung out a mile ahead was a pretty sight.

The drive early on was without incident, boring almost, according to some of the cowboys who had been on other drives. The mossy horns provided some diversion. Occasionally a range cow that had been collected in the brush country had the notion to leave the herd and simply walked away. If it didn't respond to a cowboy's attempt to return the errant bovine to the column, it was roped and tied by the neck to a docile cow that had been part of a herd since leaving the Rio Grande. The two would be separated only when the range cow was semi-domesticated.

After the third day, Josh was moved from drag up to the flank position. A rider at this position on each side of the cow column was tasked with keeping the herd compact and moving ahead. Josh was right proud that he had been moved while the other two beginning drag riders had remained in that position. He was puzzled what he had done to warrant the quick move.

The next day appeared the best of days thus far. The drive began under a high gray overcast, and the cattle were almost frisky in the brisk cool breeze. The cows appeared to be in such good condition that cowboys were hard pressed to keep the herd compact and moving. So it went in the morning and the afternoon.

At dusk, the herd was thrown onto the pasture Andy had chosen for the bedding ground. It was a choice location with good grass and a creek nearby, but he did not appear to be content. Josh was headed for the remuda but stopped when he saw Andy sitting his horse quietly, looking westward.

Josh followed his gaze. "Weather?" said Josh.

"Don't like the looks of the dark clouds at the horizon."

Black clouds in the west churned, enlarging and moving slowly eastward. Tiny flashes of lightning briefly illuminated the clouds, and an occasional short, forked bolt shot from the dark mass. The angry cloud enlarged and moved faster, accompanied by brighter lightning flashes and low, rolling thunder.

Andy turned in the saddle and shouted toward the herd. "Weather coming! Be ready!" He rode to the bedding ground, shouting the warning. He reined up and looked to the west. The breeze had stopped completely, and the still air suddenly became warm and humid. Riders who had been enjoying the cool breeze only moments ago now wiped sweat from their faces with bandanas.

The black cloud moved and enlarged until it was directly overhead, boiling and lowering. Thunderclaps became louder, and lightning flashes more frequent and brighter. At the same time, a thick mist rose from the ground, reducing visibility and blurring the herd and other riders.

Josh watched wide-eyed as electrical streaks danced about the ears of his horse and the horses nearby and the horns of cattle, sparkling, glittering, briefly illuminating shapes and bodies. "What th' hell is happening?" he said to no one in particular.

"Stick with 'em, pard, later," said Harley, riding alongside, dodging terrified longhorns that charged horses and other cows.

Suddenly a massive lightning flash lit up the entire meadow, then vanished, and the night was blacker than before. Any cattle that were not already in motion, moved off the bedding ground, first at a lumbering trot, then advancing to a hard run.

Andy shouted to the darkness. "String 'em out! Turn 'em to the right! Get a mill going!" Cowboys now rode in total darkness, hoping their horses did not step in a hole, likely breaking a leg and injuring, possibly killing, the rider.

Cowboys, experienced and heeding Andy's shouts, were able to turn the stampeding column in a wide arc to the right until the lead steers curved back and merged with the bulk of the herd. The resulting mill soon calmed as the storm clouds softened and moved off. The ground fog evaporated, and a cooling breeze picked up. Cowboys looked up at a bright moon that suddenly illuminated the meadow and the milling herd, now settling, some already bedding down.

Josh sat his horse beside Harley. He inhaled deeply. "Whew. What hell was goin' on?"

Josh saw Harley's smile in the bright moonlight. "St. Elmo's fire," Harley said. "I ain't got the faintest idea who St. Elmo is or what he has to do with what happens like that during storms, but that's what it's called. The hissing and sparking don't seem to hurt the animals or people. That don't mean that lightning cain't hurt people. Lightning kills people. I was in a lightning storm where a boy was killed. Sad business. I was knocked off my horse in that same storm and knocked plumb unconscious. I lay on the ground while a couple of hands and a hard rain woke me up."

Jenny served a late supper. Exhausted hands sat mute at the campfire, eating. There would likely be no stories, jawing and singing at the campfire this evening.

On the other hand, Harley could not pass up an opportunity. "That was a bad storm, sure enough, but at least we didn't git any hail. Hailstorms are the worst, and I've been through the worst. Couple years ago, when I was working in the panhandle, we had a hailstorm to end all hailstorms. The hailstones were as big as your fist and so thick you couldn't see five feet. That storm killed two dozen cows, half a dozen horses, and two cowboys. It woulda killed me if I hadn't took my saddle off my horse and put my head and shoulders under it. Real story, '65 in the panhandle, you can check on it." He looked around for confirmation.

Cowboys stared glassy-eyed at Harley. They stood, grunting, walked to the chuck wagon, dropped plates and cups in the wash pan. Pulling bedrolls from the wagon, they staggered back to the fire circle where they dropped their beds.

Josh walked with Paul toward the chuck wagon. "Any idea how many we lost?" Josh said.

"Can't say. We got 'em into a mill pretty quick, considering, but the boys said they saw a few that didn't follow the rules and broke away from the column. We'll have a look in the morning." He drew on his cigarette. "We were lucky. Any stampede's bad, but I'll always compare my experience with the story I heard about a herd in Texas just last year.

"A night storm just like we had, lightning and

thunder and St. Elmo's fire, set a herd of two thousand head running. They stampeded over a cliff into a gully, and every head was lost. Every head." He dropped the cigarette and smashed it with a boot. "Every head."

Josh dropped his plate into the wash bucket and offered to help Jenny. She told him to get the bed ready before he collapsed. She finished up and crawled into bed beside him. She kissed him and said they could skip playtime tonight and do double duty tomorrow night.

"Okay," he said. After a long moment: "Jenny?"
"Josh?"
"Did you ever hear of St. Elmo's fire?"
"No. What's that?"

He proceeded to tell her about St. Elmo's fire so animatedly that she decided that he had completely recovered from the day's ordeal and was up to playtime after all.

Chapter Five

ANDY ANNOUNCED at breakfast that they would not stop at noon for dinner. He wanted to reach Red River tomorrow if possible, and they had to make good time today. Several cowboys, listening to this, commenced stuffing biscuits into coat pockets. By supper time, they expected to be exhausted and starving. Jenny always cooked enough sourdough biscuits before breakfast to last all day, so the supply was ample.

Andy stood with Jenny and Josh beside the chuck wagon. "Jenny, I told you a while back that I hoped to get you restocked before crossing the Red. An old hand in Fort Worth, the same who gave me the sketch map, told me about this little crossroads settlement a few miles south of the Red called Eagle Springs. It should be just four or five miles east of here. Seems it was an Indian village until settlers began moving in and making farms. This friend didn't know for sure, but he said that there should be a store selling groceries and other goods to these settlers.

"We'll give it a shot. I want you and Josh, and one

more hand—take Petey—to drive the chuck wagon to Eagle Springs. This Fort Worth friend said there was a wagon road that ran from the settlement to the Red. You should be able to drive there and meet us at the Red before sunset. Sound okay?"

"Sure," she said.

"Okay, move out. It's gonna be a long day."

"Thanks for bringin' me along," said Petey. "It's nice to be doin' somethin' else than following cows." Petey and Josh rode alongside the wagon driven by Jenny.

"We brought you along so you could protect us," said Josh. "Keep your six-shooter loaded and handy." He smiled.

Petey frowned. "You expectin' trouble?"

"Nah, just be ready. We don't know what to expect when we go someplace we don't know."

"I'll be ready for anything, Josh." He grinned, straightened tall in the saddle.

After little more than an hour, they saw a cluster of buildings ahead. Eagle Springs? Extensive fields of growing crops surrounding the town suggested a thriving settlement.

They rolled down the dusty road between a line of four buildings on the right side and three on the other. A sign on the last building on the right identified it as Enfield Mercantile. Jenny pulled up in front of the store. Josh and Petey dismounted and tied their reins to the hitching rail.

The street was empty but for two bewhiskered men across the street, dressed roughly in soiled shirts and trousers of skins. They stood motionless on the boardwalk, staring at the wagon and the newcomers. The reins of two horses and a packhorse were tied to the rail before them.

"Petey, go inside with Jenny," said Josh. "I'll stay." He leaned against the wagon as Jenny and Petey went into the store.

The two men walked slowly across the road, looking with considerable interest at the mules and wagon.

"Nice outfit you got there," said one of the men.

"Yeah, it suits us."

"Who you with?"

"We're the chuck wagon for a cattle outfit a few miles west. We're heading for Abilene. You fellas farm hereabouts?"

"Farm?" He looked at his companion, laughed. "Hell, no. We hunt buffalo. Hunting's been pretty good up in Indian Territory. We had a load of tobacco to pay off the bucks who think the buffalo belongs to them."

"They do like their tobacco."

The buffalo hunter rubbed his whiskered chin, staring at the wagon. "Problem is, we lost most of our packhorses to the savages. Now we got no way to get the hides to the railroad. We need packhorses. Or a wagon."

"Yeah, you got a problem. I hear most tribes in the Territory have plenty of horses. We lost some of our mounts in a stampede and hope to buy some from Indians. Might find our lost horses among theirs."

"We're not on the best of terms with bands where we been huntin.' They wouldn't likely give us the time of day." He looked back at the wagon. "How about selling us your wagon?"

Josh straightened. He looked toward the store, back

to the speaker. "Couldn't do that. A dozen hungry cowboys in camp would lynch us."

The man nodded, stepped back, looked at the wagon again. He turned and walked to his companion. They strolled across the street toward their horses, talking softly.

Josh stepped up on the boardwalk to the door of the mercantile. Opening it, he saw Jenny and Petey at the counter. "Jenny, are you about done? We need to get on the road." He waved to the man behind the counter who returned the wave.

Jenny turned. "Done. Come help."

Josh strode to the counter, hefted a bag, while Petey picked up a large sack, and Jenny took a smaller bag from the counter.

"Thanks, folks," said the grocer. "I'd appreciate it if you'd pass the word to other drovers that we're here."

"We'll do that," said Josh over his shoulder as he hustled to the door. He held the door open for the others. They stowed the goods behind the driver's seat, and Jenny climbed up. Josh and Petey mounted, and they moved off, Jenny turning the team around in the street to head west.

The two buffalo hunters, standing on the boardwalk where their horses were tied, watched the wagon and riders pull away. Josh moved his mount up beside the wagon seat. Petey rode on the other side of the wagon.

"What did we get?" Josh said.

"Got a good sack of flour, dried apples, some spring onions, a little keg of molasses, and a sack of potatoes that we'll have to use soon. They don't look too good. We also got something I didn't expect. Eggs!

Three dozen. Storekeeper got 'em just this morning from a farmer who's growing his hen herd. We were lucky, and the boys will enjoy eggs for breakfast. And how about apple pie for supper?"

"Yeah!" Petey said.

"That's all good. Now listen, I expect trouble." He told them about his encounter with the buffalo hunters. "Ready, Petey?"

Petey grinned, patted his six-shooter's holster. "Ready, boss!"

A light rain began to fall. Josh pulled his hat down and his collar up. The rain settled the dust on the road, and the mules' hooves soon sent up tiny bursts of wet dust.

They had hardly left Eagle Springs behind when the two buffalo hunters walked their horses from behind a sagebrush thicket into the road ahead of the mule team. They held pistols leveled loosely on Josh and Petey. Jenny pulled up.

"I tried to buy the wagon," said a hunter, "but you weren't havin' it. Now I'll just take it off your hands for nothin.'" He grinned. Jenny glared at him.

He looked up at Jenny, the pistol still pointing at Josh. "I just might decide to take your mule skinner with me. The boys will be happier with her than the wagon."

His companion snorted. "Alvord, I thank that's a good idea. Let's do it. She might give us some pointers on drivin' mules. Been a long time since I done that. She might also be of service in other ways. I ain't done that in a long time too." He grinned at Jenny who glared at him.

"Slow down, Baumgartner," said Alvord. "I'll decide on what's going on here."

Baumgartner frowned, turned aside.

"We're taking the wagon and the driver," said Alvord, "and I also think it's a good idea to take the boys along as well. Otherwise, I'd have to shoot 'em on the spot since they might decide to come after us soon as we git outta sight. They can help load the hides. Then we can decide what happens with 'em."

He spoke to Josh and Petey. "Here's what we're gonna do. You two boys are going to put your six-shooters in the wagon, real careful. Some of the boys in our camp need pistols. Then you're gonna ride beside the mules, one on each side. Me and Baumgartner here are going to ride behind you, one on each side, with our pistols aimed at your backside." He looked up at Jenny. "Little missy, I'll give you directions on where to go, and you do it, or we'll shoot your boys. Everybody understand?" Josh and Petey nodded. Jenny simply glared at him. He smiled.

When the four riders were in position, Alvord pointed northward off the trail. "Missy, see that break in the line of trees I'm pointin' at?" She nodded. "Drive to the break. No funny stuff, remember if you want these boys to keep breathin' natural. Now go."

Jenny looked at Josh who sat his horse on the left side of the team. He nodded. She shook the reins, pulling to the right off the trail, pointing at the indicated break in the line of trees.

"Looky what I got!" called Alvord. Half a dozen scruffy men dressed in worn and soiled skin shirts and pants stood at the remains of a campfire, watching the approach of the wagon. A stack of buffalo hides taller than a man rose behind them. Bits and pieces of a shoddy camp were scattered about.

"I do declare," said a man at the fire circle, grinning broadly, "a wagon pulled by a team of fat mules and a pretty piece of merchandise."

At Alvord's instruction, Jenny pulled up at the stack of hides and waited. He dispatched others to tie Josh and Petey to a tree trunk near the fire circle where a man was building a fire. Dismounting, Alvord handed his reins to a young hunter who had not taken his eyes off Jenny since she drove into camp.

Alvord walked to the wagon and looked up at Jenny. "Missy, I'm gonna have to tie you with the others for now. Not for long. We're gonna talk and do some other stuff, you and me, a while later." He grinned, looked aside. "For now, I'm hungry enough to eat a bear's insides."

Alvord slapped the boy who stood nearby, still staring at Jenny where she sat on the wagon seat. "Close your mouth, Eddie. Your jaw's gonna fall off. Tie her near the others, not with 'em, but near."

Eddie rubbed his cheek. "Don't talk to me like that, boss. I ain't a kid."

Alvord frowned, hands on hips, leaning toward him. "You ain't a kid? You're a snot-nose baby. And you can stop lookin' at this woman like you'd like to have a piece of her. She'd eat you up and spit you out." Alvord walked away.

Eddie reached up for Jenny. She brushed his hand aside and climbed down. He motioned toward the tree where Josh and Petey were tied. He walked her to a tree about six feet from them. "Sit here," he said, "I gotta tie you up. Sorry." She frowned, glanced at Josh.

. . .

The sun disappeared behind the surrounding wood, and soon the only visible images were those illuminated by firelight. The three captives watched the hunters silently chewing on roast meat they had pulled from skewers over the fire. Juices dripped from mouths to shirt fronts and trousers. They wiped mouths with sleeves and rubbed greasy hands on trouser legs.

Alvord leaned back, stretched, and yawned. He looked toward Jenny. "Missy, I had some good fun planned with you for this night, but I'm bushed and need to head for the barn. You wait right there, and I'll be back for you tomorrow, maybe before breakfast." This was met by snickers from the other men sitting around the fire.

"She's been waitin' for some fun, boss," said Baumgartner. "Maybe I oughta satisfy her while—"

Alvord's face turned red. "Stay away from her, Baumgartner! Everbody! I git her first! You yahoos can have a piece after I've finished. If I find anybody touches her tonight, I'll cut him up. Got it? Everbody?"

The hunters nodded between bites. "Just havin' a little fun, boss," said Baumgartner softly, staring into the fire, wiping his mouth.

Alvord struggled up, stumbled from the fire circle, and disappeared in the bushes beyond the firelight.

"Sumbitch cain't talk to me like that," said Baumgartner softly.

Jenny was suddenly wide awake with a pistol muzzle pushed into her cheek. In the soft moonlight, she saw the man holding the pistol bending over her.

Baumgartner whispered in her ear. "Don't you

make a noise, or you're dead. And I'll shoot your two friends as well." While holding the pistol at her cheek, he worked on untying the rope with the other hand. That done, he pulled her up and guided her past the wagon to the bushes. Breathing heavily, he reached under her arm and touched a breast. She pushed his hand away, and he grasped her arm.

Inside the dense bushes, he pushed her roughly to the ground, still pointing the gun at her. In the darkness, he was a black specter, hovering over her. Holding the pistol at her belly, he bent and worked on the buttons to her trousers with a trembling hand and pulled the pants down.

While he fumbled with the buttons on his trousers, she raised a knee, reached inside a boot, and pulled out the six-shooter. He was pushing his pants down when she fired, striking him in the chest, blowing him backward.

The camp was suddenly alive with shouts and rushing about.

"Who shot?" It was Alvord. "Where's the woman?" He shouted into the darkness. "If you're alive, say somethin.' Don't do nothin' funny, or your two men are gonna die."

A long moment passed. "Here," Jenny called. She stood, pulled up her pants, and buttoned them. Pushing the pistol back in her boot, she walked from the bushes. In the bright moonlight, she saw Alvord and the others standing near the fire circle, watching her. She also saw Josh and Petey still sitting, tied to the tree, silently watching her.

Alvord walked past her into the bushes. He came out a moment later, laughing. He walked past Jenny to the fire circle. "Baumgartner's in there laying on his back, with his pants down and a bullet hole in his belly." He turned to Jenny. "You are somethin' else, missy. Where'd you get the gun?" She said nothing, just glared at him.

"Oh, my," he said. "We plumb forgot about the two six-shooters we put in the wagon when we first met these folks." He held out his hand. "Let's have it."

She just stared at him.

"You don't understand, do you? I could take that gun off you, but if you don't do what I say, I'll kill these two right now, then I'll let every man in this camp have a piece of you before I kill you. Now, do I get that gun?"

She bent, pulled the six-shooter from her boot, and handed it to him.

"That's better." He took the pistol and tossed it toward the hunters at the fire. He spoke to the group. "Now me and this fireball are goin' out there outta sight of you yahoos, and we're gonna rassle. After I finish, she's yours." The others laughed and shouted, slapping backs and shoulders. One man did a little impromptu dance.

Alvord looked to the east. "Sun's comin,' and we'll need to get on our way. Pull all the stuff outta the wagon, and git the hides loaded. Soon as we get done with the breakfast fun, we need to git away. Some-body's gonna come lookin' for these people." Alvord gripped Jenny's arm tightly and walked toward the bushes.

Suddenly shots and yells and the sounds of galloping horses rose below the camp. Alvord released Jenny and ran toward the fire circle where the other buffalo hunters rushed about in confusion. Jenny ran toward camp behind him.

Six cowboys galloped into the camp, six-shooters pointing at the hunters, and reined up sliding. Hunters who had found their guns dropped them and raised their hands.

The cowboys saw Josh and Petey where they were tied. "Where's Jenny?" said Paul.

"Right here," Jenny said, as she walked into camp, "and that's the top dog over there," pointing at Alvord. She walked toward Josh and Petey. "Give me a hand, somebody." She worked on the knots that held Josh. Pedro dismounted hurriedly and went to untie Petey.

Josh struggled up, leaning momentarily on the tree trunk. Then he walked slowly to Alvord. "The best thing that ever happened to you, you son of a bitch, was these boys riding into your camp. Because if they hadn't, I was going to get loose somehow, and I was going to cut you into little pieces."

Alvord sneered. "Yeah, you talk big when you got all the guns."

Josh glared at him, then turned aside. He held out a hand to Jenny. "Jenny, give me my gun, and give him yours."

"What're you doing, Josh?" said Petey. "He's a mad dog. You shoot mad dogs." The other cowboys had dismounted and still had pistols trained on the hunters. They mumbled their agreement.

Jenny retrieved Josh's six-shooter from the wagon and walked back to him. She looked him in the eye, paused a moment, then handed the gun to him. Josh motioned with his head toward Alvord.

She walked to the hunters at the fire circle. "Who's got it?" A hunter handed her a pistol. She examined it, confirmed that it was her six-shooter. She went to

Alvord and offered it to him. He looked at it, looked up at Josh, and took the pistol.

Paul frowned. "Don't do this, Josh. It makes no sense. He ain't worth it. Just shoot him and be done with it."

Josh pondered. "Now how are we gonna do this?" After a moment, he pointed at Alvord. "You go over to the hides, and I'll stay right here. Everybody else move back. We're going to face away from each other. Paul, you count to three. On three, we turn around and fire away." He pointed at Alvord. "Got it?"

Alvord frowned. "Yeah." He walked to the hides, faced away from the camp.

"You sure about this?" said Jenny. He nodded, walked to the fire circle, and stood there, facing away from Alvord.

"All right, all set?" said Paul. He looked back at Josh. "I sure don't like this, Josh. It's madness.

"Count," said Josh.

Paul shook his head. "On my count of three, after I say 'three,' turn and fire." He turned toward Josh, who faced away from him. "Josh, this is crazy. You don't need to do this. Just shoot the bastard, and it's finished."

"Count," Josh said.

The silence was complete in the camp. Only soft birdsong from somewhere in the nearby treetops broke the silence.

Paul shook his head. "Okay. Ready? One. . . two. . ."

Alvord whirled around and fired. But the pistol didn't fire, it only clicked. Alvord's jaw dropped. Josh turned around slowly and leveled on Alvord.

Suddenly a six-shooter barked, and Alvord

collapsed. Everyone turned to see Eddie lowering his six-shooter. "Sumbitch," he said softly and dropped the pistol to the ground.

Paul looked from Eddie to Josh, who held his six-shooter at his side. "We're done here," said Paul. He spoke to the hunters. "You fellas are lucky we don't take your horses and shoot the lot of you. But I guess you're trying to make a livin' and fell in with the wrong boss. We're taking all your guns, and we'll drop 'em on our track a couple of miles from here. I suppose you may need 'em. And you still got them hides to transport. Good luck with that since you ain't got no wagon now."

While the cowboys collected all the guns in camp, the hunters paced about the fire circle, forlorn, looking blankly at each other.

Josh and Jenny went to the mules that grazed on a patch of grass outside camp. They removed hobbles and walked them to the wagon where they worked on putting them in harness.

"How'd you arrange that?" Josh said.

"You don't think I would give him a loaded gun, do you?" She smiled. "After I shot the fool, I knew they would take me and my gun. I dumped the shells before they came for me."

He smiled, shook his head. "Jenny, Jenny, you are somethin' else. I'll never figure you out. And that's good." He went to her, put his arms around her, and held her. She dropped the lines and hugged him.

"I had to be sure you would ride with me back to the herd," she said. "I wouldn't want to have to choose between Harwood and Toby to take your place."

"Miss, uh, Jenny?"

Jenny and Josh turned to see Eddie.

"Eddie, is it?" said Josh.

"Yes, that's right, Eddie."

"You did me a service, Eddie. I was about to kill that fella, and I'm afraid it would have haunted me the rest of my life."

"It won't bother me at all. He was a animal. I think most of the other boys agree with me, but I'm not sure of that. I don't know what's gonna happen to me when you leave."

Josh and Jenny waited.

"Would you let me go with you? I'd work for nothin,' just somethin' to eat. I know cows. I grew up on a farm. I wouldn't be no trouble. I got a horse. Please, can I?"

Josh and Jenny looked at each other. She nodded. "I'll talk to Paul," Josh said to her. He spoke to Eddie. "Get your horse and anything else you own. Come back here and help Jenny. She'll tell you what to do. I'm not saying you're going with us. I'll talk with the boss."

Eddie grinned and ran toward the camp.

Jenny finished harnessing the mules and climbed up. She drove the wagon to the fire circle where cowboys were mounting. The hunters stood aside, some still looking confused, others glaring in anger at the cowboys.

Eddie walked into camp, leading his horse, a small sack tied behind the saddle. He kept his distance from the other hunters.

"What're you doing, kid?" said a frowning hunter.

Eddie looked toward Josh, who sat his horse beside the wagon. Josh nodded. Eddie mounted in a hurry and walked his horse to the wagon.

Eddie turned to the hunters. "I'm leavin' you to it, boys. You don't need me, and I sure don't need you."

Paul led off, and the other cowboys followed. Jenny pulled in behind. Eddie rode with Josh beside the wagon.

"This ain't the end of this!" shouted one of the hunters.

Josh pulled up, pondered. "Keep moving," he said to no one in particular. He turned his horse back toward the camp. Eddie and Petey rode after him.

Josh reined up before the hunters who still stood beside the dead fire. Petey and Eddie rode up on each side of him.

"Who said that?" Josh said.

The hunters moved away from a stocky bewhiskered man who didn't move, his chin slightly upraised, glaring at Josh.

"You gonna shoot me now. Go ahead. I ain't affeered of you. What do I have to live for? Aside from the chance to come for you."

"No, I'm not planning to shoot you. Just wanted a good look at the one who might come looking for me so I can shoot him down on the spot. No second thoughts next time." He reined his horse around and set out at a lope down the slope. Petey and Eddie followed. Eddie looked over his shoulder at the camp, grinning.

The three riders slowed beside the wagon. Josh nodded to Jenny. Just before reaching the road, the cowboys dropped the load of pistols they had collected in camp. Jenny pulled onto the road, and the riders followed.

Josh rode up beside Paul at the front. "How'd you find us?" Josh said.

"You can thank Mother Nature. Your wagon tracks were still visible from yesterday's rain. They were the only tracks on the road, so we figured they had to be yours. We saw where you turned off the road and moved up the slope. The tracks disappeared in the grass, but it was pretty clear that you were headed for the break in that line of oaks."

"Much obliged. That affair was not going to end well. I'll be glad to get back to work. A couple of hours ago, I couldn't have said that."

"We'll all need to get back to work. We're holding the herd with the few boys that aren't riding with us right here. Sorry to tell you this, Josh, but the boys are going to be a lot happier to see Jenny than you. There's a lot of hungry cowboys right here and in camp. Harley said he would have a dressed antelope ready for the fire pit."

"I heard that," said Jenny over her shoulder. "I'm as anxious as the boys. You may have to delay another day, just so the boys can eat everything I'm planning to cook."

"Yahoo," yelled Pedro. Other riders whooped and shouted.

"THERE THEY ARE," said Jenny. They saw the herd being held a couple hundred yards from the river. As they approached, cowboys at the herd saw them and called and waved. Andy rode toward the entourage and waited. Jenny pulled up beside him.

Andy smiled. He looked from Josh and Petey up to Jenny on the wagon seat. "I am so glad to see the lot of you. We couldn't figure what might have happened. I expect we're going to be delayed at the Red, so that will give you time to rest up and the boys to fill their bellies with Jenny's vittles. Go ahead, Jenny. There's a shady spot just off the bank. Josh and Paul, ride with me, and we'll talk."

"Eddie," said Josh, "stay with Jenny for now. We'll talk later." Eddie waved and rode up beside the wagon.

Jenny shook the lines, moving toward the herd. All the cowboys but Andy, Paul, and Josh rode with her.

The trio rode at a slow pace while Josh talked about Eagle Springs and the buffalo hunters.

"You were lucky," said Andy, "we were all lucky, that it ended well. For you, I mean. Sorry about the two you had to shoot. I hate to see that, hate to see anybody killed, even the really bad 'uns. I hope the rest of the hunters make it."

Josh told him about Eddie, and Andy agreed to the arrangement, with the clear understanding that Josh was responsible for turning him into a cowboy. Josh told about the hunter who declared the affair wasn't over. "I doubt it will come to anything but thought you oughta know."

"Sounds like those boys are going to have too much on their hands to cause any trouble," said Andy, "especially since they lost the two head men and still have that load of hides on their hands and no way to get them to a railroad."

As they approached the herd, Jenny pulled aside and stopped at a scattering of pecan trees. She jumped down from the wagon. "Eddie, tie your horse and come over here. Watch me taking care of the team. I might call on you to help. When I finish that, I'm gonna scrounge in the wagon for some cowboy clothes and get you out of those skins. You're gonna take the clothes to the river and wash yourself. You stink so bad you're gonna run off the cows."

Eddie grinned. "Anything you say, Jenny."

Andy, Paul, and Josh rode by the herd, responded to waves and greetings, and soon reined up on the riverbank. A couple of cowboys on the bank greeted them, and a few others rode up beside them.

"You see what we got ahead of us here," said Andy. Usually a wide, placid, shallow stream, with water flowing in a series of channels between sandbars, the Red now was a mile wide and a deep, raging torrent in the main channel. Uprooted brush and trees were carried in the flow. "Must've rained upcountry for days to produce this." He looked up at the cloudless sky. The sun was directly overhead. "We'll see about crossing tomorrow. Maybe it'll go down overnight."

He turned to the cowboys sitting their horses on the bank. "Now I wouldn't want you to get bored this afternoon, boys, so let's do what we need to do to cross tomorrow if it doesn't go down. We may have to float the wagon, so we need four good size dry tree trunks."

The hands looked at each other, grimaced, and grumbled. "Here it comes," Andy said. He grinned. "If you don't like the work afoot, then you'd best get it done as quickly as possible so you can get mounted again. Axes and ropes in the wagon. There's plenty of down stuff along the bank. Now git!

"Paul, take Josh and scout out the best crossing. Two fords, actually. One for a normal crossing in case the flow is down and it's fordable, another if we have to float the wagon and swim the animals. Have a good look out for quicksand. I'm told there's lots of it." Andy looked up at the sky, then westward. No clouds in sight.

Paul and Josh rode to the bank and turned downstream. They studied the bluff banks, the red soil that gave the water its light hue and colored the timber at streamside and bits of dry driftwood lodged at the high-water mark in the lower branches of trees.

Meanwhile, the other hands pulled up at the chuck wagon, still grumbling. They dismounted and tied reins to wagon wheels. Jenny was leaning into the back of the wagon and withdrew, frowning.

"What's going on? It's not dinner time," she said.

"Jenny, we need axes and shovels," said Harley. "We got to do some hand labor." He turned to the other cowboys. "Actually, I'm the senior hand here, so you boys are going to swing the axes, and I'm going to drag the trunks to the crossing. I don't s'pose anybody's got a problem with that." He smiled.

"You may be senior in age, you old geezer," Toby said, "but you ain't the senior in brains. We'll take turns at everything we got to do." Harley smiled.

Jenny crawled into the wagon and handed out two axes and a couple of shovels. She withdrew and then handed out three coils of rope. "That do it?"

"That should do it," said Harley. He parceled out the tools and rope to the others. "Let's git on it and git it over with." He and the others walked to horses, mounted, and rode off.

All except Toby. He remained beside the wagon, holding a coil of rope.

"Need something else?" Jenny said.

"Sure do. Jenny, seeing as there's nobody here but you and me, what do you say we—"

Jenny put hands on hips. "Toby, there's no 'you and me' here, and you need to ride on and get to work."

"Jenny, Josh's nowhere in sight, and—"

"Josh? What's Josh got to do with anything?"

"Aw, Jenny, everbody knows what's goin' on, but I thought—"

Jenny stepped toward him. "You thought nothin,' Toby. Now get on that horse and get on your way. I told the whole bunch I could take care of myself, and you're about to test me."

Toby raised a hand, palm toward Jenny, and stepped backwards. "Okay, okay, just havin' a little fun. Didn't mean to get you all riled up. It's just if you ever decide you want to have a little fun, just tell me." He smiled.

Jenny relaxed. "Okay, Toby. Be on your way. I'll have a little somethin' to nibble on in a while. You behave yourself till then."

He nodded, smiling, and turned to go. He threw back over his shoulder, "nibblin' is sorta what I had in mind, Jenny." He jumped aside, barely avoiding Jenny's kick at his backside.

"Git outta here, Toby," barely suppressing a giggle.

He went to his horse, mounted, and set out at a lope toward the river, laughing out loud.

She shook her head, picked up short lengths of wood from the stack at the fire circle, and began setting a fire.

IT WAS A LATE DINNER, but one that the hands would talk about for days. Jenny fed them chunks of roasted antelope, beans, fried onions and potatoes, fried eggs, plenty of biscuits, and hot coffee. To top off the feast, apple cobbler and a biscuit drizzled with molasses.

Talk was subdued as cowboys bent over their

plates. Only when they were finished and depositing their plates in the wash bucket did they find their tongues. They thanked Jenny and told her how much they had missed her.

"You didn't miss me," she said. "You missed my cooking."

"Well, yeah," said Charley, "that too. But we worried all the same. I'm so glad to see you that I would hug you if I didn't think I would get hit over the head with a piece of firewood." He turned and pulled a face in Josh's direction. Josh smiled and waved a fork.

Jenny took Charley's plate, dropped it in the bucket, reached out, and hugged him. He was so surprised, he recoiled, then relaxed and cautiously hugged her. He turned back to the others, some standing and some still sitting at the fire circle. He cocked his head, smiling.

Petey and Eddie left the campfire together. Josh had persuaded Petey to take on the task of teaching Eddie the fine art of cowboying. They began at the beginning that afternoon, riding drag together as Petey, the old hand now described the different positions around the herd occupied by riders. He also told him something about each of the hands, how to get along with them and how to stay out of their way.

"Cows sometimes are just like people," said Petey, warming to his role as teacher. "They find a place in the herd they like, and they take up that place ever time they're on the trail. It might be at the front, or halfway back, or dragging at the back. You'll come to recognize certain cows by color and gait. Ain't terribly important, but it's fun to get to know particular cows."

That night, Jenny and Josh lay wide awake after playtime. "I was afraid we were going to pack it in," he said. "I didn't see how they could let us go." He rolled over and touched her cheek. "But I hadn't counted on this little fireball taking control. You saved us both."

"No, I just bought us a little time till the outfit showed up and saved us. Gotta give Eddie some credit as well, at least in giving us some peace of mind. I'll have to think of some way to thank him properly."

"Give him more apple cobbler and nothing more, hear?"

She smiled, kissed him.

Chapter Six

AT FIRST LIGHT, Andy and Paul sat their horses at the ford Paul and Josh had chosen yesterday. "Looks pretty good to me right now," said Andy, "but I don't like the looks of them clouds," gesturing westward with a nod of his head. "Anyway, I'm thinking we should be able to get across before any new water hits us. Let's get the herd moving."

They rode at a gallop the short distance to camp where all cowboys not watching the herd sat around the campfire, breakfast plates in laps. The two riders pulled up at the gathering.

"Okay, boys, break it up, and get your horses! We're crossing, right now."

"You mean that manual labor we done yesterday gittin' logs for floatin' the wagon was done for nothin'?" said Harley.

"We may need the timber yet," Andy said. "But if we hurry, we may not need 'em. We got dark clouds out west, and we could be on the north side of the Red before any new water hits us. If you plan to take off your saddle and your britches, do it just before we cross and put 'em in the wagon. Okay, let's git on it!"

Tim scowled. "Hey boss, I ain't finished my breakfast."

Andy frowned. "Tim, my boy, did I *ask* you to help move this herd, or did I *tell* you to help move this herd? Timmy, you ain't got the sense of a young jackass. You plan to give us a hand today, or do we review our working relationship?"

Tim stood, grunting. "Okay, boss, if you put it that way." He grinned and walked toward the chuck wagon. The others stood, hurried to the wagon, and deposited their plates and utensils in the wash bucket. They hurried toward the remuda.

"Josh!" Andy called. Josh stopped, turned. "Help Jenny get ready. We'll cross the wagon first. A wagon crossing sometimes helps motivate the cows to follow." Josh nodded and walked back toward the wagon. "Move out quick," Andy said to Josh. "The herd's gonna be right behind you." Andy walked away, mumbling.

Jenny had put the mules in harness before breakfast, anticipating an early start. Josh helped her load cooking and camp gear in the wagon and secure anything loose. They checked utensils and gear that hung from the sides of the wagon. She climbed up to the wagon seat and pulled the lines from the brake handle. He stood on the ground, watching, smiling.

She looked down at him. After a quiet moment: "Aren't you forgetting something, like your horse?"

He pulled a face, turned, and ran toward the remuda where mounted cowboys were already riding toward the herd. Most of the cows were already up and grazing and were easily put in motion toward the river, about three hundred yards distant.

Jenny shook the lines and put the mules into a fast walk toward the river. Andy and two others, standing on the riverbank, watched the wagon coming, Josh riding alongside. He held the reins of Jenny's saddle horse. Just in case, she had told him. She instructed him to tie the horse to the back of the wagon with a short lariat. When he said all this was unnecessary, she silenced him with a stern look.

"Okay, here's where we are," said Andy. "The flow was down at first light when I checked it but seems to have risen a couple of inches since then. We shoulda skipped breakfast. My fault. Anyway, we should be okay. Josh and Charley will ride on each side of the team. Jenny, when I give the signal, push the team right on in. Head a little upstream. Helps to counter the current. God forbid, but if you start floating, try to point the team a bit upstream against the current."

Jenny was aghast. "You think we might be floating? Andy, my stuff'll get wet!"

"Well, Jenny, I wish I could build a dam to prevent that, but it's a little late. You just drive that wagon across as best you can, and maybe you won't get your shoes wet. Look there." He pointed at the north bank. "There's a couple of mounted fellas on the north bank to help if you need it. Head right for 'em"

He shouted to the men on the north bank. "We're comin' over!" The two cowboys sat their jittery horses at the water's edge, waving.

"Go, Jenny!" shouted Andy. She looked nervously at Josh who sat his horse beside the left lead mule. He nodded to her.

She shook the lines. "Walk up, mules, walk up!"

The team pulled down the gentle slope to water's edge where they hesitated. She shook the lines hard, and they stepped into the shallows. They kept pulling steadily until they were belly deep.

Jenny looked over the side at the current pushing and flowing through the wagon spokes, the water level gradually moving up on the wheel. "Josh," she called, her voice wavering. He turned in the saddle. "I can't swim," she said, barely audible.

Josh looked back at Jenny. He saw a face he had never seen before. She was terrified. "Just stay in that wagon seat," he said. "No swimming today." He turned back to the front, gently slapped the mules' hindquarters with his quirt.

"Josh, I'm floating!" The wagon bed had lifted and slid gently to the side with the current. The mules were swimming, necks stretched, heads high and eyes bulging. Josh's horse swam alongside, and he quirted the mule alongside, shouting encouragement. "C'mon, mule! C'mon, mule!"

"Dammit, my stuff's gonna get wet!" said Jenny. "Walk up, jennies, git going!"

Pushed by the current, the mules swam slightly upstream, heading for the open space on the far bank where the two waiting cowboys sat their horses at water's edge. Jenny shook the lines again and again. Josh pushed his swimming horse in front of the mules, hoping they would follow.

Josh's horse, then the team, finally found footing in the shallows and moved slowly up the incline to the grassy bench. At the top, Josh called to Jenny. "Pull it aside. They'll be putting the herd in right away." With that, he kicked his horse down from the bank and into the water.

•

"Come back here! I need help!" Jenny called.

He waved over his shoulder just as his horse plunged into the current.

On the south side, Andy spoke to the half dozen hands sitting their horses beside him. "All right, the wagon's over, and the damn water's rising. Let's git on it!"

The cowboys galloped to the herd that was being held a hundred yards away. In short order, the hands had the herd up and moving toward the crossing, cowboys riding alongside the bunched cattle. The herd had been watered at a hole the previous day, so they were not rushing to the river at the smell of water, which they would do if they were thirsty.

As the front of the herd approached the bank, Andy shouted. "You point men, bunch 'em, push 'em!" The rider on each side of the front of the column moved inward, yelling, bunching the column, and pushing them down the embankment to water's edge. The lead cattle stepped into the water, then abruptly turned aside and lunged back up the embankment.

Andy clenched his eyes, opened them. "Damn it, we got no time for this. Paul! Git the lead steer on a rope and bring him to the front. The herd should follow him." He looked upstream and shook his head. The current had increased noticeably.

Paul found the docile steer that customarily was in the lead during the drive. He put a rope on him and rode to the front of the milling herd just back from the bank. As he rode by the herd, a few cows filed in behind him, then others, and soon the entire herd was moving. Paul rode into the shallows, and the lead steer placidly followed. A few cows walked gingerly after him.

Josh rode up the bank from the stream and reined up beside Andy. "From the other side, I could see a few miles upstream. There's lots of floating logs and tree limbs in eddies along the banks. If the current picks up, this stuff is going to come down on us."

Andy nodded. He shouted to the hands. "The herd's moving! Keep 'em bunched. Water's coming up. Let's get 'em over. Watch out for floating stuff!"

"Look out!" Josh shouted. A large floating branch swept by immediately in front of Paul. He and the lead cow took no notice as if this was what they did every day, but the cows behind shied and broke out of line. Cowboys on each side of the column quickly pushed them back into the moving column.

"Current's picking up!" shouted Andy. "Move 'em! Move 'em!"

The herd moved in good order into the water toward the north shore at the opening in the brush where cows were lunging up the bank. Midway in the stream, they lost footing and were floating. The line of swimming animals, heads thrusting upward, eyes bulging and flared nostrils, curled downstream, but by instinct, they followed the cows in front and swam for the opening. Small branches and woody debris swept by in the current, sometimes striking animals, causing some shying, but hardly interrupting their progress.

Then: "Look out! Here comes a whole tree!" shouted Josh. He was in mid-stream and first saw the huge, green-leafed pecan tree that must have been uprooted and washed from the bank by the heavy rains. He had been watching upstream and saw the tree when it swept around a turning in the stream.

It was strangely quiet as the floating tree crashed into the column at the deepest part of the stream, scattering cows and cowboys. All were swallowed momentarily in the leafy mass, submerging, surfacing, gasping, cows bellowing, heads held high and eyes bulging.

The quiet was broken as cowboys in the water shouted their distress, and those on both shores shouted encouragement and instructions to everyone else on how to save hands and cows.

A cowboy bobbed to the surface and grabbed his mount's tail as the horse swam frantically toward the shore, bumping into cows that flailed and swam in every direction. Another cowboy held tightly to his saddle horn as the horse made for the shore.

Then it was over as quickly as it began. The two cowboys who had their horses to thank for saving their lives made the shore and quickly became famous as they breathlessly recounted their narrow escapes. The column continued crossing in good order.

On the north shore, Josh had hardly dismounted when Jenny grabbed him and held him tightly. "Don't do that again, hear?" she said.

Josh raised her chin and kissed her. "Tell that to Andy, sweetheart. I suppose we'll have more streams to cross before we reach the railhead."

"Okay, listen up." Andy waited until all who were not watching the herd grazing placidly nearby had gathered. Jenny and Josh walked over. "The Red is usually shallow with a slack current," Andy said. "We were lucky today." The others murmured agreement. There would be stories told around the campfire this evening that would be changed and magnified over time, told over and over on this drive and other drives to follow.

Jenny had listened without hearing. She had been

looking around the group and back to the river. "Where's Tim?"

Andy's head came up. He looked at the group, one by one. "Charley, Toby, Harley, cross and search the banks downstream. The rest of you, everbody that's not watching the herd, search the north bank downstream. Git on it!"

The cowboys ran to their horses, mounted, and began the search. As they moved down the bank, they occasionally dismounted to search through the heavy brush at water's edge.

Jenny ran to the wagon and untied her horse. She mounted and galloped on the bank downstream.

Josh kicked his horse to a gallop after her. "Where you going?" Josh yelled.

She ignored his call. After a five-minute ride, she pulled up quickly, her horse sliding. She dismounted, pointed. "It's the tree." Josh dismounted and walked to where she stood in the shallows. They searched the branches, pulling a branch aside, pushing another.

And there he was. Tim, what had been Tim, was entangled in a mass of small branches, offshoots from a larger branch. Josh helped her untangle the body, pull it from the water, lift it and place it over his saddle. Jenny mounted, and he climbed up behind her, holding his horse's reins with its sorrowful burden.

Back in camp, Tim's body was lifted gently from the saddle and lowered to the ground. The cowboys said not a word, just looked at what had been their pal, Tim. There were not many dry eyes among the hands. This was the first long drive for most of the cowboys, and most had not seen a dead body anywhere but at a church funeral.

Andy held his hat by the brim. "Timmy, Timmy,

Timmy. We hardly knew you. I don't think you knew how much I cared for you, 'cause I was so hard on you. But I loved you, son." He shook his head slowly, without taking his eyes from the body.

The hands stood quiet, holding hats, looking from Andy to the body, at the meadow and the river, the sky.

Josh broke the silence. "Boss, I saw three graves just down the bank." He pointed downstream. "One of 'em was new, this year for sure."

Andy stared at the body, wiped his cheek with a hand. "We'll bury him there." He pulled a bandanna from a back pocket, stooped, and opened it gently over Tim's upturned face.

Dawn and a light breeze flapped the loose canvas on the chuck wagon. Josh leaned against the side of the wagon, watching Jenny packing dishes and cooking gear in the back. He had helped her wash dishes and pack leftover kindling and chips in the tarp slung under the wagon. His horse's reins were tied to a wagon wheel.

"The boss wouldn't let anyone help with the digging," Josh said. "He said he wanted to do it, and he would do it. Some offered, and he just shook his head and said nothing. Can't figure the guy out."

She raised the tailgate and tied it. "I think he's feeling guilty like he should have done more for Tim, him being so young and new at all this. He seemed calmer when we were all gathered at the graveside, especially when Charley said the Lord's Prayer. Andy had his head bowed and eyes closed tight the whole time."

"He wouldn't have been so moved if he had heard

what Charley said when I turned my horse into the remuda later."

She paused, her hand still on the tailgate. "What?"

"Charley said he recited the Lord's Prayer so much when he was a churchgoer that he knows it so well, he could say it in his sleep. Then he said, 'course, it's all superstition and nonsense.' I don't think the boss would be happy to hear that."

"No, he wouldn't. Best you and Charley keep it to yourselves." She walked up to the team, already in harness. "I gotta go."

He hadn't moved. He stared toward the river. "Makes you stop and think about what we're doing here. What the point is of our being here. We take a herd of cows to Kansas and get paid off. Then what? Go back to Texas, collect another herd and drive it to Kansas? And then another?"

She stared into the wagon interior a moment, then turned to him. She reached and took a handful of shirt, pulled him to her, and kissed him. "You have an upset stomach or somethin,' honey? I have a few comments I could add to this conversation, but if I do it now, I may just about get out of sight when I have to stop for nooning. You just keep these thoughts in mind, and tonight I'll suggest a few things a body can do while making a living." She untied his horse's reins and handed them to him. She kissed him, climbed up on the wagon seat, shook the lines, and the mules pulled away.

He watched the wagon move into the track, then mounted hurriedly and rode at a lope toward the bedding ground where cowboys were getting the cows up.

. . .

"Hell, it don't look no different to me," said Toby. "I thought this Indian Territory was gonna look different somehow. Looks just like Texas to me."

Toby and Josh stood in the shade of a huge pin oak. They had strolled over to the shade after depositing their dinner dishes in the pail at the wagon. Now they watched Jenny washing dishes, putting things away inside the wagon and on hooks on the wagon side. Josh, as usual, had asked if he could help. As usual, she waved him off and said she had everything under control. That was before Harwood ambled over and began to give her more attention than she wanted. Josh couldn't hear the conversation, but he knew Jenny's temperament enough to know that she was not pleased with the exchange. Nor with the smoke from Harwood's cigarette.

"I think I'll walk over to the chuck wagon for a cup of cold coffee," Josh said.

Toby grinned. "Yeah, maybe the conversation over there will produce enough heat to warm it up for you."

Josh strolled toward the chuck wagon. He wanted to give Harwood time to see him coming. Harwood saw him, leaned against the side of the wagon, chin lifted ever so slightly, and watched him come.

Josh nodded to Harwood, walked to Jenny. "Anything I can do to help get you on the road? I see Andy rousing up the hands lounging at the shade tree."

"I'm fine, just about ready to leave. You go and help Andy rousing the hands." She gestured toward Harwood. "Take him with you."

Harwood stepped away from the wagon. "It's 'Harwood,' missy, not 'him.'" He was not smiling.

Josh stepped in front of him. "'Harwood,' it is.

Harwood, it's time for you and me to get about our business and leave Jenny to hers."

"I'll decide when I'm leaving." He glared at Josh.

Josh waited, standing between Harwood and Jenny who ignored both of them as she busied herself, hanging cooking gear on the side of the wagon.

Josh waited, shifted. "Decided yet?"

Harwood dropped the cigarette, smashed it with a foot. He walked slowly around the wagon toward the remuda, his chin raised.

Jenny watched him go. "He makes me nervous."

PART of the herd grazed placidly in good grass in a meadow. Cowboys easily moved cattle from the stream to the meadow. All had been well watered in bunches and would graze until sunset.

Josh stood with Andy and Charley near the chuck wagon where Jenny was washing the supper dishes. Andy studied a paper he held. "This would be Beaver Creek. We might end up wishing we had crossed this evening since it's low water. High banks, but I saw a good ford. I don't see any clouds out west, so we shouldn't have a problem tomorrow."

"What's that you got?" Josh said, pointing at the paper Andy held.

"Sketch map an old fella gave me last winter in Fort Worth. He and a couple of others rode to Kansas last fall, thinking he might put a herd together to drive up there this spring. They had a brush with some Indians who didn't think much of his plan, so he decided to forget it and gave the map to me." He looked up. "I think we can take care of ourselves.

"Actually, there's not supposed to be any Indian

problems. A year or so ago, when I was first thinking that I might want to drive a herd to Kansas, I looked into the Indian situation. Seems there was a treaty signed in 1865 between the federal government, and the tribes, in Indian Territory that set up reservations for all the tribes. The government would give the tribes all sorts of assistance. Sounded like it would prevent any problems with Indians, but so far as I could find out, the reservations were never set up, and the Indians now are still mad about that and as wild as ever. We'll have to be on our toes."

Dusk. Anticipating a long, dry drive the next day, cowboys had wandered away from the campfire earlier than usual, strolled to the bushes, came back, and made their beds. Jenny finished putting away the clean dishes, stirred the cooking fire to ignite any burnable fuel, and watched the last small flames die.

She went to the wagon, crawled under to the bed that was already laid out. She did not see Harwood, standing in deep shadow under two large pecan trees, watching her.

A low ceiling partially obscured the moon, and the weak moonlight barely sketched the outlines of the wagon. Harwood walked slowly to the wagon, stepping carefully to make no noise. Reaching the wagon, he touched the side and bent to his knees beside the bed. He leaned over the tousled head.

He whispered. "Yeah, I'm comin' in there. You ready for me?"

There was a rustling as the covers were pushed back.

"Ready," said Josh. "What you got in mind?"

Harwood jerked back, banged his head hard on the wagon bottom. Scooting backward awkwardly, he jumped up and ran from the wagon and was swallowed by the darkness. He missed the laughter from beneath the wagon.

Next morning, the cows were positively frisky, having been well watered and fed the previous evening. They were driven across the stream at the ford, shallow all the way but for a narrow channel of swift water that was swimming, no problem for the herd.

Then everything changed. The sun was piercing and the prairie dry. By noon, the herd was dragging and strung out, tongues hanging, and lowing pitifully. Cowboys looked to the skies, hoping for clouds and a cooling breeze. Andy passed the word to all hands that they would skip nooning and sent the chuckwagon ahead. He also sent two pairs of hands ahead to look for water.

Cattle began to wander away from the column and did not respond to the cowboys' efforts to control them. Cows bumped into each other, wavered, stumbling before gaining their balance.

"What's happening, Charley?" said Josh. They rode beside the slow-moving herd and could only watch the scattering of the column.

"They're going blind."

"Blind?"

"It's temporary. Well, it's temporary if they get water soon. If they don't get water, then it's pretty serious." He straightened, looking ahead. "Here come the boys who were ahead looking for water. What th' hell? Why are they running?"

Two cowboys came galloping hard, whipping and spurring their mounts.

"Stampede! Stampede!"

The riders pulled up, sliding, at the front of the column. Harley gasped. "Boss, they're coming hard in the middle of the trail, right at us!"

Andy turned in the saddle and shouted down the column. "Stampede coming from the north! Turn 'em to the right! Let's get 'em off the trail far as we can! Git on it!"

The hands on the left side of the column began pushing the cows to the right, with little success. The cows hardly responded to the shouts and quirts. Cowboys at the front pulled pistols and shot into the ground at the cows' feet, still with little success.

"Look out!" The stampeding horde crashed into the almost-stationary column, scattering animals and cowboys. Andy's cattle were carried along with the stampeding herd on the back trail. The pace of the rush was slowed by the exhausted herd, but all attempts to turn or slow the column failed. Cows that seemed to be blind were carried along by the rushing bodies on each side.

Josh rode alongside the herd, trying to prevent cows from scattering. He crowded a huge steer, quirting it. Suddenly the steer veered off toward him and crashed into his mount, slightly lifting the horse and throwing horse and rider to the ground. As the horse fell on its side, Josh's leg was pinned underneath the horse's body. The mare's legs thrashed as she tried to roll over and regain her feet.

Josh pushed on the horse and beat his fist on the horse's side. "Get off! Dammit, get off!"

The steer that had upended the horse stood spraddle-legged beside the downed horse, eying her and pawing the ground. Josh fumbled for his pistol as the cow lowered its head.

The steer charged, and Josh fired. The steer's legs buckled, and the longhorn rammed into the horse's belly, pushing the horse's body against Josh's.

Paul and Harley pulled up at that moment and dismounted quickly, hopefully, ground tying their horses. Harley grabbed the downed mount's reins, pulling gently and encouraging it to stand while Paul joined Josh in pushing on the horse, rolling it until Josh was able to extricate his leg.

Josh and his mount found their feet at the same time. He took the reins from Harley and stroked the mare's neck. His rescuers had recovered their reins and watched.

"Can you ride?" said Paul.

"Yeah, think I can. We'll see about my horse. I think she's okay."

"Let's see what we can do," Paul said. The last of the herd had passed and now was a cloud of dust rising from the trail in the south.

CATTLE STOOD in the shallows of Beaver Creek where they had watered the previous evening. The line of thirsty cows stretched a half mile in each direction from the ford. Cattle that couldn't squeeze into the line pushed from behind until a cow that had slaked its thirst clambered up the bank to the meadow above.

It wasn't the best way to water a herd. Ideally, cowboys would push the lead cows downstream where they would drink clear water. Cows that followed would reach the stream a bit upstream where they would drink clear water, then continue until the end of the herd reached water upstream of all, and all would have a chance at clear water. But this thirsty herd was in too much hurry for the proper routine.

As cows left the stream, cowboys from both outfits pushed them to a meadow of good grass bordered by a mixed stand of redbud and laurel trees.

Andy and Sam, boss of the other herd, sat their horses near the ford. They agreed that it was too late to separate the herds this evening. They would camp together, share night herd duties, and work on the separating after breakfast.

"Bad business," said Sam. "Still don't know what set 'em off. Might've been wolves. One of the boys saw a pack at the edge of the woods where we stopped for dinner. The trail ran close to those woods, but we figured the wolves, being nervous animals, would run when we got close. They didn't. We had no sooner set off after dinner than the cows got nervous, and that's when they started running. Still don't know whether it was the wolves or something else. Anyway, here we are. Sorry, we ran into you back there."

"No apology necessary, Sam. Happens. I've heard all sorts of stories about what causes stampedes. Night herder sneezing, accidental firing of a six-shooter, a horse snorting in the middle of the night, even a strange smell. Fella told me that his herd stampeded one night when the cows caught the scent of a panther that was creeping up on a deer carcass hanging from a tree near the chuck wagon.

"Naw, it might just as well been my herd that ran into yours. I don't think either of us lost many head. Looked like they ran straight down the trail. We had some cows that was goin' blind from the heat, but I think we got back to water in time to save 'em.

"Sam, I was surprised to see your herd. I thought we was the first herd headin' for Kansas this year. Anybody ahead of you?"

"I didn't see anybody. I think I'm first. Do you have a buyer? I don't."

"Nope. Looks like we're casting the same dice. I yield first place to you, but I'll be hot on your heels. If you find a buyer, tell 'im there's a good herd of fat cows a day behind." They both smiled. Sam reached over, clapped Andy on the back, and rode away at a lope toward his camp.

After a late supper, cowboys from both camps assigned to night herd began the ride around the combined herd. Singing and whistling wafted to the camps from a half dozen riders.

Josh and Paul stood with three cowboys from Sam's outfit, after introductions and handshakes, smoking and recounting the day's spectacle, enjoying the cool breeze that had come up at sundown.

Paul listened, frowned. "That singing by one of your hands is fixin' to scare our cows. Somebody outta tell him to whistle instead."

"Yeah, our cows must be used to him," said Bennie from the other outfit. "Say, you boys have got one on us. I was wandering in your camp earlier and saw you brought your own doxie with you. She is a purty little thang. I s'pose you wouldn't mind if I mosey out to the woods with her for an hour or so later. I ain't even seen a woman for over a month."

Josh pondered a moment. How do I respond to this moron? "What we've got on you is that we have the best cookie west of the Mississippi. She's no doxie; she's our cook."

Bennie smiled. "Course she is. I saw her at the chuck wagon. But surely you boys don't let that get in the way of a little fun after the dishes are done." He grinned.

Paul changed the subject, asking where Sam got his cows, how he put the outfit together, where were the cowboys from. He glanced aside at Josh who was not listening. Josh had not taken his eyes off Benny who stared at the chuck wagon where Jenny was washing dishes.

Small talk finished, the group broke up, and hands strolled toward their separate camps.

JENNY THREW a couple of chips and short boughs on the fire which flared up when the fuel caught. She pulled the skillet from the wash bucket and shook the water from it.

"Don't you have any help with the washing up?" said Benny. He grinned.

She jumped, saw him, picked up a cloth, and rubbed the skillet. "I don't need any help."

"Tell you what. How 'bout if I help you finish up, and we take a walk? It's a nice evening, and we can make it even nicer."

She rolled her eyes, opened them, and turned to him. "If you got funny business in mind, sonny, you're barking up the wrong tree."

He smiled. "It ain't so much funny business I got in mind, but some serious business that I been missing a long time. What do you say we take a little walk to the woods?"

"Get lost, Benny! I got no time for this!"

He grabbed her arm and pulled her, squeezing her breast with the other hand. She swung the skillet, aiming for his head. He ducked aside, and the skillet struck his shoulder hard.

"Ow! Goddamit, you bitch, I'll—"

He was suddenly pulled backwards. Josh spun him around and landed a hard blow to his head, another to his belly, and again to his head as he stumbled backward and collapsed to the ground.

Jenny watched, wide-eyed. "Were you there all this time?"

"I was. You were brilliant."

"You were watching? He might've hurt me."

He removed the skillet from her hand and set it on the fireplace grate. He took her cheeks in his hands. "No one's going to hurt you. You are one fierce woman. If I hadn't been here to save him, you probably would have killed him." He smiled, pulled her to him, and hugged her.

She leaned back. "Yeah, just stay close in case you need my help." She smiled, kissed him.

Cowboys sat around the dying campfire, exchanging comment on the run and the aftermath. A dry piece of wood and a couple of buffalo chips tossed on the fire caused a momentary burst of flame, which changed to a flickering blue.

Harley told the story about Josh's encounter with the steer a third time, as cowboys left the fire and others sat down. "I tell you, Josh, you was lucky. Or a damn good shot. I never saw a critter that big put down with a single pistol shot. If you hadn't got him right between the eyes and messed up his brain, he woulda messed up your horse, and maybe you." There was a murmur of agreement around the fire.

Jenny sat beside Josh, her leg touching his, ignoring the looks from cowboys, sipping from her coffee cup. Unlike the hands who drank coffee with supper, she had hers after cleaning up and joining the others at the campfire.

Harley finished rolling a cigarette, picked up a short length of glowing kindling, and lit the cigarette. He inhaled until the tip glowed. "Reminds me of what happened one time when we was huntin' up on the Canadian." Some cowboys looked at each other and rolled their eyes.

"We was huntin' deer, ya see, and we followed a four-pointer into a narrow brushy ravine, and the four-pointer disappeared into the brush." Three listeners fell on their backs. "We moved up a few steps and stopped. Then we heard a sort of snuffling." The boys on their backs began to snore. "Then the biggest grizzly bear you ever saw busted out of that thicket and came for us." Two more cowboys collapsed on their backs, snoring loudly.

Petey, eyes wide, leaned toward Harley. "What happened, Harley?"

Harley looked hard at Petey. "Hell, what do ya think happened? He killed ever' one of us."

"But . . ." Petey frowned, looked around. All the snoring cowboys now sat upright, grinning.

"Hell with you, Harley." Petey looked around again. He grinned.

The hands sat quiet, staring into the dying fire, drawing on cigarettes, exhaling wisps of smoke.

"Jenny?" Everyone turned to Toby. "Jenny, I do like

your cooking, everbody knows that, but would you make us some son of a bitch stew sometime?"

Jenny recoiled, frowning. *"What?"*

"Son of a bitch stew. It's so good. Any of you fellas had son of a bitch stew?" A few others nodded.

"Doesn't sound good to me," said Jenny. "Sounds nasty."

"Oh, well," said Toby, "some folks call it son of a gun stew."

"Sounds better, but still not very tasty. What's in it?"

Toby frowned, pondering. "Well . . . I don't know. Harley, do you know?"

Harley nodded. "Yes, I know." He pulled out his tobacco pouch, extracted a paper, and tamped some tobacco on it. He licked the paper and rolled the cigarette. He lit it from an ember and inhaled.

"Then say it!" said Charley. "You do this all the time, you old geezer, make us wait for you to finish a thought. Say it!"

Harley smiled at Charley. "Since you ask so nicely, I'll tell you. A cookie who made a fine son of a b— . . . son of a gun stew told me what's in it. It's got some meat, liver, heart, brains sweetbreads, and tongue. He said you can use wild meat or beef, but beef is best."

"Hmm," Jenny said. "Sounds like junk food to me, but I'll think about it if anybody else thinks it's any good." A general murmuring of agreement followed this pronouncement.

"I'll give it a shot," she said, "if somebody else does the butchering and tasting and will take the blame if it poisons anybody."

"On the subject of cowboy appetites," said Harley, "anyone hear about the little boy who saw a bunch of cowboys settin' on the ground around a campfire who asked his mama if cowboys eat grass? His mama said: 'No dear, cowboys don't eat grass. They're partly human,'" Harley guffawed, slapped his leg, and looked around. A couple of hands chuckled; most frowned.

Jenny and Josh lay on their backs on the pallet, a quilt pulled up to their shoulders. They breathed deeply. A bead of perspiration rolled down her cheek. He turned to face her, pulled the cover down to expose a breast. He leaned down and kissed the nipple. She giggled, pulled the cover up, and turned to him. She leaned over and kissed him.

"I like Petey," she said. "He's so innocent."

"Yeah, he's a nice fella. But he's in the wrong business, being innocent. Bad guys take advantage of anyone who's not as tough as they are. One thing he's got going for him, he's got a fine pistol, and he's a great shot. Hope he's never tested."

She raised up on an elbow, studied his face in the bright moonlight. "What about you, Josh Nesbitt? You ever been tested? I know so little about you."

He lay back. "I have." He told her about incidents on the riverboat that led to gunfights and the deaths of two men at his hands, innocent of all but drinking too much and owning short tempers. "They could have killed me with the same justification. I still see their faces in dreams and waking hours when I'm not occupied, when I'm alone."

She kissed him. "I'll take care of that."

. . .

Sam and Andy sat their horses, watching their outfits separating the mixed bunch into their separate herds. The work began immediately after breakfast and was almost finished.

"I'll move my herd out soon as my Segundo gives me the word," Sam said. "After all the trouble I've given you, I really should let you go first."

"You're not to blame for what's happened. You move out, and I'll be right behind you."

"Benny's going to eat dust at drag a long time until I can decide whether to feed him to the wolves or keep him."

"No harm done. We still got our cookie, and she's as feisty as ever. She's a wonder, believe me. Sorry, you didn't get to sample her cooking."

"My loss." Sam looked toward his herd. His cowboys were riding around the herd, preparing for the departure. He turned back to Andy. "Listen, when we cut our cows outta the mixed bunch, we could have missed some of your animals. If we find any cows with your brand, I'll keep a record when I sell the herd, and I'll get the sale price to you."

"That's mighty good of you," said Andy. "I'll do the same."

Sam waved toward his herd. "My Segundo just signaled. We're off." He extended a hand, and Andy shook it.

"Vaya con dios, my friend," said Andy.

Sam raised a hand in goodbye and set out at a lope toward his herd.

Chapter Seven

"If this is Indian country, where are all the Indians?" said Petey. He sat near the chuck wagon with three others in the shade of a cluster of tall redbud trees. Dry remnants of blossoms fell like pink snowflakes from the branches. The cowboys held empty plates.

"Let's get the dishes in, boys," said Paul. "Andy said this was going to be a short nooning. We won't be in a hurry, but we need to get moving." They had not moved the herd this morning from the bedding ground as early as usual or as fast. Andy said they would not push the cattle, giving them plenty of time to graze. He would give Sam ample time to move well ahead. He wanted no more mixing.

Now, dinner finished, Paul stood at the fire circle where cowboys scraped the last bit of beans to their mouths. He looked at the grazing herd and walked toward the remuda. He stopped, looked at a line of horse apple trees west of the herd. "Petey, you wanted to see Indians. Well, here they come." They watched a half dozen Indians riding slowly from the trees toward the campground. All were men, finely dressed, feathers in their hair, riding stout ponies.

Jenny and Josh, standing beside the chuck wagon, watched the Indians come, then ride around the wagon, their faces blank. Cowboys, sitting or standing at the campfire watched, unsure whether to draw pistols or wait for Andy's reaction.

Andy held up his left hand in greeting, his right hand near his holster. He stepped up to an Indian who stopped his horse. Andy smiled. "What're you fellows up to?"

After a long moment, the Indian replied. "T'back-uh."

The cowboys exhaled. They looked at each other, smiling.

Andy went to the chuck wagon, reached into the bed at the front, and pulled out a small sack. He walked to the Indian and offered the sack to him. The rider took the sack, nodded, looked around at the other Indians who smiled.

The cowboys relaxed commented to each other. Toby pulled fixings from a pocket and offered it to an Indian who took it, nodding. Charley and Harley followed suit, offering fixings to riders. All acknowledged with nods, a hesitant smile.

Then they were gone. The Indians rode off at a lope toward the copse where they had emerged and disappeared into the deep shade.

"Well, that was an interesting first meeting with the wildlife," said Andy. He started to walk away.

"Boss, did you notice how they kept looking around," said Josh. "Not as if they were really interested in what they were looking at, just looking around casually at something new. I think they were taking note of what we've got here."

"Hmm. Didn't notice. Seemed pretty friendly to me. Which might not mean a thing. Friendly Indians can be as dangerous as the bad 'uns. The bad 'uns will stampede your horses and try to get away with them. The friendlies will run your horses off and come back the next day, saying they found these horses and will you give us a reward for returning them.

"But you might be right. Pass the word to the boys. We'll double the night riders. And tell all the hands to have a saddled mount handy."

Some cowboys continued scraping at the remains of dinner on their plates. Some made signs of getting up. Harley didn't move. "Seeing them Indians reminds me of something I heard some time back," he said. The hands looked at Harley and relaxed. Charley rolled his eyes.

"I believe them Indians was Comanche," Harley said. He paused, looking up. The others at the fire circle stared at him. He stirred the embers with a smoldering stick.

"Well," said Petey, "what about it?"

Harley looked at Petey. "Well, seeing as how you ask." He tossed the dry stick onto the embers, and it sprouted tiny flames. "The Comanche are an interesting Indian. They believe that the spirit of a Comanche who has died lives forever in a land where everybody is young and has plenty of game and fast horses. They believe that most Comanches go into this afterlife, but an exception is a warrior that is scalped in battle. Comanche warriors scalp their enemies to prevent them getting into this happy afterlife. And they fight fierce over a fallen brother to prevent his scalp from being taken."

Petey leaned toward Harley. "Wow. How do you know this, Harley?"

"Well, my young friend, there's somethin' I've never told you. I was stolen as a child from my parents down in west Texas by a Comanche raiding party. They took me back to their village and raised me like one of their own. When I was old enough, I went on raiding parties, and in one raid, I was knocked off my horse by an Apache who cut me with a scalping knife before my brothers killed him."

"Wow. That must have been scary," Petey said, wide-eyed.

"Scary? You know why I have this bushy head of hair? It's to cover up—"

Half a dozen cowboys lunged at Harley, playfully punching him, laughing, rolling him on the ground. Harley pushed them away, laughing.

"What . . ." Petey frowned, tense, then relaxed, smiled.

THE HERD HAD HARDLY BEEN THROWN onto the trail when a dozen riders approached at a walk from the north. The riders watched the chuckwagon pass, staring at Jenny. She ignored them, shook the lines.

Andy spoke to Paul who rode with him at the head of the column. "What is it this time? I thought we were driving on a pretty new trail. But it seems everybody west of the Mississippi knows this trail, and everybody wants a piece of the action. I wonder what these fellows have in mind." Andy grimaced. "Stay with the herd. I'll get Josh to ride up with me. Alert all the hands to watch what's goin' on and check their six-shooters are loaded."

He turned and beckoned to Josh, who was riding at the right point position, to join him. Josh kicked his horse to a lope and pulled up beside Andy. "Let's see what these yahoos have to say," Andy said. He motioned ahead at the riders. "I'm sure they ain't a welcoming committee sent down from Abilene."

The two sets of riders pulled up when they met. The herd continued to stream by as hands frowned at the strangers.

"Howdy fellas," said Andy. "I don't s'pose you're out on a ride for pleasure this fine day. What's up?"

The rider at the front nodded. "We're sent down here by the state of Kansas to inspect herds bound for the state."

"Inspecting for what exactly?" said Andy.

"The government has heard that there's some rustling bein' done on the trail. We're inspecting herds to see if any herd includes any brands that don't belong to 'em and to collect unbranded range cattle in the herd that have drifted from Kansas ranches."

Andy just stared at the speaker, looked aside at Josh, back to the speaker. "Show me your authority. You need to show me a paper."

The speaker stiffened. He glanced back at his companions who looked at him, their faces blank. A couple of young riders looked aside nervously.

Andy leaned forward in his saddle, glaring. "That's the biggest bunch of bullshit I've heard in a mighty long time," said Andy. "If there's any rustlers about, you're headin' up the lot."

Both Andy and Josh rested hands on six-shooter holsters.

The speaker looked back at his men for support, but they simply stared at him or looked away.

The speaker jerked his reins hard to the right, and the horse whirled around. "Goddam pussies," he mumbled and kicked his horse into a gallop. The others followed.

Andy and Josh laughed. "I'll bet that's his first attempt at rustling. He'll want to put together a different bunch if he's to try it again."

THE HEAVY OVERCAST at sundown lingered and obscured the moon, leaving the camp in almost total darkness. Only enough weak moonlight seeped through the ceiling to outline the shape of the chuck wagon and the dark mass of the herd, most lying down and sleeping, or standing, chewing cuds. The only sounds were the singing and whistling of the night riders, occasional muted conversation when the cowboys, riding in opposite directions, met and kibbitzed a moment before moving on.

Jenny raised her head from the bedroll. She nudged Josh. He blinked, rolled over to face her, reached for a breast. She pushed his hand away and sat up.

"Listen. Did you hear that?" she said. He raised up and heard the muffled neighing of a horse, then the light shuffling sounds of hooves.

"The remuda. Somebody's at the remuda." He threw back the covers, grabbed his pants and boots, and scrambled from beneath the wagon. He shouted. "The remuda! Somebody's at the remuda, Indians or somebody! Everybody up!"

Cowboys rolled out of covers, pulled on boots, and

ran to tethered or hobbled horses, skipping as they buttoned up and jammed feet into boots. Mounting, they rode toward where the remuda was held, guessing in the darkness. Some shouted some fired pistols in the air, announcing to the Indians that the cowboys were on them.

As they approached the ground where the remuda had been held, the dark overcast thinned and parted, and a weak moon revealed an empty meadow.

Josh pulled up, shouted at the half dozen cowboys behind him. "Pull up! Quiet!" He strained to hear. The others reined up and tried to control their mounts that stomped and whirled. Josh listened and heard the muffled sound of running horses.

"This way!" He kicked his horse into a gallop toward a break in the brush. Pulling his pistol, he fired a couple of shots in the air, hoping to send a signal to the Indians that they were onto them, fearing he was adding to the flight of the remuda. *Don't step in a hole; don't step in a hole!*

After a wild ride of five minutes, Josh pulled up. The others behind him reined up. "There they are," he said. In the soft moonlight, they saw the horses milling at the edge of a thick copse of dark trees and bushes. "Easy, boys, go easy. Let's show 'em that the excitement is over, and we're just going easy back to the bedding ground."

The hands rode slowly to the horses, talking softly. They circled them and commenced moving them back toward the herd.

Cowboys sat around the breakfast campfire, working on their plates of beans, beef, and biscuits. They looked up at Josh, plate in hand, who had walked from the remuda to the chuck wagon. He sat down heavily, grunting.

"How many did we lose?" Andy said.

"Looks like we lost twenty or thirty," said Josh. "Are we going to make it to Abilene with this lot?" He looked at Andy.

Andy rubbed his chin. "Well, it means that each hand has fewer horses and is going to have to be especially careful with his mounts. You know, we might be able to buy some horses from the Indians. I'm told most bands have lots more horses than they need. They're pretty proud of their horses, but maybe we can coax a few from them. Who knows, maybe we can buy some of the beasts we just lost. Never know what to expect from the wild bucks."

"Wild bucks is it?" said Charley. Everyone turned to him. Charley hardly ever spoke at campfires, usually listening or ignoring the conversation, as if he were not interested or was above idle chatter. Any comment from Charley warranted attention.

"I think some of you need to be educated on the subject of the local inhabitants. Before the war, some of the tribes was raising cattle and shipping 'em to markets, north and east. I'm told they had a regular trade with buyers in Missouri and Illinois."

"You mean Indians kept cattle and sold 'em just like we're doing?" said Toby.

"They did. They kept cattle, drove cattle up north, and sold 'em, years before us Texans were doing the same thing. So I'm told.

"What's more, did you boys know these wild Indians fought on both sides in the Civil War? Yeah, them that fought on the side of the rebels even owned black slaves. That makes them civilized, in some people's view. Now in some parts of Indian Territory, they plant cotton and corn, and they got half a dozen different kinds of churches. I hear they got newspapers and regular towns where they live in houses just like you and me.

"On the other hand, I'm told, some Indians in the Territory decide they want to live in the old ways, and they stay away from the towns, live in teepees, and dress in the old style. And they beg wohaws from the drovers. These are the wild bucks we see."

He smiled, pulled out his tobacco pouch, and began making a cigarette. The cowboys around the fire waited, but he said no more.

"How do you know all this, Charley?" said Toby.

Charley lit the cigarette from a glowing stick he fetched from the fire. He inhaled, exhaled a stream of smoke. "Talked with a soldier couple of days before we left Fort Worth. Seems he was stationed at a fort In Indian Territory. He said that the Territory Indians had their own little civil war. Them that sympathized with the North and them that sympathized with the South fought some battles against each other. Some joined the Union army, and some fought with the Confederates. He said they are still working all that out in the Territory today. So it seems the wild bucks and their people ain't so different from the rest of us." He inhaled again and lapsed into silence, staring into the embers.

"You make them Indians sound almost like regular people," said Petey.

Charley looked at Petey. "You know what these Indians I'm talking about are called? Some people call 'em The Five Civilized Tribes. Yeah."

Harley nodded. "That's most interestin,' Charley. Talking about differences reminds me of a different sort of drive I was on couple of years ago to New Mexico." He pulled a tobacco sack from his pocket and commenced rolling a cigarette.

Charley rolled his eyes, raised his chin. Toby closed his eyes, snorted, fell backwards to the ground.

"The boss had a wanderin' eye in town, and his wife knew it. She decided that he set off on cattle drives at least a couple times a year to get away from her and do some hanky-panky somewhere. So she decided to find out.

"On this particular drive—we was driving a herd to New Mexico—we had hardly passed the county line when this buggy catches up with us, and there was Caldonie as pretty as you please, driving that buggy. Well, Caldonie was a pretty woman, but she wasn't smiling. What she expected to find out, I had no idea.

"Anyway, after a couple of days, she got bored and tired of cowboy food and announced that she was going home. The boss kissed her goodbye and had to send a couple of his hands to ride with her to be sure she got home safe." Harley took a glowing stick from the fire and lit the cigarette. He inhaled deeply, stared into the embers.

"Well, did the boss usually do some hanky-panky on his drives?" said Petey.

Harley looked aside at Petey, smiled. He pulled on the cigarette. "If Miss Caldonie had stayed with us just a few more hours, she would have seen the boss's disappointment in not bein' able to go into a Weatherford saloon where he was acquainted with a pretty young woman he called 'Puss'."

Harley removed the cigarette from his mouth, examined it closely, admiring his craftmanship.

"Damn it, Harley," said Petey, "when he got to Weatherford, did he go into the saloon and see Puss?"

Harley flicked the butt into the fire, stood, stretched, and walked toward the bushes.

"Wow. I never seen buffalo before," said Petey. He and Josh sat their horses in a broad meadow bordered by thin stands of trees on the right and left. They stared at a small herd of buffalo a few hundred yards ahead, grazing at the edge of a row of elms. The riders were downwind and had not spooked the herd.

"You'll likely see a lot more before this drive is finished," said Josh. "The line of trees behind the buffalo suggests water. I would really like to report back to Andy that we found a good place to water the herd." Andy had dispatched two pairs of cowboys ahead after breakfast to search for water. He directed Josh and Petey to ride in a northwesterly direction, which would take them slightly west of the trail.

"The buffalo pose a problem," said Josh. "Looks to be no more than fifty head, but if the cows smell them, or if the buffalo see the cows, the herd and the buffalo likely would bolt in opposite directions, but they might not. We need to try to prevent any sort of meeting."

"Josh, why don't we kill us a buffalo? Sure would be happy to have a buffalo steak. The boys sure would be happy too."

Josh frowned. "What're you going to kill your buffalo with? That pea-shooter on your hip?"

"Hell, you killed a big longhorn with your six-shooter."

"That was a lucky shot. Got him right in the eye. I couldn't do that again in a thousand years. We'll save the buffalo hunting for another time. Right now, we need to move that bunch off the trail, so they don't mix with our herd. Let's ride up there nice and slow now. When they see us, they should move away, hopefully into the timber off to the west."

Pop! Then, pop, pop. The two riders pulled up suddenly at the distant sounds of shots. The buffalo recoiled in unison and were immediately in motion.

"Damn," said Josh. "That's rifle fire, hunters. Coming from the woods, I think. The herd's coming right at us." He pondered just a moment. "Petey, listen, do this. We're going to run with 'em. We'll try to turn 'em to the right, that's west. Get as close as you can, not too close, or you're in trouble. Fire at the ground close to their feet. The sound might turn 'em.

"Okay! They're on us! Go!"

Josh and Petey kicked their horses to a gallop alongside the leaders of the herd. They fired their pistols near the heads of the leaders and into the ground ahead of the stampeding herd. Petey dropped back as Josh plunged ahead.

"They're turning!" Josh shouted. The buffalo in the lead had responded to the shots and veered to the right, and the herd followed. The buffalo galloped on into a break in the timber and were soon swallowed by the forest.

Josh reined up. He pulled a bandanna from a pocket and wiped his face. Pushing the bandanna in the pocket, he turned in the saddle. "Whew, that was no fun. Are you . . . ?"

Petey was nowhere in sight. Josh saw only the

empty meadow, a wide path of trampled grass, and the gouges of running hooves down the center.

What th' hell?

Then he saw him, far back on the trail, standing beside his horse and staring at the prostrate buffalo at his feet. Josh rode to him and stopped. Petey looked up, grinning from ear to ear.

"I'll be damned. Didn't think it was possible," Josh said.

"Hell, Josh, I did it just like you did. Right in the eye. One shot, and he tumbled. Bumped against my horse and almost knocked us over." He couldn't stop grinning.

Josh shook his head. "Petey, you're a wonder. Buffalo steaks tonight. You're right, the boys will love it. Now, we need to take a quick ride to that line of trees back there and confirm that there's a creek in there. Mount up. That animal's not going anywhere. Take care up there. We need to be sure the hunters are not still around."

They mounted and rode at a lope to the copse where the buffalo had been grazing. Sure enough, they found a creek of clear water bordered by low brush. They found no evidence of the hunters.

They set out down the back trail toward the herd, bearing good news on two counts. Good water for the herd and buffalo steaks for the hands.

After riding but a half hour, Josh pulled up. Petey reined up and looked back at Josh who was staring at an oak copse a hundred yards off the trail.

"What is it?" said Petey.

"Indians, I think. In the shade, watching us."

The Indians walked their horses slowly from the shade. "Them's Comanche," said Petey. "They're all dressed up for battle. Look at all the paint and feathers. I'll bet they're young 'uns lookin' to prove how tough they are."

Suddenly the three warriors kicked their ponies into a hard gallop toward Josh and Petey. They held pistols above their heads. One warrior lowered the pistol and fired toward Josh and Petey.

Petey pulled his six-shooter, yelled, and kicked his horse into a gallop directly for the charging Indians.

"Petey! What th' hell!"

Galloping head on, Petey fired. An Indian dropped his pistol and toppled from his horse. The distance between the galloping horses narrowed. Both Indians fired at Petey. He returned fire, and another warrior slid from his mount. The remaining Indian peeled off and raced aside for the trees.

Petey reined up, watching the fleeing Indian. He pushed his six-shooter into the holster and wheeled his horse around, trotted to Josh, and pulled up.

"Petey, you're mad. What in hell got into you?"

"I knew an old ranger who had fought Indians most of his life. He said the best way to fight Indians is to do what they do, go right at 'em. They don't expect it from whites. If they don't kill you first, you'll scare hell out of 'em."

Josh shook his head. "I'll remember that. First thing I'll remember is to be sure you're beside me. C'mon, let's finish up here. We need to ride"

They rode south on the trail. "Where'd you learn to shoot?" said Josh.

"My pa. My pa wore a six-shooter like it was a pair uh pants. Put it on every morning even if he didn't plan to leave the house. He did leave the house ever' few days and sometimes was gone for a day or two.

He'd usually come home with a sack of some kind with all sorts of stuff. When Ma and I asked him where he got the stuff, he'd always say, 'never mind.' He got really mad if we asked any more. We decided he probably stole it.

"Anyway, Pa gave me a gun when I was five. Not a toy gun, a real gun. He had me shootin' bottles and targets, and I was a pretty good shot before I was seven or eight. He said I better learn to shoot, or I wouldn't see twenty."

"How old are you?"

"Nineteen, I think."

"Did your pa use his gun for anything besides shooting at bottles and targets?"

"Probably. He didn't come home from one of his trips. We never saw him again. A deputy brought his horse and an empty sack tied to the horn. The sack had blood on it."

"We got off easy," said Andy. "If you and Petey hadn't been up ahead, we would've had buffalo crashing right into the middle of the herd. Makes me wonder. We need to tell the boys who ride ahead each morning looking for water to also look for buffalo. If they see any that are not running at 'em, they should be able to push them off the trail. Help me spread that word." Josh nodded.

Andy shook his head when Josh told him about the encounter with the Indians. "That boy is a mystery. Everbody thinks he is a bit simple, but I think he has more going on in that head than we suspect. I wouldn't mind at all having him beside me if we get into trouble."

Petey rode with the chuck wagon till Jenny pulled up at the buffalo carcass. He used the butcher knife Jenny handed him to cut off slabs of meat. After stowing the meat in the wagon, he rode back to the herd.

Hands enjoyed the buffalo steaks that evening and were quick to thank Jenny.

"Thank Petey," said Jenny. "He brought it in." The cowboys listened to Petey tell about how he downed the beast with a single shot from his six-shooter.

"Uh six-shooter?" said Alonzo. This required another telling of the story.

"That's not all Petey hunted today," said Josh. "Petey hunts Indians as well as buffalo. Tell 'em, Petey."

Petey recounted the story of the encounter with the three young warriors. The cowboys looked at Josh, who sat apart with Jenny, wondering if Petey had learned too much from Harley. Josh nodded.

Josh and Jenny stood, said good night to the hands, and walked around the wagon to the cooking fire. They refilled coffee cups and sat near the fire circle.

"Well, the boys were happy with the buffalo steaks," said Josh.

"Yeah, me too. But it's too bad we didn't have time to dry the rest. Hate to waste all that good meat." She leaned against Josh, sipping her coffee. A pleasant cooling breeze had come up at sunset, and Jenny now tossed dry sticks and chips on the embers.

"The hands like your meals sure enough, but the buffalo was a good change. And don't worry about all that meat left on the carcass. Somebody will find it, two-legged or four legged. It won't be wasted."

Jenny drew her knees up, wrapped arms around her legs, stared into the flames. "Josh?"

"Jenny?"

"Josh, what's gonna happen after we deliver these cows?" She turned abruptly and looked at him over her arm. "I don't mean . . . I don't mean—"

"I know what you don't mean. I don't know. I can tell you this, my little cookie sweetheart, I'm not letting you out of my sight."

She looked back at the fire. "Yeah, I know. You like my cooking." She leaned into him and nudged him with a shoulder.

"Well, there's that. And a few other things. Like these two right here. He reached around her shoulders and grabbed a breast with each hand.

She struggled, giggling, pushing his hands away. Then she twisted toward him, put her arms around his neck, and held him tightly, sobbing.

He leaned back. "Hey, hey, where did that come from? What's wrong?" She choked back a sob that became a hint of a smile.

She wiped her cheek with a hand. "I don't know. I'm so happy, I'm afraid something is going to happen to ruin it."

He wiped her cheeks with his hands, held her cheeks, and kissed her. "Nothing bad is going to happen to you, sweetheart, only good things." He brightened. "You said at the beginning of this drive that you signed on because you wanted to see a train. Remember? We're gonna see one. If the railroad hasn't reached Abilene by the time we get there, we'll ride east till we see one. Hell, we may ride all the way to Chicago!"

"Hmm. Don't know if I want to go to Chicago for

any reason." She wrapped her arms around her upraised knees. "Maybe I'll see one in Fort Worth. People were saying that the railroad would come to Fort Worth in just a few years."

"We'll see about that." He leaned over, kissed her cheek. "I've got the first night herd ride tonight. I expect you'll be sleeping when I get back. I just might wake you up."

"You better."

JOSH'S EYES OPENED WIDE. He heard a low rumbling, like water boiling in a kettle. Then a flash of sheet lightning lit up the campground like midday. Jenny sat upright abruptly.

"What is it?" she said.

"Afraid we're going to have a bad one. It's—"

He was interrupted by an explosive burst of thunder and a series of lightning flashes then forked lightning that struck in the woods just off the trail. And then the heavens opened, dumping sheets of rain on the camp.

The herd was up milling and beginning to wander. Then a simultaneous burst of thunder and sheet lightning set them off. They broke from the bedding ground, trotted at first, but soon were running.

Cowboys were out of their beds and finding their horses, mounting and trying to hold the cattle. They soon gave up to confusion and darkness. If the cattle had stampeded and run in a loose column, they might be able to control them, but this was no longer a herd, only loose cattle running in all directions. The outfit would wait for daylight.

. . .

At first light, hands who had sat their horses all night in the rain looked around. The bedding ground was empty. There was not a cow in sight.

"All right, everyone over here!" Andy called, and all rode to him. "Jenny is already fixing breakfast. Finish up quick and come back here."

After standing around the chuck wagon, wolfing down leftover chunks of buffalo, fried eggs, beans, and coffee, hands mounted and gathered at the appointed place.

"This is gonna take some time. We'll hunt in pairs, and we'll ride out in every direction. Two hands will stay in camp to tend to cows that are driven in. Jenny has meat and biscuits ready. You may be out all day. Take care. Some of the locals may take this opportunity to pick up a cow or two. Use your judgment on whether to fight 'em off or let 'em take it. Your life is not worth a cow or two."

Andy set to naming pairs and pointing to the sector each pair would search. "Josh, take Petey and Eddie. Eddie might as well get to know the hard part of cowboyin.'"

Josh, Petey, and Eddie sat their horses atop a low ridge of grass and stony outcropping, looking out over a plain of rolling grassland, broken by low parallel ridges. They saw not a single cow or any other animal.

Josh wiped his forehead with a hand. "Strange. It's like we rode into a different country this morning. We're no more'n a couple of hours from the bedding ground, and it's nothing like we've seen."

"I don't see no cows," Petey said. "Which way do we go from here?"

Josh squeezed his eyes shut, then opened them. "I don't know. We left the campground in a northwest direction, so we should move northward, but . . ." He shook his head. *Which way is north?*

"Look," said Eddie. He pointed. A dark mass moved from behind a ridge, gradually expanded, and materialized as five riders. The riders stopped, looked directly at the three cowboys.

"Indians," Josh said. "They see us."

The Indians rode slowly toward the three cowboys, then stopped in the swale below the ridge. They sat quietly, looking up at the cowboys.

"They're in rifle range," said Petey. "Do we shoot 'em? We could pick off every one of 'em."

"Yeah, we could, but that might not be a good idea," Josh said. "They may be a scout for a larger force behind that would hear the shots, and we'd be dead."

No one moved, no sound broke the silence. Then a coyote trotted across the grassy slope below the cowboys.

An Indian kicked his horse into a gallop after the coyote, laughing and waving. Another charged after him, caught up, and both stopped abruptly. They turned, holding their mounts in check, side by side, then burst into a wild gallop, shouting and laughing.

"Those are kids," said Eddie. "They're racing. They're showing off. I think they're Kiowa by their dress. We hunted with the Kiowa some. We gave 'em tobacco and six-shooter shells and sugar. I learned a little Kiowa. It was easy."

Eddie stood up and stepped from behind the rock that shielded him.

"Git down! Are you crazy?" said Petey.

Eddie shouted something unintelligible. The Indians below reined up, and all looked up the slope. One shouted, and Eddie replied.

"What th' hell's going on?" said Josh.

"I said we are friends. And I said I wanted to race with 'em. Kiowas, especially kids, love to race. I'm goin' down."

"You're outta your mind, Eddie!" said Josh. "They'll cut you up in little pieces. They may be kids, but they're Indians, and they are not our friends. Their daddies may be close by."

Eddie slid down the slope behind their rocky hide and went to his horse. Untying the reins, he mounted, rode up the slope, passed Petey and Josh, and down toward the Indians. The Indians sat their horses quietly, watching him coming.

Petey shook his head. "That's the last we'll see of him in one piece."

They watched Eddie, hand upraised in greeting, come up to the Indians. The five boys crowded around him as he talked, pointing up the slope toward Josh and Petey.

They talked some more, laughing and moving their prancing horses in circles. An Indian pointed in the distance, circled his hand, and pointed at the ground before him. Eddie nodded. Then Eddie and a single Indian moved away from the group, stopped side by side, holding their skittish horses in check.

"I'll be damned," said Josh. "They're gonna race."

At a shout from one of the bystanders, Eddie and the Indian rider kicked their horses into flight. They galloped ahead a hundred yards or so, whipped around a stunted oak, and raced back to the starting point. Eddie led by a nose then was gradually overtaken, and the Indian boy won by a length.

The racers turned their heaving mounts back to the others as all laughed and shouted. Eddie dismounted, bowed to the group, raised his arm in a gesture of some sort. He handed his reins to the winning rider, loosened the girth, and slid the saddle from the horse, dropping it on the ground.

The Indians whooped, yelled, and laughed. They kicked their horses to a gallop, the race winner leading his prize, toward the ridge where they had first appeared. Then they were gone.

Josh and Petey went to their horses, mounted, and rode to Eddie who wore a mischievous grin, his saddle at his feet.

"Eddie, we might've traded your horse for our lives," Josh said. "Pretty good trade, I'd say. Good thinking. Sure glad you picked up enough Kiowa to talk to these sprouts."

"That ain't all," said Eddie. "The boy I raced said they saw some cows on a meadow couple of miles from here, up that way." He pointed. "He said they don't know how to handle cows, so didn't go after 'em. He said they would tell the men back in camp about the cows. I think he said, not sure of this, I think he said we better hurry. They all laughed at this."

"Well done, Eddie. Tie your saddle behind me, and ride with Petey. Let's go find us some cows."

"I could have beat him," Eddie said. "I pulled up just a little bit as we got close to the finish line." He grinned.

They rode over two ridges and found a herd of at least two hundred cattle, grazing peacefully on a patch of good grass. Having grazed for hours, they were moved off and herded easily.

"Be easy so they don't scatter," Josh said.

The three tired hands drove their bunch to the main herd that grew each hour with the arrival of other cattle that cowboys had rounded up and driven back to the bedding ground.

Exhausted cowboys sat at the evening campfire, silent for the most part, enjoying their supper, reward for a job well done in collecting all but fifty or so head that were judged lost, to be found by other drovers or Indians. The story of Eddie's race and loss of his horse left cowboys shaking heads and a new attitude toward the new addition to the outfit.

Chapter Eight

Josh woke to the sound of a light rain pattering against the canvas wagon cover. It was a sound he had come to enjoy, growing up in semi-arid country, a soft pat-pit-pat against a wall or side of the house or barn. Especially at night, like now, to be awakened by a sound that sent him dreaming.

The sound of rain on canvas grew louder. *Uh-oh.* Flashes of sheet lightning illuminated the campground. He sat up. A rumbling in the north was followed by explosions of thunder and forked lightning. A lightning flash showed the cows rising from the bedding ground and beginning to walk about.

He sat up, nudged Jenny. She jerked aside. "Wha"

—

"We got a stampede building," She sat up, threw back the blanket.

"Get dressed and stay here," said Josh. "I need to get out there." He dressed quickly, pulled on his boots and slicker, kissed her, and crawled from underneath the wagon.

Flashes of lightning and shouts from all quarters showed hands finding mounts and moving slowly around the herd. The cattle, pelted by the downpour, walked about, heads hanging.

Then, mixed with the sound of the heavy rain and rolling thunder and occasional loud bursts, they heard the rumble of hooves from the northern trail. Lightning flashes, now almost constant, illuminated the galloping horde bearing down on them.

"Buffalo!" Josh shouted. "Move aside! Get away! They're on us!"

The cattle whirled and set off running on the back trail as cowboys pulled away from the herd. The massive buffalo herd galloped through the camp, merging with the cattle, and all ran together as one mass. Cowboys could only listen and watch as lightning flashes showed the herd running hard, receding, vanishing. The sound of hooves lessened and died.

FINDING the scattered herd required one full day and the better part of a second. Miraculously, they had not gone far. It seems the buffalo had given up the run and veered off, leaving the bulk of the cattle herd milling about the trail. Hands were sent out east and west of the trail and located bands of cows that were easily collected and driven back to the original bedding ground.

After dinner on the second day after the stampede, the herd was thrown on the trail and headed north as if nothing unusual had happened. Jenny was late getting away from the campground and caught up with the herd. Josh had helped her clean up and pack and now rode beside the wagon.

He looked up at her on the wagon seat, staring, smiling.

"What?" she said.

"We've missed two nights of playtime. We need to catch up."

"You want me to pull off to that shady bunch of trees over there?" She pointed.

He laughed. "I s'pose we better wait till tonight. Unless you think we *should* pull over there now." He smiled.

She stared over his head at the herd.

He followed her stare, turned back to her. "What is it?"

"You see that dark beast right in the middle of the herd, straight over from here?"

He looked, frowned. "Yes, why, that looks like—"

"Yeah, a buffalo."

"Be damned. A young one, shorter than the cows, easy to miss. Looks like we might have buffalo steaks for supper."

She frowned, paused. "No."

"What do you mean, 'no'?"

"She's hardly older than a calf. I'll bet she's following a mother cow. I don't want that little 'un killed, by you or anybody else."

He looked aside, then back to Jenny. "I imagine no one else has seen the critter, or they would be after it."

"Then you get after it and get that baby out of the herd and pointed on the back trail where we lost the buffalo herd."

He frowned, cocked his head.

"If you won't do it, I will. Lend me your horse, or get mine from the remuda, and you can drive the wagon."

He looked aside, shaking his head. "You're dead set on this, are you?"

"I am."

He jerked the reins and kicked his horse to a lope toward the herd. Paul, riding point, saw him coming and reined up. Josh pulled up beside him. After a moment, Paul looked toward the wagon and laughed loud enough for Jenny to hear him. Paul shrugged his shoulders, looking toward Jenny.

Josh pointed his horse into the herd. He moved slowly, around cows, behind some, ahead of some, until he was in the center of the herd beside the buffalo calf. Much to his surprise, the calf did not bolt as wild animals normally did when confronted by people. Josh took his lariat from the saddle horn, shook out a short loop, and dropped it over the head of the calf. The calf shook its head but did not fight the loop or try to move away. Josh tightened the loop gently and led the calf from the center of the herd around and behind cows till he emerged from the column, the calf following without any fuss.

Only then did other hands see what was happening. "Hey, what th' hell!" Another: "Look what Josh found right in the middle of the herd!" "Josh, where did you find that little critter. Supper!"

When he continued to ride on the back trail, the docile calf following on a slack lariat, past the drag riders without looking aside or responding to the calls, the tone of the calls changed. "Hey, where th' hell you goin'?"

"Josh, come back here with them buffalo steaks."

"What's goin' on?"

When he was a hundred yards from the end of the herd, Josh pulled up and dismounted, ground tying his horse. He went to the calf, loosened the noose, and removed it. The calf backed up a couple of steps, head lowered, watching its captor.

"Dammit, do somethin.'" Josh waved his arms. "Beat it! Find your mama!

The calf jumped, whirled, and ran away down the back trail, prancing, kicking, dancing right and left, then settled down to a run.

Hope you're satisfied, Jenny sweetheart. You got me in a passel of trouble with the hands.

When he rode back to the herd and took his place at right flank, the cowboys he passed simply looked at him. Except Toby. "When I first saw that little critter, my mouth started watering. I could taste them steaks. Then you did what you did. Why did you do that?"

"Ask Jenny."

As she filled plates at the chuck wagon, Jenny ignored the questions at first. Finally, she stopped serving, put hands on hips. "Because I didn't want that little baby to be killed, and I didn't want her mama to lose her."

The hands were incredulous. "Jenny," said Harwood, "you talk like that calf was a person, not a dumb animal."

"Well, I've known some persons who had less brains than some dumb animals I've come across."

No one seemed to have a response, and Jenny returned to filling plates.

JOSH LAY ON HIS SIDE, facing Jenny who was on her back, eyes closed and smiling.

"Satisfied?" Josh spoke softly into her ear.

"Yes. Are you? Don't you feel good about it, returning that little baby to her mama?"

He closed his eyes, grimaced. "Not sure how long it will take for the boys to consider me sane again."

"That's all right. Gives them something to think about beside cows and saloons and whores."

"Hmm. As for that—"

"This conversation is gettin' out of hand. Go to sleep." She leaned over, kissed him, rolled back, and closed her eyes.

Nooning. After an uneventful morning drive, the outfit stopped for dinner under a warm sun, directly overhead in a cloudless sky. Cowboys sat in the shade of the chuck wagon and under a huge oak alongside. Conversation was sparse as they paid attention to their plates. Jenny and Josh sat on the ground in the shade of the serving gate at the back of the wagon.

Everyone looked up at the appearance of about two dozen Indians riding at a walk toward the campground. The Indians were bunched up, unsmiling, riding toward the camp, but seemingly oblivious of it.

Josh stood and walked to Andy who stood in the open, facing the approaching Indians. The Indians pulled up before him, and Andy raised an arm in greeting. The leader responded with an upraised arm. Andy pulled a tobacco pouch from his pocket, held it out, and signaled a spot under the shade tree to sit. The leader and three others dismounted, handed their reins to others.

Andy spoke to the cowboys sitting in the shade. "Give us some space, fellas, got to see what's comin' down here." The hands, including Paul, stood and walked toward the chuck wagon, carrying their plates.

"Paul, come sit with us. You too, Josh." The three walked to the shade, followed by the four Indians. The three cowboys sat facing the Indians. Andy offered his tobacco pouch to the leader. Paul pulled a pouch from a pocket and offered it to an Indian. The pouches were passed around, and each Indian then proceeded expertly to roll a cigarette.

Jenny walked over from the cooking fire, holding a short piece of kindling that glowed at the tip. She offered it to the Indian leader who frowned, then leaned forward and lit his cigarette. He leaned back, eyes closed, and inhaled deeply. She stepped to the others and lit their cigarettes. The Indians, those sitting and still mounted, eyed her with obvious interest.

Jenny then handed the glowing stick to Josh and walked toward the wagon. Some of the Indians watched her until she disappeared around the wagon. Indians had passed pouches back to Andy and Paul, and they rolled cigarettes and lit them.

Minutes passed. Those with cigarettes puffed contentedly. Those still sitting their horses watched the seated men and occasionally glanced toward the herd.

After a good five minutes of silence, the leader spoke. "White man have many fat cows." Andy nodded. And waited. "White man cows eat Indian grass, drink Indian water." Andy nodded. "White man cows cross Indian land." Andy nodded.

After a long pause: "White man give poor Indian brother ten fat cows."

Andy did not react. He smiled. "This white man is poor. He needs to sell these cows to feed his mother and wife and children."

Josh leaned to Paul, whispered. "Does Andy have a wife and children?"

"Nah," said Paul, whispering, still looking at the Indian leader.

"Tell you what," said Andy. "I will share with my Indian brother. I will give you two fat cows, and you can choose them."

The Indian leader stared at Andy, then turned to the Indians seated behind him and spoke rapidly. The three stood, took their reins from others, mounted, and moved off toward the herd. Some of the mounted Indians hooted and shouted. The leader, still seated, nodded to Andy, stood and mounted, and the group walked their horses toward the herd.

Suddenly, everyone, Indians and cowboys, looked up at the sound of a horse galloping from the north trail toward the camp. The rider passed the fire circle and reined up hard where the leader had been watching others in the process of choosing the two cows Andy offered. The rider spoke rapidly, breathlessly, to the leader. The leader shouted sharply to his followers who ran to their horses, mounted hurriedly, and all kicked their horses to a gallop down the back trail.

The cowboys watched the sudden flight of the Indians until they left the trail and disappeared into an oak grove.

"What th' hell's goin' on?" said Harwood. "They didn't even take the cows Andy gave 'em."

Andy frowned, still staring at the wood where the warriors had vanished. "Something ain't right. Those people were scared. I don't suppose we'll ever know." He turned back to the hands. "Party's over. Let's get back to work."

Josh walked with Andy toward the remuda. "I don't get it," said Josh. "They had enough warriors to demand the whole herd."

"They wouldn't do that. They've had enough dealings with the army in recent years to know that they would be in real trouble if they molested whites. But I'm told some hot heads still give drovers trouble. We'll need to be careful."

"Where did they learn their English?" Josh said.

"From recent contacts with the army probably, but also from their experience during the war. They had a lot of contact with whites during the war years, some with Yankees and some with rebels."

"Where did you learn to deal with Indians. You looked like an old hand."

Andy smiled. "I've talked a lot with old friends over a whiskey who have had more experience with Indians than me." He stood, brushed his pants. "Let's get this herd moving. I'm already getting' thirsty and thinking about Abilene."

Cowboys stood, tossed butts in the fire, walked to the chuck wagon. Depositing empty plates in the wash can, they walked toward the remuda, chatting and laughing.

Sudden shouts and whoops from the trail ahead brought them up. The cowboys stared at a horde of Indians in feathers and war paint galloping hard toward them.

"Oh my god," said Paul, "it's a whole Indian nation!"

About five hundred warriors rode at full gallop toward the camp. The hands, surprised, frightened, and awed, could only stand their ground and watch. The Indians were almost on them when they pulled up, still whooping and shouting. They loped and galloped around the fire circle and the chuck wagon. Some laughed and showed their riding skills, leaning to the side of their mount, holding on to the mane. Others lay on their mount's back or stood upright, riding full speed.

The cowboys were so mesmerized by the horsemen's tricks that they didn't notice at first what was happening at the herd. Warriors rode along the sides of the stationary herd, shooting arrows into cows. The hands could only watch as hundreds of whooping Indians rode around them and the chuck wagon where Jenny sat on the driver's seat, hat pulled down low over her forehead.

As the hands watched helplessly, Indians dismounted, skinned carcasses, and tied the hides on packhorses. Some cut strips of flesh from the dead cows and ate it raw. Others cut slabs of meat and packed them on horses.

The turmoil ended as quickly as it began. At a shouted signal, warriors on the ground mounted quickly. All whooped and yelled, waved bows and spears, and kicked their horses into a gallop northward on the trail. The band turned off the trail and disappeared into a stand of pines.

Utter silence. Hands looked ahead at the empty trail and at each other.

"What th' hell," said Paul.

Andy shook his head. "What th' hell is right. I thought we was done for. Sure never counted on that. We probably got off light. We're all still kickin,' and all we lost is a few animals. How many did we lose?"

"Looks like fifteen or so," said Josh. "Lots of meat

left on the carcasses. Okay if Petey and I cut off some steaks for supper?"

"Sure," Andy said. "Rest of you, get the herd settled, and let's move out. Glad they didn't go after the horses."

Cowboys walked to the remuda where Charley and Harwood with some difficulty had held skittish horses inside the rope corral during the turmoil. Mounts were soon saddled, and the herd was thrown on the trail. By the time they had begun to string out, fresh slabs of beef had been loaded into the chuck wagon, and Jenny soon pulled ahead of the column.

Josh rode beside Harley. "That explains why the first bunch hightailed it," said Harley. "That Indian that rode up and sent 'em runnin' must've sighted the mob coming this way and told his compatriots that the big bunch was comin.' I don't rightly know who's who, but the two bunches sure ain't friends.

"Fella back in Fort Worth who knows a lot more about Indian Territory than I do, told me that it's gonna get harder and harder to move cattle through Indian country. I've said it before, the Indians we're seein' are the wild 'uns. But there's lots of Indians that ain't so wild. Some seem almost civilized, 'specially in the eastern parts. This friend said that the tribes in the eastern part of the Territory had started charging a tax of ten cents or more for each beef that's passing through their lands. That's why, I'm told, cattlemen stopped driving north on the Shawnee Trail in the eastern part of the Territory and moved westward to the Chisholm Trail. Man, whatever happened to the wide-open spaces?"

. . .

Andy had come increasingly to rely on Josh's judgement and noticed that the other hands looked up to him. Occasionally he had Josh ride with him at the front, particularly when Paul was occupied elsewhere.

"We'll stop in an hour or so," said Andy. "The boys who went out earlier said we should hit a passable creek and a good patch of grass about then." He closed his eyes, inhaled deeply. "It's been a good day."

"What about that cloud?" Josh said. He motioned with his head at the dark cloud layer that seemed to rest on the western horizon.

"Hmm. Hadn't even noticed. Daydreamin,' I suppose. Bears watchin.'"

They indeed watched as the dark mass at the horizon expanded outward and upward and moved eastward toward the trail. An occasional soft distant burst of thunder was followed by a low rumbling.

"That don't look good," said Andy, "but we're stopping in a bit, and it just might pass north of us."

"I don't think so, boss." They watched as the black cloud advanced rapidly eastward and southward, obscuring the sun. A light rain began to fall, and forked lightning repeatedly shot from the cloud to the ground, followed by distant explosions of thunder.

Andy turned in his saddle and shouted. "All right, boys, here it comes! Put 'em in a tight milling. Keep 'em close!" He turned to Josh. "Looks bad. Help Jenny tie the wagon down." Josh spurred his horse to a gallop toward the chuck wagon ahead on the trail.

Before he reached the wagon, the heavens opened. Rain and sleet fell in torrents as sheets undulated and obscured the view. Josh jumped off his horse at the wagon and tied the reins to a wheel. Jenny glanced hurriedly at him as she pulled handfuls of rawhide strips from the front of the wagon and dropped them on the ground.

A stack of stakes followed. She reached back for a wooden mallet and an iron hammer. Handing the hammer to Josh, both set to work driving stakes on each side of wheels. They ran the leather strips through spokes and tied them to stakes on each side of the wheel. This done, they tightened ties on the canvas wagon top and checked the ties at front and back.

"What about the mules?" Josh said.

"I'm leaving 'em in harness. The lines are tied to low limbs, so I'm hoping that's better than throwing them with the remuda. We're going to lose some animals, Josh. This looks like the worst weather we've had."

They heard shouts at the herd and saw through sheets of rain that hands were having a hard time keeping the beeves in a slow mill.

"Josh!" said Jenny. He followed her gaze north on the trail.

"I hear it. Thought it was thunder, but it's a herd coming down hard." He turned toward the herd and shouted. "Stampede coming down from the north! Stampede from the north!" Josh hurriedly untied his horse's reins, mounted, and galloped toward the herd.

Alerted by Josh's shouts and now seeing dimly through the sheets of rain the mass of the herd bearing down on them, hands stopped in their tracks, trying to keep skittish horses in check. The noise from the stampeding herd grew louder, merging with exploding thunder and jagged bolts of lightning shooting from black clouds overhead.

Cowboys in Andy's herd turned the cows and had just begun to push them southward on the trail when the oncoming cattle crashed into the herd, and they merged into a surging column. Josh galloped along the edge of the rampaging herd, not sure what he should be doing.

The storm gathered as thunder exploded, sending some cows jumping sideways or straight up. Lightning struck among the massed cows, sending electric pulses around the herd, dancing around horns and ears. A massive lightning bolt struck a galloping group of cows not ten feet from Josh. Two cows were thrown violently sideways, and Josh had to rein hard left to avoid the rolling bodies.

Josh swayed in the saddle. It seemed they had been running forever. The rain slackened, and the thunder lessened to a distant low rumbling. A weak moon sent slivers of light through the light cloud cover. The landscape was dimly visible as shapes and shadows. Josh shook his head, throwing off fatigue.

Is this the way it is in hell?

Dim shouts came from cowboys at the head of the stampeding column. Josh caught only an occasional word over the deafening hooves at his side. ". . . ahead . . . herd . . . another herd!"

Another herd? We're running into another herd? God help us.

Riding about halfway back from the front of the massed two herds, Josh reined a bit away from the column and looked ahead. In the dim moonlight, he saw what appeared to be a herd that was being turned around in preparation for the mass of animals stampeding toward them. Within a couple of minutes, the three herds had become one. Cowboys of the three outfits rode alongside, helpless, just keeping up.

. . .

FIRST LIGHT. The cattle from the massed three herds walked with heads down and tongues hanging. Cowboys riding on each side of the column drooped in their saddles. With shouts and quirts, they pushed the lead cows into a turn and soon had the huge herd in a slow mill. Some cows stood spraddle-legged; others grazed on the wet grass; still more lay down. Sam and Andy sat their horses near the herd.

"Didn't expect to see you till some Abilene saloon," said Andy.

"Same here," Sam said.

"I s'pose the storm set 'em off?"

"Never seen anything like it. I lost five cows to lightning. Maybe more. We'll know when we head back up the trail. I had a cowboy knocked clean out of his saddle by lightning. I thought he was dead and pulled up. But he jumped up and just looked around, rubbing his leg. He was pretty dazed but seems okay now. We looked for his horse, but that little mare is prob'ly halfway to Texas by now. How did you come out?"

"Won't know till we get organized," Andy said. "We'll—

"Here comes Fred, the boss of the herd behind you. I met him when we started the mill." Sam waved to the approaching rider who pulled up beside them. "Fred, Andy."

Fred touched his hat. "Knew there was at least one herd in front of me, but sure didn't want to meet you two on these terms. How do you think we oughta handle this?"

"Let's let 'em cool down the rest of the day," Andy said. "Grass here is pretty good. One of my boys told me that there's a passable creek in that wood yonder."

He pointed at a line of trees a couple hundred yards off the trail. "They smell it but don't seem to be anxious to run for water like they usually do. We can push 'em over there by bunches during the day." He inhaled heavily. "Then we'll see if we can break this lot here into three herds and search the neighborhood for strays. I wager there's more out there than there is here. This is gonna take a while."

As soon as he was satisfied that the massed herds were under control, Josh rode back to the chuck wagon. As he approached, Jenny, leaning against the side of the wagon, watched him come. Before he arrived, she stepped away from the wagon. He had hardly dismounted when she grabbed him, and they embraced. He started to pull back, but she held him.

"I worried about you, Josh Nesbitt. I was afraid I would never see you alive again." She choked back a sob.

He took her cheeks in his hands and kissed her. "Everything's fine now. The boys are sorting things out back there, but it's gonna take some time. Looks like we'll be here a few days, collecting the cows that strayed and separating the bunch into three herds."

He looked at the wagon. The stakes and ties had been removed from the wheels. The mules were hobbled in a patch of grass nearby. A bucket of water lay between them.

"You sure have things under control here. Let's get the wagon down to the herd. We'll find you a shady spot. You'll be stationary for some days."

"This delay means we're gonna run out of a lot of things," she said. "I'll ask around and see if anybody knows whether there is someplace short of Abilene where we can stock up. We might have to send a couple of hands ahead with packhorses."

"Good idea. If we can find a dead cow to butcher that's not already putrid, we'll have beef. Otherwise, I'll hunt for meat." He took a step toward the mules. "I'll get the mules." He pulled a face and jumped aside to avoid her swing.

Jenny pulled the wagon into the shade of a stand of maple trees. Josh dismounted, went to the water barrel on the wagon side, took a cup from a hook, and dipped it into the barrel. He looked up to see Pedro coming.

"You were ahead on the trail?" said Pedro. "Did you see Alonzo? I can't find him. Nobody has seen him. Have you seen him, Miss Jenny?"

"No. When did you last see him?"

"He was riding beside me when the other herd hit us. It was dark, and I could hardly see anything in the rain." Pedro drooped. His face was contorted as he fought back tears.

Josh put a hand on Pedro's shoulder. "Pedro, I'll tell all the others in all the outfits to keep a lookout for him. We'll find him."

Pedro nodded, turned away, and walked toward the herd. He wiped his eyes with a sleeve.

After an agonizing, exhausting, frustrating week, the job was finished. Hands from the three outfits had scoured the countryside for miles in all directions, collecting cattle in meadows, in ravines, in sheltered woods, in bunches and singles. After consolidating the cattle into one large herd, cowboys rode through the mass, cutting out their brands and pushing them into three distinct herds.

During the week, exhausted cowboys sat around evening campfires, ate their supper with little conversation, crawled into their beds, and dropped off to sleep in an instant. The last evening, after finishing the separation of the herds, campfire gatherings were back to the usual, with a good measure of yarning and raucous laughter. They visited the other camps, confirming new friendships and offering good-lucks and be-carefuls with plenty of handshakes and back-slapping.

The three bosses agreed that they would move out in the original order, Sam first, then Andy followed by Fred. They would leave a suitable interval between herds to avoid mingling.

Before heading for his bed at the chuck wagon, Josh found Andy and asked if he could ride ahead of Sam's herd to look for Alonzo. He asked if he could take Pedro with him.

Andy frowned. "Think that's a good idea?"

"Pedro is worried to distraction. I think he should know as soon as possible."

"Yeah, I guess." He pondered, looked aside. "Alonzo didn't run away. He's too close to Pedro." He looked up into the dark sky. "I figure you'll find him."

Josh found Pedro and told him to be ready to ride at first light. Riding to the remuda, he selected one of his string and put a halter on it. He rode to the chuck wagon, leading the other horse. Hobbling the horses near the mules, also hobbled, he crawled under the wagon to the bedroll.

"About time," Jenny said. "I was afraid you had signed on with another outfit."

He pulled her to him and kissed her lips, gently squeezed a breast, kissed her again. He lay back. "If I tried that, they would tell me I can't sign on unless I bring the cookie with me. Those boys have sampled too many of your offerings." He rolled over to face her. "They haven' been sampling anything that belongs to you besides your cooking, have they?"

"Hmm. I'd be lyin' if I said I hadn't had a few offers when you were nowhere in sight."

"Who were they? I'll kill 'em. I'll kill 'em all."

"Then who's gonna drive all them cows to Abilene?"

"That many? Well, I suppose I'll have to leave 'em be. We gotta get those herds to Abilene." He kissed her. "You liar."

She pulled back. "You think so? Shall I call roll tomorrow morning when we see all them cowboys ridin' by?" She pinched his cheeks, kissed him, pulled him to her. "C'mon, you can sample anything you like."

JOSH ROLLED out of the bedroll at first light. He kissed Jenny who jerked the cover up over her head. Pulling his boots on, he crawled from the wagon, stood and tucked the shirt into his pants, and buttoned up. He saddled his mount and rode to Pedro who was already sitting his horse, waiting for him. Josh handed him a couple of biscuits from the small bag that Jenny had given him last evening, and they set out.

"Why are you bringing the other horse?" said Pedro. He looked at the horse that Josh led. A small bundle was tied on its back.

Josh pondered. "We might do some hunting on the

way back. I've seen lots of antelope and deer on my morning rides looking for water. Would be nice to have some fresh wild meat after all that half-spoiled beef."

They passed Sam's herd, waved to cowboys who stood and sat around their chuckwagon, eating an early breakfast. After but fifteen minutes, they had left outfits and herds behind and were alone on the trail.

They had no difficulty retracing their route. The trail had dried out from the storm a week ago, but it was still deeply gouged from the hooves of thousands of stampeding cattle. After a half hour riding, they might have thought themselves the only persons in the universe. The trail at this distance from Sam's herd was still marked with the track of running cattle, but the prairie on each side of the trail was green and lush. Only a few scattered maples and small crabapples broke the view.

Pedro stared at a distant line of trees. "There's probably a creek over there," he said. "Maybe Alonzo needed to drink, and he went there."

Josh was not looking at the wood. He stared at a fragment of color in the center of the trail ahead. As they approached, the color became a dark blue cloth streaked with mud.

Pedro still stared at the wood. "Can we ride over—"

"He's not in the woods, Pedro," Josh said.

Pedro looked at Josh, frowning. Then he saw it. They rode a bit further, then pulled up, scattering a dozen crows from what had been Alonzo. They dismounted and stared at the body. It had been trampled repeatedly until it was but a layer of cloth and crushed flesh and bone. Wolves and vultures and crows had left little inside the cloth that resembled human remains.

Pedro stood over the body, in shock, eyes bulging and jaw hanging. He dropped to his knees, sobbing, rocking back and forth. He touched the blue fabric. "Era mi mejor amigo. Era mi paisano. Era como hermano." He beat his fists on the ground. "Porque nos fuimos de San Antonio? Maldito sea este arreo de ganado!" [He was my best friend. He was my countryman. He was like my brother. Why did we leave San Antonio? Damn this cattle drive!]

Josh put his hands on Pedro's shoulders. "C'mon, cowboy. C'mon, Pedro. We need to get back to the outfit. We'll take Alonzo with us and have a proper burial." Josh helped him stand. He untied the bundle from the packhorse's back and pulled out a canvas sheet. Unrolling it, he laid it beside the remains.

"Give me a hand, Pedro." They stooped and lifted the body that was no thicker than a folded blanket and placed it gently on the sheet, folding the canvas over it. Josh lifted the bundle, draped it over the horse, and tied it down.

Pedro drooped, head hanging. Josh rested a hand on his shoulder. "Sorry, cowboy." They mounted and rode south on the trail.

After a half hour's ride, they passed Sam's herd. Cowboys watched them and their sorrowful burden. A couple of hands removed hats as they passed. Another half hour and they passed the chuck wagon. Jenny pulled up and watched them pass. She waved, and Josh nodded. She shook the lines and moved on.

After supper, they buried Alonzo under a low white dogwood tree that still bore a few blossoms. Spent blossoms covered the ground. Cowboys removed their hats, and Charley recited the Lord's Prayer. Andy asked Pedro if he would like to say anything. Pedro, tears streaming down his cheeks, shook his bowed head vigorously.

As they walked from the burial site, Josh told Pedro that Andy said he was going to give Alonzo's pay to him, if that was okay with him. Without looking at Josh, Pedro nodded and said he would take it and give it to Alonzo's poor parents.

Josh put an arm around Pedro's shoulders. "Sad business," Josh said.

Chapter Nine

THE DAYS that followed were so pleasant and ordered that the memory of the stampede was virtually forgotten. Andy had lost thirty cows and half a dozen horses, but while scouring the countryside for his beeves, cowboys had collected about twenty branded cows that belonged to somebody else and half a dozen unbranded range cows. He would take the branded cows to Abilene and try to locate the owner. The unbranded would be useful to give to Indian suppliants or to slaughter for beef.

The branded cows were a bit of a mystery since he still thought Sam's herd was the first on the trail this year, and the brand didn't belong to him. Could they belong to local tribes that had begun identifying their herds with brands? If so, he had no intention of searching for these owners.

They rode through lush grasslands, often stopping early in the evening, preferably near a creek, to let the cattle graze and water. They knew that cattle that were well-fed and watered bedded down more peacefully and drove more easily the next day.

Cowboys with some leisure time usually had no trouble taking fish from streams. They walked into the woods and shot deer and turkey. The game and fish were given to Jenny who was happy to add the wild foods to the menu. The foragers also often found blackberries and plums which they usually ate on the spot, but enough were delivered to Jenny to provide the makings for pies, always a treat for the hands that craved variety from the usual chuck wagon fare.

"Now what?" Josh sat with others around the chuck wagon, just finishing off a dinner of beef, beans, potatoes, and biscuits. All stared at a party of ten men riding slowly, silently, toward the camp. The only sound was the lazy slapping of canvas on the bows of the chuck wagon from the light breeze.

"I'll get Andy," said Petey. "He's back with Charley at the remuda." He jumped up and ran toward the remuda.

The ten men pulled up near the cowboys who were all on their feet now, holding plates and waiting.

"Sorry to interrupt your dinner," said the rider at the front. "We got business with the trail boss."

"He's with the remuda," said Josh. "We've sent for him."

The leader looked around. "Could I trouble you for some water? Hot and dry today."

"Over here," said Toby. He walked to the chuck wagon, dropped his dishes in the wash bucket, and took a couple of cups from hooks on the side of the wagon next to the water barrel. "Come over and help yourselves."

Half a dozen riders dismounted and handed their reins to others who remained mounted. They walked to the wagon, filled cups and drank, took full cups to the others.

Josh studied the visitors. He was puzzled. Anyone who rode into a strange camp usually introduced themselves and stated their business. He turned and saw Andy striding over.

"I'm the trail boss. What can we do for you?"

"We're inspecting for ticks, and we need to look at your herd. The charge for this service is twenty-five cents a head, and I'd appreciate it if you would get the payment ready for me to collect when we've done."

Andy didn't move. He simply stared at the leader. Finally: "What's your authority for this service? Who do you work for?"

"Territory of Kansas."

"We're not in Kansas. We're in Indian Territory."

"Well, they send us south to prevent any herds carrying ticks to enter Kansas." He took the reins from the mounted cowboy who held them. "We ain't got time to talk about this. Now you just tell your boys to keep the herd bunched, and we'll get to work."

Andy and the hands didn't move. They were all standing now. "Show me a paper that gives you authority to inspect my herd," said Andy.

"I've got the paper, I've told you I have the authority, and I'll do what I said we're gonna do. Now tell your hands to control the herd while we do our work!"

During this conversation, the riders all dismounted and lined out behind the leader, facing Andy's cowboys who had gradually spread out behind Andy.

Andy spoke slowly and softly. "No, you won't do anything with my herd. I think you're a bunch of crooked rascals with no authority and no aim but to rob honest people."

The leader reached for his pistol. "By God, I'll—"

"Hey! Look at me!"

Everyone looked suddenly toward the chuck wagon where Jenny stood, a shotgun leveled on the leader.

"First gun drawn by any of you lot," she said, "and this scattergun's gonna ruin a lotta pretty hats and the brains under 'em!"

The leader's hand hovered above his pistol grip as he stared at Jenny. "She wouldn't—"

"Yeah, she would, man," said Josh slowly. "Don't test her."

The leader and his men looked at each other, trying to decide. While the leader and his men hesitated, Andy and his hands drew their pistols and leveled on the visitors.

"Be on your way, fellas," said Andy, "and be glad you still have heads on your shoulders. If you'll look again, you'll notice she hasn't lowered that shotgun and still has that look in her eyes. She might pull that trigger yet. We have a hard time keeping that woman in check. She's a mean 'un."

The riders scrambled to their horses, mounted and drummed their mounts' bellies, galloping up the trail and disappearing into the woods.

The outfit to a man turned to Jenny. She lowered the shotgun and smiled. Josh walked to her. "Where did you find the shells?"

"Shells?"

Josh took the shotgun and broke it. The chamber

was empty. The hands laughed, slapped backs, gathering up their plates and cups.

"That's our cookie!" shouted Harley. "Don't nobody cross our cookie!'

Josh put the shotgun in the wagon behind the seat. He went back to Jenny, took her cheeks in his hands. "Jenny, Jenny, Jenny, what am I going to do with this woman?"

She put her hands to his cheeks, pinched, and held on. "Josh, Josh, Josh," she said softly, "you come to bed tonight as soon as you finish your supper, and I'll tell you what you can do with this woman."

Josh stood at the morning cook fire, watching Jenny pull away and onto the trail. She waved from the wagon seat without looking back. He waved, knowing she did not see him. He felt a sense of loss, as he always did when she set out after breakfast was finished. He shook his head, walked toward the remuda where other hands were saddling up and riding off to the herd.

He rode point this morning. Andy, riding in front at the trail boss position, looked back over his shoulder and waved. His head raised, Josh looked up into a clear, powder blue sky. A soft breeze cooled his cheek. He smiled, marveling at his good fortune. Riding with good comrades, the end of the drive in sight, in love with a wonderful woman who loved him as much as he loved her. At least, he hoped she did.

"Josh!"

He started, looked up abruptly. He had been

dozing. He looked at Andy who pointed ahead. A wagon was stopped in the center of the trail. The team stood still, and the lines lay on the ground beside the team.

"Get up there," said Andy, "looks like our wagon."

Josh spurred his mount to a gallop toward the wagon. He touched his six-shooter. He reined up beside the team. It was the outfit's chuck wagon. The wagon seat was empty. Josh looked around frantically, his gut suddenly on fire. He searched for any sign of struggle, any clue to what had happened. He saw nothing. Only the empty wagon seat on a chuck wagon that otherwise was exactly as it had left camp after breakfast.

Josh looked up at hoofbeats. Harley and Petey pulled up beside him.

"Andy sent us to help," said Harley. "We'll find the bastards."

Petey dismounted and walked to the side of the trail where the hoofprints of moving cattle ended. He studied the ground.

"Here they are. Three horses. They seem to be walking." He followed the prints, searching the ground, then looked up. "They seem to be heading for those trees over there." He pointed at a dense grove of oak, the ground underneath the trees crowded with sage.

"I'll kill the sons-uh-bitches," said Josh softly. "I won't ask questions. I'll kill the sons-uh- bitches. If they've harmed her, they're gonna beg me to kill 'em."

"Softly, boys, softly," said Harley. "They're probably not too smart. They might've stopped right over there in the woods. Go easy."

Josh nodded. He walked his horse over the prints. Petey mounted, and he and Harley followed.

As they moved into the shaded woods, the prints became more pronounced in wet ground and easier to follow. Josh pulled his six-shooter, and Harley and Petey drew their pistols. They stopped at a small clearing, then saw hoofprints leaving the wood and entering a meadow.

"I'm going to follow the prints best I can," said Josh. He pushed his six-shooter into its holster. "Harley, move off to the right a bit, and you, Petey, off a bit to the left. Keep in sight if you can. Let's move as fast as we can, but careful not to spook 'em. Go."

They set out at a slow lope, fanning out, moving ahead toward a low rising a hundred yards away.

As he topped the rising, Josh saw them. Two men sat on a log at a small fire. The third stood over Jenny who sat cross-legged on the ground beside the fire, her hands tied behind her.

"You sons-uh-bitches! I'll kill you!" Josh spurred his horse down the slope, drawing his pistol as his horse brushed against dense sage bushes.

The two men at the fire jumped up and ran toward horses tied to saplings behind them. The man standing over Jenny drew his pistol and brought it up toward Josh. Jenny quickly struggled to her feet and lunged at the man. At that moment, Josh's shot struck him in the chest, and he collapsed into the fire.

The man's companions meanwhile had pulled pistols from saddlebags and leveled on Josh. Each man suddenly was blown backward by shots from Harley and Petey and fell beside their mounts.

Josh pulled up beside the campfire. He dismounted, holstering the six-shooter. He lifted Jenny from the ground, pulled her to him, and held her tightly.

"Hey, you're gonna squeeze the life outta me. Lighten up. I'm not goin' anywhere."

He released her, took her cheeks in his hands and kissed her, then pulled back and looked into her eyes. "My, but you're a piece of trouble."

"Thanks, boys," said Jenny to Harley and Petey, who stood nearby, holding their horses' reins.

"Glad to be of service, Missy," said Harley. Petey grinned, nodded.

"Harley," said Josh, "appreciate it if you would ride back to the herd and report to Andy. Petey and I will stay with Jenny at the wagon in case these yahoos have any friends as dumb as them. We're waiting for the herd to catch us. Dinner will be a little late."

Harley mounted and kicked his horse to a gallop back to the trail. Petey and Josh mounted, and Josh pulled Jenny up behind him. She put her arms around his waist and held him tighter than necessary to hold on.

They reined up at the wagon. Dismounting, they tied reins to wheels. Jenny climbed up to the wagon seat and reached behind the seat inside the wagon. She bought out a handful of biscuits.

"Anybody for a biscuit?"

"I sure would," said Petey. She handed him a couple of biscuits. He took them and wandered away, munching on the flaky bread.

She offered a couple of biscuits to Josh. He took them without seeing them. He saw only her face, her eyes, her lips, and her hair. His eyes were misty.

She looked toward Petey as he strolled on the meadow. Turning back to Josh, she took his face in her hands. "Honey, everything's okay. I'm here."

"Yeah. I'm still shaking, I'm so mad. I could have

ripped those sons-uh-bitches to shreds. I would still be shredding them if they had hurt you."

"Well, they didn't. They talked about what they planned to do, but you got there in time. I was wishing all the time I had the shotgun, but that would only have got me killed. I actually reached for it when they stopped me but thought better of it. I recognized the leader of the bunch from yesterday."

"Here comes the herd," said Josh. Petey walked back to the wagon. "We'll ride with the herd and stop for nooning as usual. Harley will have told everybody about what happened, and they'll expect a late dinner."

THERE WERE no repercussions from the encounter the previous day, but Andy decided that henceforth one or two hands would ride with Jenny each time she drove ahead to get ready for the next meal. He figured the hands selected for the task would be delighted. They would have Jenny's company and no work to do. Unless they were accosted by strangers.

Josh and Petey left this morning after a hurried breakfast to search for water, an everyday task. Another pair of hands rode in a slightly different direction, still not far from the intended trail. Now Josh and Petey sat their horses looking across a grassy meadow into a wood of scattered sycamore and elm.

"What do you make of that?" said Petey. They stared at a bunch of cows, standing in the shade. A few grazed, and others stood motionless.

"Let's have a look," Josh said. They rode to the wood, slowly, trying not to disturb the cows, and reined up short of the wood. "Must be fifty head or so. Most are branded, but I don't recognize it. Number of range cattle as well. I'll ride a bit deeper into the wood to see if there's water back there. The cows came here for some reason more than shade. You stay here and discourage any that want to wander off."

Josh rode into the wood, taking care not to disturb the cows. He confirmed his assumption with the discovery of a narrow creek bordered by dense brush. Riding from the copse, he waved to Petey. "It's a creek, all right. Okay, let's move them out, slowly, and back to the herd. Andy's going to be real happy."

Andy indeed was happy. Yesterday afternoon's drive was dry, and they had a hard time bedding the herd. All hands had been on edge. They knew that a thirsty herd is more likely to stampede than one that is fed and watered before bedding down. So, Josh and Petey's discovery was welcome news.

The small herd they drove in was welcome as well. "I don't recognize the brand," Andy said. "Must be a herd in front of Sam. I thought he was first this year. We'll keep 'em with us and turn 'em over if we find the owner. The range cattle can come in handy. Any time Jenny needs beef, we'll kill an unbranded cow. We can also give them to Indians who ask us politely for a cow."

They hadn't long to wait for the next Indian visit. The hands had hardly turned in their supper dishes at the chuck wagon and begun to roll cigarettes around the campfire when they saw a band of twenty warriors galloping toward camp. The cowboys quickly pocketed their tobacco pouches, stood, and touched their pistol grips.

The Indians reined in, the horses dancing and

settling. The warrior at the head dismounted, Andy stepped toward him, raised an arm in greeting.

The Indian responded with a raised arm. "How."

"How," Andy said.

The Indian looked past Andy at the herd. "White brother have much fine cattle. Give poor John five fat cow."

Andy relaxed, smiled, looked past the speaker. "Poor John has many fine horses. I think Poor John not poor. I give two fat cows. Take your pick." He waved toward the herd. "Take cows no brand." He described a brand by tracing a circle and square with a finger in the air. "Do you understand? No brand." The Indian nodded. Andy pulled his tobacco pouch from a pocket and offered it to him. The Indian took it, showed it to the mounted warriors. They nodded, some with upraised arms.

"Poor John, how many herds in front of us?" He pointed to his herd, then pointed up the trail, showed two and three upraised fingers.

"I understand. Two, maybe three. I see two."

"Good. Okay, take your cows. Two, no brands."

The warrior nodded, mounted, and led his men toward the herd at a walk.

"Whoo," said Toby. "Josh, your strays come in handy already. Glad they took the strays and not my scalp."

"Speaking of scalps," Paul said. He waited for Jenny who walked toward the campfire, coffee cup on hand. "Jenny, cookies I have known usually cut hair. Would you be willing to take that on? I'm gettin' pretty wooly, and I wouldn't trust my scalp to any of the yahoos in this outfit. Would you be willin' to give me a trimming?"

Jenny frowned. "Hmm. I suppose I could give it a try if you're willing to take the result with no complaint." She looked him over, right to left. "Yeah, you do need some work on that hair. Pretty soon, it's gonna be hard to see your eyes." She looked around, pointed. "Sit on that rock there, and I'll get my tools." She handed her cup to Josh who sat at the fire circle.

"Now?" said Paul.

She stopped, put hands on hips, scowled. "Now. Unless you were trying to suggest that I'm not a proper cookie that sometimes cuts hair. Hmm?"

Paul reached his hands out, palms toward Jenny. "No, no, not at all. I really want a haircut." After a moment, she turned and walked toward the wagon. She rustled around in the wagon front and came back with scissors and comb. She stood before Paul on his rock, scissors in one hand and comb in the other.

She set to work, pulling the comb through his hair, snipping, then combing, studying her work, then snipping, and the hair fell to his shoulders and in his lap. She leaned back, frowning, appraising, then combed and snipped again. Cowboys by now had gathered around barber and customer, grinning, jaws hanging. Occasionally, Jenny looked at them, frowned, and they turned sober, straightening, occasionally pulling a face.

Finally, Jenny straightened, flexed her back. "All right, you're done."

Paul stood, ran fingers through his hair, removing loose hairs. He turned to the circle of cowboys.

Petey grinned from ear to ear. "Boy, you look like uh porkypine, Paul." The others snickered and guffawed.

Jenny turned on Petey, glaring, eyes squinting. "You're next."

Petey recoiled, open-mouthed. "I don't need no haircut."

"Yeah, you do. You got a head that looks like a horse tail and might scare the cows into a stampede. Sit down." She pointed at the rock.

"Aw, Jenny—" He writhed.

"Sit down. In addition to cutting hair, you might remember that I also fix breakfast, dinner, and supper. Sit down!"

He slumped and sat on the rock, as the hands gathered around.

Jenny looked him over, scissors and comb in hand, and set to combing and snipping, combing and snipping, combing and snipping. Cowboys looked on, eyes widening, jaws hanging.

As he watched the cut hair falling before his eyes, Petey's face dropped, in despair, it seemed, and acceptance.

After ten minutes of combing and snipping, Jenny stepped back, squinting and appraising. She looked at the line of cowboys, now silent, open-mouthed, looking at each other.

"Be damned," said Charley. "That looks like a head of hair that was cut by a barber." Sober mutterings of agreement from the others.

"Would you do me next," said Freddie, "it's been months since my Mama cut my hair. He ran the fingers of both hands through the heavy mop. It was the first time Jenny had heard the boy from the Rio Grande drive speak.

"Me too," said Pedro.

Jenny smiled. "You two will be first tomorrow after supper. If we're near water, wash your hair. That goes for anybody else who wants a cut down the line. I don't want to deal with any more dirty mops.

"And you, Harley. Your hair looks like a Texas tornado landed on top. You need to get in line for a trim."

"Me? Ah, no, missy." He ran the fingers of both hands slowly through his hair, his chin uplifted. "I believe in the Sampson idea about hair. My strength is in my hair. If I lost my hair, I would be weak as all these shorthairs around me."

This explanation was followed by laughter, rough comment, and no little backslapping. Jenny sat down beside Josh and retrieved her coffee cup. She sipped, made a face.

"Want me to get a fresh cup for you?" Josh said. She shook her head.

The hands were unusually quiet, smoking and staring into the flames.

Harley flipped his cigarette butt into the fire. "You know, Jenny's mention of stampede a minute ago reminds me of what happened to the outfit I was with a few years ago on a drive to Colorado." A few hands leaned toward Harley in anticipation. A few others looked at each other, rolled their eyes. One cowboy flopped on his back and began snoring.

"We was driving about two thousand head, and everything went real easy for the first month. No problems with finding grass or water, no problems with the herd at all. Then everything changed. A light breeze come up, and it was nice on that hot day. Then the breeze turned to a wind, and the wind turned into a proper storm. Then we saw right in the middle of the trail ahead, a little twister, swirling the dust and leaves and patties and little pieces of wood.

"Then all hell broke loose. That twister got bigger and faster and turned into a proper tornado. It moved toward us, and there was nothin' we could do. We just sat our horses and watched it come. This twister come on right into the herd, scattering cows and horses in every direction.

"Then the strangest thing happened. About two dozen cows and a cowboy who was ridin' beside 'em was lifted up in the air, swirled around higher and higher until they was right over our heads. And there they hung in the air, the two dozen cows and the cowboy spaced out like they was standing there in the air, but we saw 'em from the bottom, their legs stretched out and standing on nothin.' Then they spun faster and higher and just disappeared. All of us on the ground just looked at each other and shook our heads.

"Well, we collected all the cows that the tornado had scattered and threw 'em back on the trail."

Harley pulled out his tobacco pouch and commenced rolling a cigarette. The hands watched silently. He picked up a stick from the fire and lit the smoke.

Petey writhed. "C'mon, Harley, tell us what happened to the cows and cowboys in the air."

Harley looked at Petey. He inhaled deeply, exhaled a stream of smoke. "Oh, yeah. We kept moving the herd up the trail. Then we turned around a big stand of pines, and there they was. There was the two dozen cows grazing peacefully right in the middle of the trail and the cowboy setting his horse right beside 'em."

Three cowboys fell backward on the ground and snored loudly.

Petey frowned. "But, Harley, that don't"

Harley tossed his cigarette into the flames. "Bedtime, fellas." He stood, gripped his pants at the waist, and slid them side to side. "Early start tomorrow." Others at the fire stood, threw butts into the fire.

Petey didn't move. "Dammit, Harley."

JOSH AND HARLEY rode ahead on what they thought was the trail. Josh was now considered the top water searcher and rode out most mornings looking for water. Harley, a senior of many sorts in the outfit, did not normally make the early morning ride but asked for the assignment today.

"What I really have in mind son, is not water, but buffalo. You see, some old boys back in Fort Worth told me that the most fun they ever had was roping buffalo. Now, I never done that, and I sure would like to give it a try."

Josh searched the land ahead, ignoring the comment.

"I've shot buffalo," Harley said, "but never roped one."

They rode silently, studying the trail and particularly the occasional line of brush and trees at the edge of a meadow that could suggest water.

Harley suddenly pulled up. "Josh." It was almost a whisper. "Look." Josh saw the small black mass at the edge of a wood ahead, a hundred yards off the trail on the left side, that moved slightly, then expanded and separated to become a small group of animals.

"That's buffalo, fer sure," said Harley. His hand rested on the coil of rope at his saddle. Josh noticed.

"Harley, that's not a good idea. We're doing two things on these morning rides, looking for water and moving buffalo off the trail so they won't bother the cattle.

Harley stared ahead. "They're off the trail, ain't they." He pushed his horse to a fast walk, fingering the rope coil with his right hand.

"Don't do it. If you put 'em up, and they stampede back down the trail, we're in trouble."

Harley ignored him, eyes fixed on the buffalo, seemingly hypnotized by the sight. He kicked his mount to a lope.

Josh grimaced and followed, unsure how to handle the situation and already concocting an explanation to Andy if something should go wrong.

As the riders drew closer to the small bunch of twenty or so buffalo, the animals' heads came up, and they began to trot away alongside the line of trees. Harley kicked his horse to a full gallop, meanwhile lifting the coil from his saddle with his right hand and beginning to open a loop.

Josh followed, helplessly, knowing Harley was determined and now committed.

Harley reined alongside a young cow at the edge of the galloping bunch on his left. The cow swerved toward the horse that shied, then recovered, and Harley moved the mount closer. He held the loop at his right side, leaned forward, and swung it awkwardly in front of his mount's head leftward at the buffalo. The loop dropped over the buffalo's head and slipped down to the neck. Harley pulled on the noose and reined slightly to the right.

Then all hell broke loose. When the noose tightened around the cow's neck, she swerved to the left, and the rope struck the horse's breast. The horse suddenly broke stride, and the rope slid down, entangling the horse's legs. The mount stumbled and fell, throwing Harley over his head, and horse and rider tumbled.

Josh had watched with a mounting fear. Galloping just behind Harley, Josh had shouted to him, knowing that nothing would stop him now. When horse and rider fell, Josh pulled up hard, dismounted quickly, and ran to the prostrate Harley. He knelt beside him. Harley lay on his back, still, facing up and eyes closed.

Josh was paralyzed. *What do I do now?*

Harley's eyes opened slowly, fluttered. He saw Josh. "Damn, that was no fun," softly, a whisper. He smiled a hint of a smile. "Am I dead?"

"No, you aren't dead, you old geezer. But you might be after Andy gets through with you."

Josh helped him sit up. Harley braced himself, shook his head. "Well, we won't tell him what happened, will we? Help me stand." Josh slipped his hands under Harley's armpits and pulled him up, grunting with the effort.

Harley shook his head, ran fingers through his hair. He examined the ripped shirt front, the muddy smears on his trousers, felt the purple bruises on his cheeks. He turned to Josh. "You know what happened, don't you? Damn horse stepped in a prairie dog hole. They're all over the place. Been afeared my horse was going to step in one. And sure enough, it did." He leaned toward Josh, almost nose to nose. "You saw that, didn't you?"

Josh smiled. "Sure, Harley, sure I did." He looked ahead at the empty meadows on each side of the trail. "Good thing the buffalo ran ahead and not back toward the herd. Then I'd let you do the talking with Andy."

Back at the herd, Josh reported to Andy that they had found no water. Andy accepted this report, studying Harley while he listened to Josh.

"Well?" said Andy.

"Damn horse stepped in a prairie dog hole," Harley said. "Little critters are all over the place. Surprised it hasn't happened before to somebody."

Andy looked him over again, head to toe. "I don't recall you need to run your horse when looking for water. This didn't happen walking your horse."

Harley looked aside at Josh. "Well, we knew you wanted a report as soon as possible, so we ran a bit to hurry it all up." He looked quickly back at Josh.

Andy looked one to the other, shook his head. "Git to the herd."

At nooning, Josh stood in the wagon shade with Jenny. "I don't feel sorry for old Harley," she said. "I feel sorry for the poor buffalo that will have to drag that rope around till it falls off or chokes her to death. Poor thing."

AT SUPPER THAT EVENING, all the hands wanted to talk about was Harley's story about the prairie dogs that nobody believed. Yet, they continued to ask him about it, prodding him to tell the story again, laughing and joking.

"Tell us what really happened," said Toby. "I thank your horse got tired of an old wooly geezer on his back and just plain threw you." Laughter all around.

Harley ignored him. He spooned potatoes to his mouth, chewed slowly, gazing into the fire. Josh sat across the campfire and watched him. He had never seen him like this. Harley always had something pithy to say, especially when he was the butt of conversation. But now, nothing.

Harwood grinned, leaned toward Harley. "Old man, I think . . ."

Harley looked up at Josh, gestured aside with a slight movement of his head. He stood and walked to the chuck wagon, dropped his plate into the bucket, and walked from the wagon to the edge of firelight. Josh went to the wagon, deposited his plate, and walked to Harley.

Harley stared into the darkness. Josh waited.

Harley turned to him. "Did you ever hear about the blue mustang mare?"

Josh shook his head. "No."

Harley inhaled deeply. "I've heard about the blue mustang since I was a little kid. When I grew up, I supposed it was just a story people told to sound like they knew something you didn't, something mysterious, to make you think about something outside your head."

"Never heard of it."

"I hadn't thought about the blue mustang for some years now, but I never forgot about it."

"Where's this going, Harley?"

Harley turned to him; a face Josh had not seen before. "I saw the blue mustang mare up there today." His eyes opened wide, and he leaned toward Josh. "I saw her, Josh. Just when I was about to toss the loop over that buffalo, I saw her at the edge of the wood beyond the herd. That's why I messed up my toss. I was tossing at the buffalo, but I was watching the mare. She stood there stock still, not moving, watching me just like I was watching her."

Harley's excitement had grown with the telling of

the story, and Josh worried. Had his old comrade begun to drift? Had a childhood fantasy become his reality?

Josh waited.

"Then my horse got tangled in the rope, and we tumbled. Soon as I hit the ground, I looked for the blue mustang, but she was gone. Then I blacked out." He shook his head, looked up into the darkness.

He turned to Josh. "I'm going out tomorrow before breakfast. Come with me. I'll clear it with Andy. We're looking for water."

Josh hesitated. "Sure you want to do this? Maybe—"

"I'm not tetched, Josh," softly. "I saw her. You comin'?"

"Sure."

THEY RODE at a walk following the line of the wood. Josh said they needed to ride into the trees, looking for the stream that a wood often suggested.

"Not yet. I don't want to frighten her. If she's watching us, we would spook her if we rode in." They rode a parallel course to the wood, fifty yards from the line of sycamore and maple trees.

Nothing. Josh was becoming impatient. They had been riding an hour and had yet to do what they were supposed to do, look for water. He became convinced the line of lush timber signaled water.

Josh removed his hat, pulled out a bandanna, and wiped his face and head. "Harley, it's gettin' awful hot. We need to check the wood for water and get back to the herd."

"Yeah, suppose so."

They reined toward the line of trees. Harley drooped, studying his horse's ears.

Josh suddenly pulled back on his reins, causing his mount to jerk her head upward and shake her head.

My god! My god! "Harley!" It was a whisper that brought Harley's head up. He reined up. They stared, open-mouthed, at a horse, unmistakably blue, at the edge of the wood. The blue mustang mare was alone, rigid as a statue, watching the two intruders.

"Is it real?" Josh said, a whisper.

Harley sat his horse, his body relaxed and his face serene. He smiled, just a hint of a smile. "Oh, yes, she's real. I've seen her in my head, in my dreams, enough to know she's real."

"What do we do now?"

"Just what we're doin'."

"Don't you want to get her?"

Harley turned to Josh. He spoke slowly, softly. "We do that, and she would be just another saddle horse. She needs to go free, stay free." With that, Harley spurred his mount, reined to the right, and galloped along the line of the trees, Josh following. The blue mustang burst into flight, galloping along the line of trees, matching Harley's gait.

After a five-minute furious gallop, Harley shouted toward the mustang and waved an arm. The mare turned and disappeared into the dark wood.

Harley pulled up, and Josh reined up beside him. Harley looked at him, turned away, and wiped a tear. "We don't say nothin' to the boys, okay?" Josh nodded.

They stared at the wood where the blue mustang mare had vanished, then turned and rode down the back trail.

Chapter Ten

"WHAT'S WRONG? IS IT ME?" Jenny lay on her side, facing Josh who was on his back, staring at the dark underside of the wagon bed. Playtime had been more a habit than the usual, almost frantic, breathless coupling.

"No, sweetheart, it's not you. It's me. And that damn blue horse." He turned to face her and told her about the blue mustang mare.

"I never heard this story," she said. "Sounds like a ghost story. You know, I've been wondering lately if old Harley was beginning to drift a little. He has the strangest look on his face sometimes, like he's not here, but somewhere else."

"But I saw that horse, Jenny! At least, I think I did. Could Harley have seen that blue mustang because he wanted to see it? And could I have followed along and thought I saw it too? It was hot that morning. Could we both have been suffering from the heat?"

She touched his cheek. "I don't know, honey, and now you're giving me a headache. Give me a kiss, and we'll go to sleep and try not to dream about blue horses." She rolled on her side, facing away, and scooted back against him.

He closed his eyes, breathed deeply, opened his eyes. "I almost expected that blue horse to sprout wings and—"

She jumped, rolled over, and pounced on him, her hand over his mouth. "Stop it! If you don't be quiet, I'm going to get up and . . . and . . . go sleep with Harwood! Will you be quiet?"

He mumbled an okay. She removed her hand, kissed him, and lay back.

Josh frowned. *Harwood?*

BREAKFAST WAS FINISHED, the chuck wagon was packed up, mules hitched, and Jenny climbed up to the seat. Standing beside the team, Josh watched her pull away.

The herd had been watered last evening just before bedding down on good grass. The combination of water and good grass was the recipe for a contented herd. Andy gave the word this morning to get the herd up slowly, throw them on the trail gently, and let them move at their own pace for a time, grazing as they moved ahead.

They had gone but a few miles at this pace when everyone in the outfit saw riders ahead coming at a brisk gallop directly for the herd, raising a cloud of dust that obscured their features.

"Easy!" Andy shouted to the hands. "Easy, be ready!" Andy was riding at the front of the column. Josh was behind him at point.

As the riders drew closer, they materialized as Indians, about twenty, in buckskins and feathers in their hair. When it appeared they would collide with Andy, they pulled up hard.

The Indian at the front raised an arm as his excited horse pranced and settled. "How," he said.

Andy raised his arm. "How." He waited for a response and received none. "What can I do for you this fine morning? I suspect I know what you want me to do this fine morning." He smiled.

The Indian at the front who had greeted Andy turned to those behind him and spoke rapidly. A number of them replied sharply, and the leader turned back to Andy.

"Wohaw," the Indian said.

"Yes, that's what I figured. You want a wohaw." He turned to Josh who had ridden up beside him. "Or two or three or five wohaw." He figured the Indian didn't understand a word beyond "wohaw."

"Wohaw?" said Josh.

"That's what some Indians call a cow. They've heard ox-drivers shouting at their team, and they think that's what they call their cows."

The Indian pointed at the herd. "Plenty wohaw." He pointed at his chest. "Five wohaw."

Andy smiled grimly. "Oh, it's five wohaws now, is it?" Andy shouted to Paul who rode point opposite Josh. "Paul, keep 'em moving. I'm going to have a smoke with the chief here. Josh, you stay with me." Andy pulled a tobacco pouch from a pocket and showed it to the Indian. The Indian nodded and said something to those behind him.

Andy and Josh dismounted and tied their reins to a low buckthorn. The chief and two others dismounted, handing reins to others who remained mounted. Andy sat on the ground and motioned to the others to sit. He pulled a second pouch from a pocket and handed the two pouches to the chief. He and the other two Indians proceeded to roll smokes which Andy lit with a lucifer. He retrieved a pouch, rolled a cigarette, and lit it. He offered the pouch to Josh who declined.

The smokers puffed contentedly, silently, staring at the land, the sky, the herd, ignoring all but the smokes they held. Ten minutes passed.

"Josh," said Andy, "you're gonna take one or two of these bucks and cut out two unbranded strays for 'em. I'm counting on them being okay with that, but we'll see."

Andy stood, followed by Josh. He dropped his smoke and crushed it with a boot. The Indians stood and waited. "Two wohaw, chief." He held up two fingers. "Send a couple of your boys with my man." He pointed to the Indians behind the chief, and he pointed to Josh. Then he pointed at the herd. He held up two fingers again. "Two wohaw."

He turned to Josh. "Now we'll see if we're gonna have trouble with this arrangement." He glanced aside at the chief who stared at him, unmoving. After a moment, the chief spoke to the men behind him, and two stepped aside. One pointed at the herd. Josh and the two Indians mounted and rode toward the herd.

The chief still stood with Andy. His face betrayed no emotion, carried no signal. He took his reins from the Indian who held them and mounted. The group rode toward the herd where they waited at the side, watching Josh and the two Indians enter the column.

After delivering the strays to the Indians, Josh rode to Andy. They watched the group riding up the trail. An occasional whoop and shout rose from the group.

Andy chuckled. "I don't know whether those

shouts mean 'hooray-we-got-the-cows,' or do they mean 'we'll-come-back-for-the-others.' We'll need to keep our eyes open."

Dusk. The hands sat around the campfire, finishing supper, scraping plates, and sopping up gravy with biscuits. Jenny sat beside Josh, sipping from a coffee cup.

"I swear, Jenny," said Charley, "you're gonna have to start servin' us on bigger plates or let us come through the line twice."

"You're welcome to come back to the cook fire as long as there's anything in the pot," she said, "but you'll have to serve yourself. By the time you come back for seconds, I'll be sittin' right here."

Charley waved his fork in reply. He glanced at Andy. "What's that you got, Andy?"

He looked up. "My sketch map. I figure we're in central Kansas now, and we got a decision to make. And that decision depends on where the railhead is. We still don't know whether it's in Junction City or Abilene. And I expect we'll only find buyers at the railhead."

He grimaced and looked up. "Paul, I want you to ride ahead in the morning and see if you can find out anything about this. Take Josh with you. There's at least two herds ahead of us. See if they know anything. Find out where they're heading. Better take some vittles and bedrolls in case you have to spend a night or two out."

"I wouldn't mind spendin' a night or two out," said Harwood, "that is if I had a bottle to keep me company." He looked aside at Andy, grinning.

"I know Andy's ban on alcohol in camp is not too popular," said Harley, "but sounds pretty good to me. I'm reminded of what happened on a drive couple of years ago."

Cowboys looked at each other. One flopped back and began snoring.

"Cookie bought a bottle at a town where he had taken the chuck wagon in to buy supplies. That night, after everbody was in bed, he drank that bottle, all of it, and turned into a madman. He took an ax and took to chopping off the heads of sleeping cowboys. He killed four boys this way and was headed for me when I woke up and saw him over me with the ax raised. I jumped up and yelled, and he ran away to the woods. We put up a guard the next few nights to be sure this madman didn't come back."

Loud snoring accompanied the end of Harley's story.

Jenny leaned against Josh, then stood. "C'mon, I need to work on these vittles that Andy says you need to take with you tomorrow." Josh stood and walked with Jenny toward the wagon. The hands, as usual, watched them go, silent for the most part.

At the wagon, Jenny grasped the front of his shirt, pulled him to her, and kissed him. "What am I going to do about playtime?" She cocked her head, smiling. "Maybe I'll ask one of the boys to visit me while you're gone."

"If I see any of the boys grinning for no reason when I get back, I'll kill 'im, and I'll thrash you."

"Sure you will." She peered into the back of the wagon. "I'll be up early tomorrow to fix some biscuits and whatever else I can rustle up for your pack. You'll need to count on hunting for your meat." She turned back. "But that's tomorrow. We need to turn in now for you-know-what."

PAUL AND JOSH rode out at first light. They alternated between a walk and a lope, trying to cover ground, pushing ahead of the herd. In late afternoon, they saw a herd ahead, watering at a narrow stream. They rode toward a cluster of cowboys sitting their horses near the stream, watching them come.

"Didn't expect to see you boys any time soon." The speaker was Sam, boss of the outfit whose herd had stampeded and merged with Andy's herd.

"Didn't expect to have to ride up this way," said Paul.

"I suspect you're going to ask me a question that I can't answer."

"Yep. But I hoped you would have an answer. The railhead."

"I know nothing about that.," said Sam." We've just about decided to send somebody ahead to find out. I'm heading for Abilene at the moment, but I could change that to Junction City real fast if I hear something different."

"That's about where we are too. We'll spend the night with you, if that's all right, and be off tomorrow."

"The camp's yours. Supper and a campfire and breakfast."

"Thankee. We'll be off after breakfast. Your boys are welcome to ride with us, or we'll send word if we learn anything. Any idea how many herds ahead of you?"

"There's one for sure, and that may be the only

one. I was going to send a couple of boys ahead, but I suppose you'll be visiting them."

"Probably. I'm hoping for Abilene. I heard before leaving Fort Worth that the farmers around Junction City are not happy about the prospects of cattle coming in there, trampling their crops and getting the local stock excited."

Paul and Josh waved goodbye to Sam and his boys at first light and set out before the herd was thrown onto the trail. They again alternated between a walk and lope and soon left Sam's herd behind.

For the rest of the day, they saw no animals but a herd of antelope that ran across the trail ahead, stopping in the middle of the trail to stare at the intruders. Then, they bolted and were gone. Later, a small herd of a few buffalo stood at the far side of a meadow, motionless, watching the riders pass.

The riders stopped before sundown on the banks of a shallow stream of clear water that was hidden by dense brush. Josh walked along the bank hardly a minute and bagged two fat rabbits with his rifle. By the time he had them skinned and gutted, Paul had a fire going and a spit set up.

They roasted the carcasses over the fire and tore cooked strips from the hot flesh, eating silently, hot fat dripping from their hands.

When they were finished, Paul wiped his hands on his trouser legs. He drank from his canteen and offered it to Josh. Josh waved him away, picked up his own canteen, and drank.

"When all this is finished, what's happening with you?" said Paul.

"Jenny."

Paul smiled. "I understand."

"What about you?"

Paul leaned back; his eyes closed. "Dunno. I've done a few drives now, and I don't think I want to do this forever." He opened his eyes and stared at the flames. "I've heard that some boys who have come up the trail have stayed to open ranches in Colorado and Wyoming. If we don't find a buyer, maybe Andy will decide to do the same. Even if we do find a buyer, maybe I'll ask for my pay in cows and start my own place." He turned to Josh. "What do you think?"

Josh frowned. "Hmm. Never thought of that. Sounds interesting. Pretty scary, too. You'd be settling on lands the Indians think belong to them."

"True enough, but there would be others around, ranchers and farmers. And the army couldn't be far behind as those lands are being settled up. Wouldn't be long before towns would appear. Think on it. We could be in at the beginning."

Josh stared into the embers as his mind raced.

JOSH SAT up and watched the sun just beginning to send its rays through the stand of scattered oaks. He stood and walked off the trail to relieve himself. Coming back, he patted his mount on the back where she was hobbled.

Paul stood beside his saddle, which had served as a pillow. He waved to Josh, scratched his head vigorously with both hands, then bent to pull a sack from the saddlebag. He took out some strips of jerky, handed a couple to Josh who acknowledged with a nod.

They stopped last evening and camped just off the

trail, expecting no one would disturb their sleep. Now they stood quiet, watching the day come, chewing the salty dried beef. Paul studied the piece he held. "Well, it ain't like Jenny's cooking, but I've gotta say it's the best jerky I ever tasted."

Josh smiled. "No surprise there since it's Jenny's jerky."

Andy nodded. "Ready?"

"Yep." They wiped hands on trousers and picked up saddles and blankets. Josh stopped. "Hold on." Andy stopped and followed his gaze.

A throng of people emerged from a wood ahead and moved toward the trail. Some were mounted, leading packhorses, but most were afoot. The people walked slowly, men and women carrying packs. Children also carried small bags, calling dogs that cavorted about the column.

"What do we have here?" said Paul.

They watched in silence. "I wager that's a whole village moving," said Josh.

The people walked southward, came abreast, and walked on, looking aside at the two strangers. A man left the throng and walked toward Andy and Josh. He came up to them, raised a hand in greeting.

The man wore a loincloth and leggings of tanned hides and a light brown cotton shirt. His hat appeared to be army issue. He wore a rawhide necklace of elk teeth.

"Can you tell me how far to water?" the Indian said.

Josh pointed to the south. "About two hours walk. There's a creek just off the trail on the right side. Good water. Do you want water?"

The man nodded. Josh pointed to the ground, and

the man sat. Paul sat beside him while Josh fetched a canteen from his saddlebag and offered it to the man who drank deeply.

"Where do you go? Josh said.

"We are Wichita. We are returning to our home. We were driven from our lands in Indian Territory by Confederates in their war. We went north and settled on the Little Arkansas. Jesse Chisholm set up a trading post at our settlement. Do you know Jesse Chisholm?"

"We have heard of him," said Paul. "Why are you leaving your settlement?"

"Americans are moving to Kansas where we live. They do not want us to live there. So we are going back to our home in Indian Territory now that the big war is over. We hope the other tribes there will not bother us."

"Your English is good," said Josh.

"I work for the army in Indian Territory before we had to leave. And I work for Jesse Chisholm in his store." He stood. "Now I must leave. My people will need me. We hunt for food, and I am the best shot." He smiled.

"What is your name?" said Andy.

"I am Onacona."

"Onacona, I am Paul, and this here is Josh. On this trail, you will pass two herds. The boss of the first herd is Sam, and the boss of the second herd is Andy. Tell them Paul and Josh said Onacona is a good man and tell them Paul and Josh said to give you three cows."

Onacona nodded, twice. "You are good white men, Paul and Josh. I have not known many good white men." He waved a goodbye and trotted toward the column. He slowed when he caught up with the stragglers and walked with them.

"Be damned," said Josh. "The more I see of Indians, the more I begin to understand what's been happening to them since the whites moved into their lands. It don't excuse them for what they've done to whites—I don't forget the savages killed my folks—but I begin to understand they are reacting to what the whites have done to them."

"Hmm. I hear where you're comin' from, but I've seen too much Indian killing, like your folks, to feel quite as kindly as you seem to."

"Onacona?"

"He's a good Indian, seems to know where he fits in today's world."

Josh picked up his saddle and walked toward his mount.

"Now who might they be?" said Paul. "Don't look like cowboys."

The column of Wichita had hardly disappeared down the back trail when Paul and Josh, riding at a walk, saw two riders on the trail ahead coming toward them. One of the riders waved.

The four riders met and pulled up. "Howdy, boys," said Paul. "I'm Paul, this is Josh. We got a herd of Texas longhorns a couple of days back heading this way. Who might you be, and what're you about?"

The riders beamed. "We're from Abilene, and we're looking for you. I'm John, and this is Vince," motioning toward his companion. "We're in the employ of Mr. Joseph McCoy who is setting up a cattle shipping operation in Abilene. He sent us south to assure drovers that he is ready to buy their herds, beginning right now!"

Paul looked at Josh, then back to John, the speaker. "He's set up to buy and ship now?"

"Well, he's buying now and will begin shipping soon. But that's not a problem. Mr. McCoy has bought land outside Abilene to put cows on until he can begin shipping. He's building shipping pens right now, and he'll be ready to ship in just a little while. Just come on in. He's buying right now."

"How many herds between us and Abilene?"

"Just two."

"And Mr. McCoy has enough space for those herds and ours?"

"He does indeed. Just come on in, and you'll see."

PAUL AND JOSH met the herd at the noon stop. The hands already had their dinner plates in hand and were sitting around the chuck wagon. All watched Jenny hug Josh and cling to him as he looked over her shoulder at the grinning hands.

When she pulled back, she saw the hands watching. She raised her chin. "What of it? Hurry up with those plates. I'm just about to pack up and leave you, sitting on your big fat butts!"

The hands whooped and hollered, all in good fun. Even Jenny had to laugh.

Jenny dished out plates for Paul and Josh, and they sat beside Andy. Paul told about their exchange with McCoy's men. "They were pretty happy, finding us, and we were the third herd they had met. My impression is that this McCoy is really anxious to find herds to buy. If he really has bought land to put cows on and is building shipping pens, he's invested a lot of money in all this. We should get a good price."

"You'd think so," Andy said, "but sounds like he has no competition. So nobody else is going to bid on our herd."

"But you have no choice," said Josh. "You'll have to take what he offers."

"Maybe. Maybe not. If I'm not satisfied with his price, I may decide to pass by Abilene and the train and drive on north. I heard stories in Fort Worth that people are setting up ranches in Colorado and Wyoming, and even farther, in Montana. The rumors say the demand for cattle and horses is strong for stocking ranches. We'll see what old McCoy offers."

Josh remembered his conversation with Paul last evening as they stripped slivers of meat from the roast rabbit.

"There's the first sign that we're coming up on Abilene," said Paul. He and Josh and Harley had ridden through a field of sunflowers and now sat their horses at the edge of a sizable cornfield. The slanting evening sun cast long shadows from the tall green stalks.

"I remember what an old hand who had been up this way told me about Kansas," said Harley. "He said 'there's nothin' in Kansas but sunshine, sunflowers, and sons-uh-bitches.' I wonder what we're gonna find here."

They had pulled up at a row of furrows that had been plowed around the field. Josh frowned. "What's that supposed to do?"

"No doubt, it says I own this property, and you stay off it," Paul said. "I suppose the owner would rather put up a fence but fencing up here is probably pretty scarce. I just hope we can keep our cattle out of his corn patch. They haven't been watered all day, and they haven't grazed much. They're going to think that corn is their supper." He turned in the saddle and looked down the back trail at the approaching herd. "Josh, ride back and tell 'em to push the herd a little to the west, away from this corn patch." Josh turned his mount and kicked her into a lope.

He never reached the herd. He met cows that had separated from the column and were moving toward the cornfield. He tried to turn them without much success. Other hands rode among the wanderers, trying to turn them back to the herd.

"Paul! Harley! They're coming!" Josh shouted. Harley rode toward the approaching cows, lashing out with his quirt. Paul drew his pistol and fired in the air. The shots gave the oncoming cows some pause but did not stop them as they crossed the furrows and entered the cornfield.

"Hey! Hey! Git them animals outta my corn!" The farmer, waving a shotgun over his head, ran toward the encroaching cows. He shouldered the shotgun and fired over the heads of the cows.

Josh ran toward the farmer. "Hey, man, easy with the scattergun, you're gonna hurt somebody. We're trying to get the cows out. Give us some time."

"They're destroying my corn. By god, I'll kill 'em if you cain't get 'em out!"

More hands had ridden into the corn and were pushing the cows out, slashing with their quirts and coils of rope.

Paul reined up beside Josh and the farmer. "We'll pay for the damage," said Paul. "Doesn't look like they did much."

The farmer was furious, his face contorted. "I work every daylight hour to make this farm go, and now every herd that comes by damn near ruins everything I've done."

"We'll make it up to you. We'll keep the herd moving, but the boss will come see you before we get away."

"No, no, don't leave. Keep the herd here. If you can keep them out of my corn, bring them a little closer."

Paul frowned. "What're you talking about? You tell us to get away, and now you tell us to bring the herd closer."

The farmer grimaced. "Yeah, sorry, sorry. I don't want them cows in my corn, but I surely would like them to graze over there in the pasture and bed down right there. By the time you leave in the morning, I'll have my fuel for the year. I'll guard that field of patties till they dry out and then collect 'em. Firewood's scarce around here.

"If you'll stay, I'll come to your camp this evening with fresh vegetables from my garden. Will you do that?" His anger had changed to supplication. "And you won't have to pay me nothin' for the damage to my cornfield."

"I expect we can do that. I'll head over and talk to the boss man."

The farmer beamed. He raised an arm to stop Paul. "By the way, something you need to know. Some cattle buyers from Ellsworth—that's on the rail line east of Abilene—are sending men around here to talk to farmers, trying to get us to raise hell with the drovers who are headin' to Abilene, maybe encourage 'em to head for Ellsworth instead." He smiled. "Thought you outta know."

NONE in the outfit had ever seen Abilene. All they knew was what they had heard from people who had not been there, for Abilene was a new frontier town that had no past.

They bedded the herd last night near the farmer's corn field, as he had requested, and enjoyed his fresh vegetables and milk. This morning, the farmer walked among the cow patties, some still wet and steaming, and he was a happy man. He thanked every hand he encountered and wished them luck and success in Abilene. When asked what he thought of Abilene, he replied simply that everybody in the neighborhood expected it to have a bright future if the cowboys didn't destroy it.

By mid-afternoon, the herd was put on a pasture a few miles south of town. Josh and Jenny leaned against the chuck wagon, staring at the dark compact mass in the distance that looked more like a cluster of rocks than a town.

"Doesn't look like much, does it?" said Jenny.

"The farmer said everybody thinks it has a great future."

"I can't see the future, can I?"

They looked at the herd, grazing on good grass nearby. "I'm glad Andy put us in the group going in today," Josh said. "I wouldn't want to hear about it before I see it. I expect you'll have to fix supper for the bunch that are not going in?"

"Yep, but I'm not going to let that keep me from gettin' away."

"I wonder if they have a saloon."

"I heard Harley say if they've put two boards together, they'll have a saloon." She turned to him. "I wonder if they have a whorehouse."

He chuckled. "Now that's something I'll have to investigate. Maybe I should go in now and meet you after you've finished with supper."

She pulled a face. "Oh, aren't you the big man? I can see some of these old hands in the outfit a-whoring, but you'd be scared to death."

He turned to her. "Now, that's a challenge, and you're getting me all fired up. On the other hand, why would I need to go a-whoring when I have my own pretty little whore right here in camp." He reached around and grabbed her bottom with one hand and a breast with the other.

She shrieked and pulled back, pushing his hands away. "You stay away, little man, or I'll have to tell Andy he needs to put you with the boys that are minding the herd this evening."

"Nope, we're all committed. You just be ready as soon as you get supper finished, and we'll head off to town. Andy has advanced us a few dollars that I expect to multiply at the card tables. And maybe indulge in some other pleasures as well." He smiled.

"Big talk. Maybe I'll go with you and watch. Or maybe I'll stay here and announce to the boys that since they couldn't go to Abilene this evening, Josh's little doxie is opening business right here in camp. Maybe I'll tell 'em to line up, with Harwood at the front of the line." She leaned in, her face whimsical and taunting.

He took her cheeks in his hands. "Maybe I'll stay here and watch. Do I get a cut of the proceeds?"

She leaned back, scowled. "Git away. I need to get on this early supper."

Half a dozen riders approached the outskirts of Abilene. Josh and Jenny rode a short distance behind the others. Jenny pulled up, and Josh stopped beside her.

She looked across the prairie to the west where the sun had just touched the horizon, coloring the low layers of lacy clouds a riot of pastel tints.

"Josh, I just can't take it in. I never really noticed sunsets at home. They were just the end of day. Out here, they just grab hold of me. I could live my life right here, watching that sunset every day."

She looked at him, waiting. "Well?"

He cocked his head. "Sunset, it's the end of the day. Pretty today. It's not always pretty, sometimes downright scary."

After a full minute, when she did not respond, he looked aside at her. She stared ahead, then turned to him.

"Sometimes I think my head's going to explode. Especially when I'm by myself, when I walk outside camp and leave everbody and everything behind, and it's all quiet and still. And I wonder what all this means for me. Things change too fast, Josh. I love the country so much, the wild, free, open country, that I'm afraid I'll lose it. What's going to happen? Will it always be like this? I can't believe it won't change."

He pondered, shook his head. "You are one sweet, weird woman, you know that? You think too much."

She frowned, ran her fingers through her horse's mane. "You're no help," softly.

"Well. Sure, things are gonna change, but we hope it will be for the better, but better for who? I enjoy the wide open, beautiful country as much as you, but I fear it won't be wide open in the future as much as now.

"You know how corrals are built to hold stock from wandering? Some ranchers would like to enclose not just a little corral beside the barn, but hundreds or thousands of acres. If they could do that, they wouldn't have to do annual roundups to locate stock. Their cows wouldn't mix with other men's cows.

"But building board or rail fences to enclose hundreds or thousands of acres would be too expensive. That's likely to change. I've heard they've invented wire fences that will be so much less expensive that almost anybody that runs cattle will be able to fence his place. If they do that, it will be less expensive to run a ranch, but the open range will be gone. I'm not sure how I feel about all this." He looked at the ground, frowning. "I never really thought about what all this means. Now I'm not sure I like what it means."

They sat quiet, watching the sun until it dropped below the horizon, leaving a glow where it disappeared, and the sky above slowly darkened.

"It's poetic," she said.

"What do you mean, poetic?"

She looked down. "I don't know, really. I guess I mean that the way I feel about the country is something I feel rather than something I know. You know, how poetry can move you without really understanding what the poet meant when he wrote it."

"I've not read much poetry. I didn't understand what I read."

She turned to him. "You don't like poetry?"

"Oh, didn't say that. I like what I've read the way

you like the taste of a certain food. You like it but can't describe why you like it."

"Makes sense."

They watched the glow at the horizon until it evaporated and became part of the darkness.

A weak moon dimly described the line of trees off the trail, and dimly outlined each other.

After a long silence. "You probably won't believe it," he said, "but I conjured up a few lines that look like a poem."

She looked at him, frowned. "You didn't!"

"I did, but there's no time for that now. C'mon, let's catch up." He kicked his horse to a lope. She followed, shouting.

THE ESTABLISHMENT that the riders entered was a small frontier town, hardly past its birthing. On the town's edge, they rode through a scattering of rough log buildings, presumably homes, roofed with sod. They passed a small hotel with a sign out front, The Bratton Hotel. A few horses stood in the stable out back on the creek bank. Just past the hotel, they approached the Old Man Saloon.

"Didn't I tell ya they'd have a saloon!" said Harley, wide-eyed.

"I'll stop here for a while," said a grinning Toby. "I'm dry as a bone and could use a little refreshment after that long ride from Fort Worth. Anybody with me?" Every rider except Josh and Jenny pulled up.

"C'mon, you two, let's drink to the end of this drive."

"We'll join you later," said Josh. "Gonna have a look at the town before it's too dark to see anything."

The pair continued riding down the dusty road, empty but for a few cowboys and town folk on foot, some strolling and chatting, some hurrying to be some other place.

Adjacent to the saloon, they passed shake-roofed Frontier Store. A sign in a window notified the passerby that the store sold groceries and dry goods and housed the town post office. A few other nondescript shops with no identifying signs or postings lay on each side to the end of the road that seemed to run out into the prairie.

They reined in abruptly. There before them lay parallel iron rails. The railroad. They looked both ways and saw nothing but empty rails. Josh removed his hat and scratched his head.

"Lookin' for the train, I bet." They were startled, looked aside for the speaker. An old fellow, wearing overalls and a straw hat, lounged on a bench at the side of the last building in the street. He held a pipe.

"The train is here?" said Jenny.

"If you mean, has the railroad reached Abilene, the answer is 'yes.' If you mean, where is the train, and what's it doing, the answer is that it left this morning to pick up rails and crossties at Junction City, east of here. Should be back any time now. I'm waitin' on it. I work for the railroad, you see."

"When do you expect it?" Jenny said.

"When I see it comin.' You'll hear it when it gets here. The engineer has lots of fun, scaring people who have never seen a train with his loud steam whistles just as he's pullin' in. You'll hear 'im." He grinned. "People jump outta their pants when he whistles."

"We'll head over to the saloon and come back when we hear it."

"Be careful comin' out. People jam up the saloon door comin' out, and people have been known to get hurt. Some of the drunks run the other way, scared outta their wits, but most everbody runs down here to see a train for the first time."

Josh and Jenny reined around and rode up the road to the saloon where they dismounted and tied their reins to the rail. Stepping up on the boardwalk, they went to the saloon door. They walked into what must have been the greater part of the population of Abilene. The eight gaming tables were filled, with bystanders peering over the players' shoulders. A dozen cowboys leaned against the bar, boot on the footrail, chatting loudly, laughing, and slapping backs.

"There they are," said Jenny, pointing at the boys from the outfit. Three sat at a table, holding cards. Harley and Petey, drinks in hand, stood behind the players. Harley leaned over Toby's shoulder, pointed at his cards, said something softly. Toby looked aside at Harley, lowered his cards, and said something sharply. Harley straightened, smiling.

Jenny and Josh walked to the table. Their pards saw them coming and waved. They stopped beside Harley who leaned over and whispered, then leaned back and guffawed. Neither Jenny nor Josh understood a word, due partly to the noise and partly to Harley's progress toward inebriation.

"Hey, where did you come from? Ain't seen you before."

All of the hands, sitting and standing, looked at the speaker, standing behind players at the adjacent table. He stood with two others, all three grinning and holding drinks, looking directly at Jenny.

"You been upstairs restin' all evenin,' darlin'?

Come over here, and le's have a look." His words were slurred, and he weaved forward and backward. "Ain't seen you before. C'mon over here, and le's have a look." He grinned as slobber bubbled from the side of his mouth. He took a weaving step toward Jenny.

Harley stepped in front of Jenny, gently pushing her backwards. "I won't even speak to this fella, he ain't got a brain that's working at the moment. You fellas with him better put a halter on him and lead him outside."

"You talkin' 'bout me, you old fart, you talk to me!" He threw his glass to the floor, shattering it, sending everyone nearby jumping aside and backing away.

"Fellas, can you give this moron a dousing in the water trough? Maybe that'll clear away the cobwebs."

"You . . . you sumbitch, I'll . . ." He weaved, reached around his back, and pulled out a six-shooter, leveled on Harley, the pistol unsteady and gyrating.

Harley stepped backward, holding up a hand, palm outward. "Whoa, whoa, hold on, old man!"

The drunk steadied the pistol.

The drunk's companion grabbed his arm. "No, Johnny!" Johnny pulled away and fired.

Harley's head came up, and he fell backward against Josh and Jenny. They supported him as he collapsed to the floor. Josh ran around Jenny to the shooter. He punched him hard in the face, then punched him again as he fell, then kicked him on the floor. His companions, wide-eyed, backed up.

"I didn't know he had a gun," said one. The room was deathly quiet.

"Is there a doctor in town?" Josh said to the house, looking about frantically.

Another of the shooter's companions, also drunk

and weaving, reached behind him and held his hand there. "Yeah, but why should I tell you. Ya just whupped my pard." He hiccupped, spraying spittle.

Josh reached down and pulled a pistol from his boot. He shoved the barrel into the drunk's cheek until his eyes bugged.

"I'll ask again, but only this last time. Where is the doctor's office?" The man gasped, his eyes rolled back, and he passed out, crumpling to the floor.

"Go outside, left, past three storefronts." Josh turned toward the bar where the bartender was pointing. "He's on the second floor of the mercantile, outside stairs on the side. Don't know if he's there."

Josh and Petey gently pulled Harley up, supported him under his armpits, and dragged him to the door and outside. Jenny ran ahead and opened the door. They walked on the boardwalk past the dark stores and around the last building to the staircase. As they struggled up the stair, Jenny ran to the top, three steps at a time, and pounded on the door.

Nothing. She pounded and shouted. After an agonizing minute, a light appeared in a window, and the door slowly opened. A head appeared as Jenny talked to him. The doctor looked down the stair and beckoned them to come in.

Chapter Eleven

Josh and Jenny sat on the stair. Soft moonlight dimly illuminated the outlines of the stores on the opposite side of the street and the steel rails that ran behind them.

"He's lucky," said Josh. "If the doc's right, an inch to the left, and he would be a dead man. I'm glad the doc wanted Harley to stay over. I would have worried myself sick if I had to be responsible for him in camp. I'll come back in tomorrow. If all is okay, as the doc expects, we'll ride real slow back to camp tomorrow."

"I'm coming with you."

"You don't have to do that."

"Well, I'm coming. I feel responsible for all this. You tried to talk me out of going to the saloon, but I was bullheaded and went anyway."

He put an arm around her shoulders and pulled her to him. "It's not your fault.

He leaned over and kissed her cheek. "However, I can understand why those hot-blooded drunks might want a session with my doxie." He smiled.

"Not funny right now, Josh Nesbitt. C'mon, let's get back to camp." They stood and walked slowly down the stairs. "I'm glad Petey decided to stay with Harley. And glad the doc let him stay. Petey seems to really like Harley. As grumpy as he is sometimes, I think Harley likes Petey more than just as pards, more like a father-son friendship."

At the bottom of the stair, they stepped down on the boardwalk and walked slowly toward the saloon where their horses were tied.

"Maybe we'll see the train tomorrow after we deliver the herd," said Josh.

"Forgot all about it, the train and the herd. It's gonna be strange to be in camp without a herd. I understand McCoy will meet us at his pens north of town. Whatever he can't get in the pens will go on the pasture he owns."

Josh inhaled deeply, looked up into the gloom, a few twinkling stars penetrating the cloud layer. "Yeah, and then we get paid off, and we're no longer an outfit. We're just people on our own without a job. Sounds strange."

Grasping his arm, she leaned on his shoulder. She wiped her eyes on his sleeve.

He stopped. "Hey, what's wrong?" He put his arms around her shoulders.

"I'm scared." She rubbed her face on his chest and choked back a sob.

He pulled her close and rested his cheek on top of her head, breathing in her perfume. He pulled back, held her cheeks in his hands. "Sweetheart, there's nothing for you to be afraid of. Tomorrow we're gonna talk about what's happening."

. . .

"That was a strange evening," Jenny said, "and I don't feel good about wanting to feel good, but I do anyway. Harley's going to be okay, and you didn't go upstairs at the saloon. You didn't have a chance to drink too much, so you didn't fall off your horse on the ride back to camp. You were pretty sleepy, and I had to prop you up a couple of times so you wouldn't fall."

They lay in the bedroll under the wagon, he on his back and she on her side, facing him. "I'll let you off playtime tonight, but I do want to hear about your poem if you're up to it."

He rolled on his side to face her. "Funny, I was exhausted on the ride back, but I'm wide awake now. Probably won't last long." He cleared his throat. "You sure you want to hear this?"

She just looked at him.

"Okay. If you laugh, I'll turn you over and whip your butt." He cleared his throat again and recited.

> *Keep your friends close.*
> *Hoard them like fine gold*
> *Or they will slip through your fingers,*
> *Grains of sand.*
> *I stand in a desert.*

She rose on an elbow. "Honey, that is wonderful! It's sad and wonderful. I didn't know . . ."

"Yeah, I know. You didn't know I had any thoughts beyond what I want for supper and what I want at playtime. Maybe I don't, except when I'm drunk. I was mostly drunk on the riverboat and one night decided to end it. I decided there was nothing left for me. I'd been stumbling drunk for three days, going over and over everything I had lost. My family mostly, but also all those pards in the war. I had thoughts that were not all rational or ordinary, at least, not ordinary for me. That's when I wrote the poem. In my head, that is, standing at the rail in the dark. Still haven't written it down on paper. I've just gone over it in my head so many times, I know it."

She leaned over and kissed him. "Tomorrow I'm going to write it down if you can remember it when you're cold sober." She pinched his cheek, kissed him again, rolled on her back, and closed her eyes. A moment later, she heard him breathing deeply.

Early afternoon the next day, the outfit drove the herd from the bedding ground for the last time. As they passed around the town to deliver the herd to McCoy at his pens and pasture, Josh and Jenny turned off and rode to the doctor's office. They led two horses.

Harley and Petey waved to them from the staircase where they sat on the top step. Harley's arm was in a sling, and a soft grin creased his face. They stood and walked gingerly down the stair, Harley holding to the rail as Petey gripped his other arm. Josh passed them and continued to the top where he knocked on the door.

At the bottom, Jenny brought them up to date while Josh settled with the doctor. He rejoined them at the bottom of the stair. He laid a hand on Harley's shoulder.

"Don't know how much the doc told you. He said if the bullet had been just an inch to the left, we would have picked you up in a pine box. You're lucky, pard. How does it feel?"

"It don't feel any worse than I usually feel when I get up in the morning. It don't hurt unless I do this." He raised the arm, and he winced with squinted eyes.

"Well, don't do that, you dummy," Jenny said, as she gently pushed the arm down. "Now, c'mon, I want to see this train. We'll walk. We're meeting the rest of the outfit at the station after they finish the business with McCoy."

"Look there! Here they come." Petey waved. The hands rode toward the station, Paul in the lead. A number of the cowboys waved. They disappeared behind the row of shops across from the station.

"I been looking forward to this!" said Petey. "Did I tell you the only reason I signed on for this drive was to see a train?" He grinned.

They rounded the last building in the street to reach the station and tracks.

"What th' hell?" said Petey. The tracks were empty. They squinted along the tracks eastward and saw no evidence of a train.

"What th' hell," Petey said again. "I come all the way from Texas to see a train, and all I see is empty tracks!"

Jenny looked at Josh. "I sorta wanted to see a train too."

"Don't despair, folks. Faint heart n'er won somethin' or other." They saw the overalled oldster from their previous visit sprawled on his bench. "The train is a'comin'." Checking his watch, he stood and looked eastward on the track. "It's not really on a schedule as yet, but we have a good idea of its comin's and goin's. It should be here just about . . ." He looked at his watch again. "Just about . . . right now." He pointed at the small black mass that had materialized at the far reaches of the tracks.

"It's comin'!" yelled Petey. At Petey's outburst, cowboys in their outfit and a dozen or so bystanders turned to see the approaching train. A buzz of conversation rose from the group.

The engine grew larger as it rolled toward the station, hissing, steam issuing from the black mass. Then the steam whistle shrieked, and the people jumped and backed away from the track. The overalled character on the bench guffawed, slapping his legs.

The engine pulled to a stop at the stationhouse. People looked up at the black monster that loomed above them. As wisps of steam continued to issue from the body, muted groans and rumblings seemed to escape from its bowels.

"My god," said Petey softly, eyes wide and jaw hanging. "The thang's alive." He looked at Harley, grinning. "Harley, what do you say we ride th' train back to Texas, at least as close as we can git to Texas? Whatta ya say?"

"Hmm. Well, my young friend, that might not be as dumb as it sounds. We'll have to see how close it comes to Texas and whether we could bring our horses with us. I think this shoulder might feel better on a seat in a train than on horseback. We'll do some thinking and asking."

"Yeah!"

Jenny and Josh stood back from the bunch at the tracks. She looked up at him. "Josh?"

He took her arm, and they walked to the overalled train employee. Josh pointed to the car behind the engine. "That looks like a wagon for passengers, but nobody's getting off."

"It is indeed a passenger car. They'll be gettin' down in a minute. Takes some time to get their gear together. Just one passenger car today. The cars behind it are carrying crossties and rails. The train will offload that stuff west of here, at the end of tracks."

Overalls pointed. "There they come!"

Men stepped down from the passenger car to the ground. Their dress identified them as the easterners they were. They carried cases and bags which they set down and looked around at this town they had heard so much about. Some stamped their feet, testing their balance and getting the circulation moving.

One man, after stepping down, turned and took the hand of a young woman, helping her down the steps in a full dress, adorned with lace and other frills.

"My, my, aren't you the honey," said Jenny. "Good luck with that outfit."

Cowboys and townspeople walked around the train, gawking and commenting, laughing, jumping aside at the release of steam. They asked questions of train workers and the overalled stationmaster.

Petey stood before the steps of the passenger car, looked around, and quickly climbed inside. After a couple of minutes, he stepped down, beaming, and strode to Harley and others, almost skipping.

"That would be a fine thang to do, ride the train to Texas," Petey said.

"We'll talk," said Harley.

"Okay, everbody," said Paul, speaking to the cowboys as they walked toward their horses. "Andy is treating us to dinner at the café next to the hotel. He wants to talk about what's coming up."

Josh and Jenny walked with Harley to his horse,

and each took an arm to help him mount. He tried to brush them off with a series of stop-it-I-can-do-it protests, but they persisted until he was aboard.

"Now, do you want to climb up here with me, or can I ride by myself?" Harley said with a stern look, then a hint of a smile. "Thanks, pards." He turned his mount, and Petey rode up beside him.

The hands reined up at the café, dismounted, and tied reins to the hitching rail. They crowded through the door and inside where a waitress showed them the long table reserved for them. Andy stood behind the table.

"Everybody have a seat," said Andy. "Dinner is on the way." The hands filed in pulled chairs out and sat. Filled coffee cups were on the table, and some took a cup and sipped. They looked expectantly at Andy who sat down at the end of the long table.

Andy drank from his cup, set it down, and looked around the table. "Here's where we stand." He told the hands about the settlement with McCoy. The buyer wasn't ready to ship just yet. He would put the herd on grass and fatten them up for shipment in August or September. "I won't worry about it since it's no longer my concern, and it ain't my herd. I been paid in full, and it was a good price, I gotta say."

The hands cheered, fists pumping, slapping backs, smiling broadly.

"Now about the outfit. I want to tell you that it has been a pleasure to work with you fellas." He looked at Jenny, smiled. "And you, missy." She made a face, smiled. "I'm giving each of you your favorite horse. I've sold the rest of the remuda to a Wyoming rancher I met in town, Dan Leiter by name. He and his boys will come for them tomorrow. Seems he is expanding his ranch operation and needs the horses. I've sold the chuck wagon and mules to the same fella. We'll meet him when he and his boys come to the campsite tomorrow after breakfast.

"In fact, another fella who was with this rancher said he would like to look at my herd, and if he liked what he saw, he would make me an offer. He said he had a couple of friends, ranchers in Wyoming, who were expanding their cattle operations and asked him to be on the lookout in Abilene for likely herds. I thanked him and told him I didn't own any cattle. McCoy already owned my herd.

"This McCoy is a shrewd operator. I heard that rumors are running wild in Abilene that drovers could be influenced by offers from ranchers in Montana, Colorado, and Wyoming to bypass Abilene and continue to their country where they would find a passel of buyers. I heard McCoy has hired ten men at fifty dollars a month to ride south and persuade drovers approaching Abilene to ignore all the talk and take the sure course and sell to him."

Andy smiled, leaned back. "And that's it," Andy said. "Got any questions for me?"

"Yeah, you damn reprobate, when do we get paid?" It was Charley. He smiled ever so slightly.

Andy grinned. "I suspected somebody would remember that. Tomorrow after breakfast, I'll pay off the bunch. After you're paid, clear out anything you want to keep from the wagon. Cut your horse from the remuda. The rancher who bought the remuda and chuck wagon will be here mid-morning with his boys to pick up the lot.

"Don't know about the rest of you, but when all that's done, I'm home for Texas. I would advise we stick together on the ride south. There are desperadoes out there who know that cowboys going home from a drive have cash in their saddlebags. If we stay together, we have enough guns to be sure we get home with the cash.

"I understand some of you are thinking of taking the train home. Just bear in mind that the train doesn't go all the way to Texas, and you'll be riding horseback a good part of the way. Since you won't be identified as a cowboy going home after a cattle drive, you should be okay, but you'll still be prey to bad guys."

"Make way, fellas here's dinner." A waitress walked up behind Andy, holding two plates. Another waitress behind her held two plates. They set the plates of steak, potatoes, beans, and biscuits in front of the cowboys. "Be back with the rest in a jiffy. Hot apple pie comes later." The waitresses swept away toward the kitchen.

THE RIDE back to the campsite was unhurried. There was little conversation, almost as if it had all been said, and there was nothing left to say. No need to talk about the herd, the weather, water sources, the trail, the remuda, rustlers, and renegades.

Josh and Jenny rode behind the others, out of earshot. "I'm going to miss my mules," she said. "They're like my kids. Minded me most of the time, only rarely gave me trouble. Hope this new outfit takes good care of them."

Josh smiled. "They're mules."

"Animals have feelings and moods. Don't pretend you don't know that, big man. I've heard you talking to your horse."

He glanced aside at her, frowning. "Yeah, well, I have threatened and cussed a little from time to time."

"That too, but I've heard you say some sweet things as well."

"Hmm. It's a horse."

She shook her head, kicked her mount to a gallop.

"Hey, what's th' hurry?" He drummed his horse's belly and galloped after her. They passed the others who shouted questions and encouragement to them, all in good humor.

They pulled up at the chuck wagon and dismounted. "What's the hurry?" he said.

"If you haven't noticed, it looks like rain. I'm fixing an early supper, and I want to get as much sorting done in the wagon as possible, so we won't be hard pressed tomorrow to get the wagon cleared out for the buyer.

"After you put the horses in the remuda, you might lay out the bed under the wagon and pull the tents out for the boys. Take 'em over near the fire circle, and maybe they'll set up over there. Tonight's the last playtime under the wagon, and you're likely to make enough noise to scatter the remuda."

"Oh yeah?" he said. "I just hope there's enough thunder to drown out your yips and yowls." He patted her bottom.

She swatted his hand. "Git away and git busy."

SUPPER WAS EATEN around the campfire in a light sprinkling that caused the fire to sizzle and smoke. Conversation was subdued, no yarning or bawdy tales, partly due to the rainy gloom and partly to the realization that this was the final night with the outfit. Some talked without enthusiasm of the ride home. The only bright spot in the conversation was anticipation of going back to Texas, though some were reluctant to talk about what awaited them at home.

Anticipating a wet night, hands set up tents and laid out bedrolls before supper. When the drizzle increased to light rain, they hastened to deposit dishes at the chuck wagon, run to the bushes, and back to tents.

The rainfall increased to a steady downpour. Before running from the bushes to his tent, Petey shouted to the camp that this was going to be a real Texas frog-strangler.

Jenny and Josh crawled under the wagon and into their blankets, shedding clothes until they were naked. Their love-making was matched and muted by the torrents of blowing rain that pelted the wagon's canvas and thunder that burst and rolled overhead and gradually lessened in intensity as it moved westward, rumbling, softening till it sounded like boiling water in a kettle, the sure sign that the storm was over.

Jenny and Josh lay on their sides, facing each other, gasping, then breathing deeply. He wiped her glistening forehead with the blanket.

She laid a hand on his cheek. "I hate endings."

He pulled her to him, hugged her tightly. "Nothing is ending but this cattle drive, sweetheart."

She kissed his cheek, his forehead, bit his ear lightly. She pulled back. "I loved your poem. I wish you had written more. I think you have a talent."

He rolled onto his back. After a long moment. "Josh?" she said.

"I did write another, in my head, that is."

"You did? Tell me about it."

He hesitated, then told her. At least a year after leaving the riverboat, when wandering in the wilds of central Texas, in despair, still suffering from survivor's guilt, he saw a swarm of butterflies and watched them tearfully. He saw them lift and fly away, and he was overcome with a desperate sense of loss. He had always loved butterflies as a child on the family farm. He had seen no butterflies during four years of war.

That evening in Texas, alone beside a campfire, he drank himself into a stupor and composed the butterfly poem. He had repeated it so many times in his head since then, he still knew it as he had crafted it those long years ago.

"Will you say it to me?" she said.

"I've not said it out loud since I wrote it. But I will." He closed his eyes.

> *I remember butterflies*
> *Orange, yellow, blue, purple*
> *Floating, gliding, dipping, descending*
> *Alighting, fluttering, folding, feeding*
> *Lifting, flapping, rising, soaring*
> *Receding, shimmering, blurring, dimming.*
> *I remember butterflies.*

She rose on an elbow, looked down at him. "Honey, that is beautiful! The words, I don't even know some of the words, but they are beautiful."

"Some of the words I had never used before. I must have heard the words some time or other, and they just jumped into the poem as I composed it, staggering drunk."

Chapter Twelve

AFTER BREAKFAST THE NEXT MORNING, each hand went to the remuda to select the mount Andy promised him. After the gift mounts had been selected, Andy chose three horses he would keep as packhorses for the Texas-bound bunch. After retrieving his and Jenny's mounts, Josh led them to the chuck wagon, tied reins to a wheel, and pulled saddles from the wagon.

Jenny fussed around the wagon interior, straightening, restacking, tossing out anything that had needed discarding for days. She stepped away from the wagon, turned to Josh.

"What am I doing? This is not my wagon anymore." She went to Josh, grasped his shirt, and buried her face in its folds. "I hate endings."

"That's twice you've said that, and I'll say again that nothing is ending for us. Hell, we'll buy us another wagon and a team of mules if that will make you happy." He wiped the tears from her cheek.

They looked up at the approach of four men riding toward the camp from the north. Andy waved to them, and they reined up. Andy pointed at the remuda, and three of the men rode toward it. The fourth dismounted, and Andy and he strolled as they talked, Andy pointing toward the remuda and back toward the wagon. Andy waved to Josh and Jenny, and they returned the wave.

Harley ambled over to Andy and Dan. Harley did most of the talking as they walked toward the remuda. Just before arriving, Dan stopped, nodded vigorously, and extended a hand to Harley. They shook, and Dan slapped Harley on the shoulder.

Charley walked from the remuda and joined the conversation. After ten minutes of mostly listening, Dan slapped his head and nodded, looking toward the chuck wagon where Jenny was reaching inside over the tailgate, and Josh leaned against the side of the wagon.

Harley and Dan separated from the group and walked to the chuck wagon. The others watched them go. Josh saw them coming and stood. "Jenny," he said. She turned and saw the visitors.

"Josh, Jenny, want you to meet Dan Leiter," said Harley. "He's the fella who just bought the remuda and the wagon." Leiter extended a hand, and Josh shook. Jenny nodded. "Mr. Leiter has made me an offer of employment, and I'm taking it. In fact, me and Petey are going to work for him."

"You see," said Leiter, "I'm expanding my cattle operation. You probably know I tried to buy Andy's herd, but I was too late. No matter. There's other herds coming up the trail. I'm going to get one or two before McCoy or any other Abilene buyer gets their hooks on 'em. That's one thing I'll have Harley and Petey doing next spring when the driving season gets under way. They'll hang around a good distance south of Abilene, checking over the herds. If they see a likely herd, they'll persuade the drover to talk with me before he commits to McCoy or any other Abilene buyer. Andy tells me, Harley, here is a good talker."

Josh smiled. "That he is. I'll agree to that." Harley raised his chin slightly, nodded.

"When they're not out looking for likely herds," Dan said, "Petey and Harley will be at the ranch. They'll be a welcome addition to the dozen men I already have. Those boys, mostly youngsters, are eager and willing. They're okay with horses, been riders all their lives, but they don't know a lot about cows. That's where Harley and Petey come in. Andy assures me they will be a good influence and good teachers, as well."

"That they will. I'll agree to that," said Josh. Harley made a face, nodded, smiling.

Dan looked at Harley a moment, then back to Josh. He glanced past Josh to Jenny, who leaned against the wagon, watching and listening.

"That brings me to this. Everbody I've talked to in this camp tells me that you are a top hand, Josh. And, uh, everbody in this camp tells me that you are the best cook west of the Atlantic Ocean, missy.

"So I'm making both of you an offer. Come work for me. My spread is just a few miles north of Cheyenne. That's a new town that has a lot going for it. We won't be driving cattle to market. We'll ship from the railroad that will reach Cheyenne by the end of the year. The town's already got a number of stores. It's got a church if that means anything to you."

Josh looked at Jenny whose face was blank, betraying no emotion.

Josh frowned. "That's a mighty attractive offer," he

said. "I haven't talked about it with anybody, but I've been thinking of going back to Texas and setting up a little cattle ranch of my own. Been on my mind since I joined this drive. In fact, been on my mind for years."

Dan looked down, pondered a long moment, then looked up. "Tell you what. I've got a big place, and I control more land than I'm likely to use for years. I say 'control' cause I don't own much of it. That's gonna change. The rumor is that the railroad is going to receive land grants from the federal government that they will sell to local people. This will increase the railroad's revenues and also get the land populated by ranchers and farmers who will ship on the railroad. The point is that I intend to buy a block of this railroad land to serve as headquarters and base of the ranch. I still expect to run cattle on the open range.

"Now. What do you say I advance you a little herd, and you pay me back in work and sales? You put your brand on 'em, and when the time is right for both of us, I'll help you set up your own operation, joining mine. How does that sound?"

Josh had listened intently, frowning, glancing occasionally at Jenny. "Are you going to be in camp a while?"

"We're staying for dinner. Need to get away right after."

"I'll talk to you after dinner."

Dan touched his hat to Jenny and walked away.

"Uh, Dan," said Josh, "does the town, Cheyenne, have a church? A preacher?"

Dan turned back. "It does indeed! The good people been meeting in the mercantile for some time but started building a church house last month."

Josh nodded, and Dan turned again to leave.

"They have a doctor in this town?" said Jenny.

Dan stopped. "As a matter of fact, they do! They got two doctors. An old fella, a retired army doctor who's been in town a few years. Then there's this young fella arrived couple of months ago. He's from back East, Massachusetts, I think. He is positively fascinated with the West and said he couldn't wait to move out here. Last time I talked with him, he was still excited about being here in the Wild West, he calls it.

"Talk to you later." He walked toward the remuda where his hands were looking over the horses.

They watched him go. Harley had listened silently to the conversation, his face blank. Now he turned to Josh and Jenny. He was more animated than they had ever seen him. He was excited, something new for Harley. "I really hope you'll decide to take him up on the offer. This is all new. I had planned to go back to Texas myself, but to do what? More of the same. This job is going to give new life to these old bones. I never heard you talking about wanting your own spread, Josh, but this offer is something. I've seen fellas in Texas try to set up their own places and go bust. More than one. Don't pass this up."

He turned to Jenny. "I hate to tell you, Josh, old friend, but I'll just wager that it's Jenny that he really wants. When we talked about Jenny and her cooking, he started to drool. He said he has a dozen hands and a really lousy cook that doesn't really want to cook. This cookie is just a cowhand who knew a potato from a cow pattie and how to make coffee, so he was sorta forced into the job. Dan told him he would let him get back to cowboying as soon as he found a real cook. Oh, Jenny, this fella's gonna love you for taking the job away from him.

"Take his offer. Me and Petey could make it on our own, but I would really like to have you on the place. Take it, please."

When Harley had walked away and was out of hearing, Josh and Jenny looked at each other, just looked, both frowning.

"First time I ever heard Harley say 'please'," she said. "I guess he's real serious about wanting us to stay."

Josh looked past Jenny to the woods, turned, and watched the activity at the remuda, Dan talking with his cowboys, stroking a horse's back.

He turned back to Jenny. "There's a lot to be said for Dan's offer. I know from talking to people in Texas how hard it is to start a ranch from scratch. Dan's offer is pretty generous. And it would be good to have such friends as Harley and Petey on the place. I can't think of anybody I'd like to work with more than these two fellas."

Jenny had watched him intently while he talked. "Why did you ask if Cheyenne had a church and a preacher?"

"Because we're gettin' married! And I want a preacher to do it, not some town clerk. If that's okay with you." He smiled.

She grabbed him and hugged tightly. "Yeah, it's okay, cowboy. If you didn't ask me, I was gonna ask you." She pulled away and kissed him. "This will take some getting used to, bein' married."

"I don't know about that. I've been eating your cooking, and we've had regular playtime. Doesn't that sound like married people?"

"S'pose it does."

He cocked his head. "Why did you ask Dan if Cheyenne had a doctor?"

She pinched his cheeks and leaned into his face, nose to nose. "Because I'm gonna have a baby, sweetheart. And I don't want it delivered by some cowboy."

"Baby? Baby?" He wrapped his arms around her waist, picked her up, and swung her in circles. He put her down, frowned. "How do you know?"

"I know. Women know. If I didn't want your baby, I sure wouldn't have put up with playtime almost every night."

"You sure it's mine?" He pulled a face.

She frowned. "Well, I guess it could be Harwood's or Toby's, but I wouldn't bet on it."

He rubbed her belly, then put his arms around her, resting his chin on the top of her head. "Everything's falling into place. We're getting married, we're having a baby, and we need a place to work and live. How do you feel about taking Dan up on his offer?"

"Up to you. I have nobody and no prospects in Texas. Same with you, I think. I'm willing to give Wyoming a try if you are. Up to you."

He raised her chin and kissed her. "Okay, done. I'll give Dan our decision. I think Harley and Petey will be pleased."

"Oh, my," said Ronnie, one of Dan's hands. Cowboys from both outfits sat on the ground around the chuck wagon. He stared at the filled plate on his lap: beef, beans, biscuits, fried eggs, potatoes, apple pie sweetened with molasses. "Is this special for us? You don't eat like this ever meal, do you?"

"Jenny asked me to apologize for the thin offering,"

Josh said. "We'll restock in Abilene. Then you'll see what she regularly serves up."

"My, my, my." The cowboy forked a piece of beef to his mouth and chewed, eyes closed. "Umm *umm.*"

Conversation was sparse, muted mostly since this would be the last such gathering. Josh had talked with Dan and accepted his offer, and he had told Andy's outfit of his decision. Harley and Petey were delighted. The remaining hands notified that four of their pards were heading north to new horizons, talked without enthusiasm of the forthcoming anticlimactic ride back to Texas.

Charley waved a fork at Jenny. "Jenny, dadgummit, what're we gonna eat when you're gone?"

"You're on your own, Charley. You've been there before. You'll do fine with wild meat, including a roast rabbit now and then, in spite of what Harley says about anybody that eats rabbit. I made a big batch of biscuits before breakfast that everybody can pick up after we finish here. I don't imagine they will last long."

"Sorry I'm responsible for enticing Jenny to leave you boys," said Dan, "but lemme tell you, my hands are going to benefit from your loss. And I'm going to enjoy her cooking all the way to my place. Sure glad I bought that chuck wagon and everything in it." This was met with hanging heads and good-natured grumbling all around.

When dinner was finished, and hands had dropped their plates in the wash bucket, they went to the front of the wagon and pulled out bedrolls and any personal belongings that Jenny had carried in the wagon for them. Some mumbled their thanks for all Jenny had done for them and all she had meant to them these months.

"We ain't saying goodbye just yet," she said. "Time for that later." She turned away and wiped a tear with a sleeve.

She caught Harley and Petey after they had deposited their dishes in the bucket. "Seeing as how you don't need to collect your bedrolls and personal stuff, how about helping me get the chuck wagon set to go? You could help by washing these dishes."

Harley stepped back, frowning.

"Sure we will," said Petey, smiling. He turned to Harley. "Won't we, Harley?" He frowned at his pard, turned back to Jenny. "What do we do? I never watched."

She smiled, gave instructions for heating water, washing, and putting the dishes away in the wagon. "Thanks, boys, Josh and I will find the mules and put 'em in harness. We want to be ready to pull out before the others head south."

COWBOYS PUTTERED and spent more time than necessary filling bags and tying them on the pack animals, fussing with their saddles and saddlebags. They worried aloud about what and when they would eat during the ride south. They put off goodbyes as long as possible.

When his hands signaled they were ready to throw the remuda on the trail, Dan said his goodbyes to Andy and his outfit. He thanked Andy for selling him the remuda, the wagon, and though they weren't his to give, for the four hands he had acquired from his outfit. Then he waved, mounted, and joined his men at the horse herd.

"We'll catch up," said Josh to Dan who waved.

Josh, Jenny, Harley, and Petey stood together, chatting with the boys they had worked with these months, sharing the dangers and rewards of the long drive.

"Hate to see you boys, and you, Jenny, going north when we're goin' south," said Andy, "but sounds like you've got a good opportunity with Dan. Make the best of it." He clapped Josh on the shoulder.

"Harley, you old geezer, it's been a pleasure to work with you all these years, even if you are the biggest bullshitter in the country." Andy shook Harley's hand vigorously and poked him gently in the chest. Take care of yourself." Harley, sober, blinked and nodded. "Petey, watch out for this old reprobate. You can learn a lot from him. But ignore his campfire stories." Petey smiled, glanced at Harley, who remained solemn.

"Good luck in Wyoming, Josh," Andy said. "Sounds like you got a lot goin' for you. Write to me. You have my address. Who knows what's in the future?"

Andy turned to Jenny. "Missy, I don't need to tell you how much we're gonna miss you." The other Texas-bound hands, who had listened to Andy's goodbyes, mumbled their agreement. "The outfit's already worrying about how they're gonna eat on the ride to Texas." More mumbled agreement.

She pursed her lips, nodded, blinking. "I'll miss you boys more'n you'll miss my chuck wagon." She turned away, wiping a cheek with her hand.

The two groups came together, shaking hands, slapping backs, smiling, laughing, some shedding a tear or two. Some shook hands with Jenny, others touched a hat.

"We'll probably never see you four again," said

Toby, "and that makes me sad. Jenny, can I hug you, even if old Josh here boxes my ears?"

She reached for him. "Come'ere. Toby." She put her arms around his neck as he circled her shoulders. He released, backed away, head lowered. He turned and walked toward his horse.

"Let's be off," Andy said. "We got a long ride ahead."

Andy's hands mounted, and they set out, three holding the leads of the packhorses. Some turned in the saddle for one last look and wave. Then they were gone, their horses' hooves raising dust that lifted and was carried away in the gentle breeze.

Jenny leaned against Josh, her face against his chest. She wiped her cheek with a hand. "Didn't think I could get so attached to a bunch of scruffy cowboys." She rubbed her face against his chest. "Let's get on with it." She turned and walked toward the chuck wagon.

Jenny climbed up to the seat and shook the lines. The others mounted and rode alongside. Josh turned for a last look of the old outfit, now hardly discernable on the back trail. He faced front, drew a deep breath.

He rode up beside Dan. Dan looked aside at him. "I'm real glad to have you boys join up with us. It's going to be a benefit for all of us." He pointed ahead. "We'll take the horses west of Abilene and stop a couple of miles north of town for the night. You won't have any trouble finding us. We'll be just off the trail. The cash I gave you should cover what you need, as long as you don't need to go upstairs at the saloon."

"No chance of that. We'll join you in time to fix supper."

. . .

Jenny pulled up in front of the mercantile. She set the brake and climbed down. Josh and the others tied their reins to the hitching rail.

"Don't go far," Jenny said. "I won't be long, and I'll need help loading." She walked through the open door, carrying some canvas bags.

Josh stopped at the door and looked back at Harley and Petey who stood idly beside the wagon. "Watch the wagon and the horses," Josh said. "I don't trust a solitary soul in this town. I'm gonna stretch my legs." Harley nodded, and Josh set off on the boardwalk. He had not walked fifty feet when he stopped.

Of all the people I might see in Abilene, this yahoo is the one I really didn't need to see. It was the drunk in the saloon who had shot Harley. He remembered the name, Johnny. The man walked toward him, head down. Two other men walked behind him, talking, looking toward the chuck wagon.

Johnny looked up and stopped. He frowned. "I remember you. Git outta my way. I ain't drunk this time, and I'd as soon shoot you as look at you."

"As a matter of fact," said Josh, "I swore I would shoot you down like a dog if I ever saw you again, but now I don't think it's worth wasting a bullet on you."

Johnny reached for his pistol, but Josh drew faster and had his six-shooter leveled on him before he had cleared the holster. Johnny hesitated, holding the pistol pointed at the boardwalk.

One of the men behind Johnny stepped aside and drew. He was still bringing his pistol up when a shot exploded, and he was blown backward.

Josh looked behind him to see Petey lowering his pistol. "Look out!" shouted Harley. Josh spun around to see Johnny leveling on him. Josh fired, and Johnny collapsed. The other man who had walked behind Johnny staggered aside to lean against a shop wall, trembling, his hands raised.

Harley and Petey walked toward Josh. Josh saw Jenny and an aproned storekeeper standing in front of the open mercantile door. "Everything's okay," Josh called and waved her back into the store. She and the storekeeper backed into the doorway, disappearing through the door.

Josh, Harley, and Petey looked down on the two fallen men. Johnny lay still. The other man lay on his side, groaning, holding his shoulder.

At that moment, a man stepped up on the walk. "Well, you fellas do know how to keep a man from his nap." They saw the badge on his chest.

Josh started to speak, but the man held up a hand. "I'm Sheriff Adams. You don't have to explain. Saw the whole thing. I was just about to go into the office for a little shuteye after a nice lunch, but you distracted me." He looked at the man leaning against the wall, hands still held aloft and trembling. "Bertie, why don't you go on your way. Nothing for you to do here." The man lowered his arms, nodded vigorously to the sheriff, and hurried away, alternately running and walking on the boardwalk.

"You might remember the ruckus in the saloon some days ago when this fella shot my pard here," Josh said, gesturing toward Harley.

"Yeah, I remember. Always figured Johnny would end up like this. I've had to caution the fella more than once. He had a short fuse and was short on brains. Felt a little sorry for him.

"I'll take care of this. You best be about your business and out of town quick as you can. These fellas have friends."

"Much obliged, sheriff. We'll get our groceries and be on our way. That's our wagon." He pointed.

Josh turned. "Let's go. Petey, watch the wagon while Harley and I get Jenny." Petey went to the wagon while Josh and Harley hurried through the mercantile door.

Jenny looked anxiously at them. "It's all sorted out," said Josh. "Petey is okay. I'll tell you later. Are you about done? We need to be on our way."

"Yes." She handed payment to the storekeeper while Josh and Harley picked up bags and walked through the door to the wagon. Jenny came out and climbed up on the wagon seat while Josh and Harley put the bags in the back. The three hurried to their horses, untied the reins, and mounted.

Jenny released the brake and shook the lines. The three cowboys followed, looking to each side, turning, and looking back over their shoulders.

JENNY and the three riders saw the remuda, then two fire circles as they approached camp. She stopped at the circle that she took to be the cooking fire since it was filled with dancing flames. She jumped down as two of Dan's hands walked over to help. Josh and Harley and Petey rode on to the remuda.

"Everything go okay in Abilene?" said Dan.

"No," Jenny said. "But it's settled now. Josh will tell you. I gotta get on supper if your boys will unload for me. I'll repack after supper." She gave instructions to the hands and set to work at once, taking down mixing bowls, griddles, and utensils.

Josh walked over and beckoned Dan to come to the cooking fire. "I'd like to tell you and Jenny both what happened in town." He described the shooting incident and the sheriff's appearance. "The sheriff said these fellas had friends and suggested that we make tracks as soon as possible. I suppose they could follow our tracks if they wanted to find us."

Dan frowned, pondering. "Not much we can do tonight. I don't want to move the horses at night. We're not gonna get a lot of sleep. I'll put my three men on night watch first, and you three will take the second watch." He frowned. "Damn, what am I sayin' here? I got *six* men here, don't I, not my three and you three." He smiled. "Anyway, that's what we'll do. If we see anybody coming at the remuda, or anyone threatening the camp, we'll do what we have to do."

He turned to go, then stopped and turned back. "Josh, I'm naming you my drive assistant. Is that okay?" Josh nodded. "Call us when supper's ready. I'm hungry enough to eat one of those mules raw." He walked toward the remuda.

Josh noted Jenny's smug face. "Well, well, well," she said. "A 'drive assistant,' no less. Comin' up in the world already. By the time we reach the ranch, you'll likely be foreman."

"Stop it. Let's get on supper and show these yahoos how lucky they are with their new cookie. What did we get in Abilene?"

She went to the sacks of groceries. "We got flour, sugar, eggs, butter, some fresh vegetables that won't last long. Tomatoes, cucumbers, squash, peaches, ears of corn. And look at this." She pulled a can from a bag. "Canned tomatoes. How 'bout that? I got five cans.

We'll save these for later when the fresh tomatoes are gone."

Josh took the can, turned it over and over. "What's the world comin' to? Tomatoes in a can. Next thing, you know, they'll be putting beans and corn in cans."

Dan's hands, wide-eyed, had watched Jenny fill their supper plates with beef, beans, corn, squash, and biscuits slathered with butter. For dessert, peach cobbler. They were dumbfounded, looking at each other, finally smiling ear to ear.

There was little conversation at the supper fire circle as Dan's men paid attention to their plates. Josh, Harley, and Petey ate slowly, watching the others. Jenny finally joined the group, carrying a plate and coffee cup. Dan's men watched her every step. She sat by Josh, looked around. The men stared at her.

"Well, did I pass?" she said.

The ice was broken, and all spoke at once, praising Jenny's cooking.

Dan held up a hand, and the comments stilled. "Jenny, if anybody tries to hire you away from me, you tell me, and I'll shoot 'im. I mean it." This pronouncement was followed by a fusillade of comment: you said it, boss; I'll shoot 'im too; he don't stand a chance.

"Thank you, boys," said Jenny. "Glad you liked it. Now, I want to say something about what you can do to help me." She proceeded to tell what she expected of anyone in camp who was fed from her chuck wagon. It was the same comment she had delivered to Andy's outfit at the start of the long drive. Dan's cowboys listened, nodded, glanced aside at each other.

"Okay?" Jenny said.

"Okay," Dan said, "understood. Okay, boys?" They nodded vigorously, smiling, adding their yeps, sure wills, any day.

Later, lying in their blankets under the wagon, Josh stroked her cheek. "You sure have a way of settin' up the order of things."

"I'd rather let them know what I expect than to complain later. Judging from their comments, I'm in a pretty good position to do that. Amazing how a full belly can decide how a fella acts."

There was no distinct common trail from Abilene to Cheyenne. One variation ran almost due west into Colorado before turning northward. Another was more direct, pointing northwestward from Abilene. Dan had followed the latter route to reach Abilene on his horse-buying ride but opted for the trail to Denver for the return.

They wasted no time in Denver, other than replenishing the chuck wagon and visiting the saloons. Dan declared that the town had no future since it apparently had no prospect for a railroad tying it to eastern markets.

The drive northward to Cheyenne was without incident, and the weather was pleasant in the high country. One of Dan's men opined that he didn't care how long it took to reach the ranch as long as he was eating from Jenny's chuck wagon.

Bypassing Cheyenne on an afternoon, Dan sent his cowboys ahead to a camping spot just beyond the outskirts. Dan and his three new cowboys and Jenny, driving the wagon, went into town. Jenny parked the wagon in front of the mercantile, and Dan gave his four new hands a walking introduction to the town. They rode past the new church and schoolhouse, and he proudly showed them the right of way where the railroad tracks would be laid. He added that the first train was expected to roll into Cheyenne before the end of the year.

"This town has a great future," Dan said. "I heard a town official call it 'The Empress of the Plains.' Don't know about that, but it's going to be where we will ship cattle back East. That's enough for me." At Josh's question, he showed them the church and the doctors' office above the haberdashery.

Jenny thanked Dan for the tour and pulled Petey away to go with her to the mercantile for supplies. Petey was most agreeable. Always happy to help you, Jenny, he had told her often.

"It ain't all sunshine and roses," said Dan. He and Josh rode beside the chuck wagon, now loaded with provisions. Harley and Petey brought up the rear, chatting and laughing.

Dan had been quiet for the most part since leaving Cheyenne. "We got all the makings of a good operation. Good barn and buildings, good bunch of hands —and they're going to be better working with you boys —and a good herd. We got about 40,000 head, mother cows, and steers. Now we got a good bunch of horses." He looked over at Jenny. "And I'm going to improve the cookhouse and add a new wing on the end that's going to be your house, Jenny. Uh, and Josh." He smiled, reached over, and clapped Josh on the shoulder.

"Sounds like sunshine and roses to me," said Jenny.

"Yeah, well. What I didn't tell about was the Sioux and the Dillards. Both are usually peaceful enough, but both are unpredictable for different reasons. Some of the Sioux recognize what's happening and want to move into the new world. I even got a couple of Sioux fellas working for me. Good boys who are gonna be good cowboys.

"Most of the Sioux don't agree with that assessment. They resent the whites moving into the country, threatening their way of life and encroaching on their land. There was a regular war back in '54 in Goshen County, north of here. Sioux killed thirty-one soldiers. Been peaceful since then, but the more whites move into the country, the more likelihood of trouble. But we'll hope for good relations with the Indians. Our two Sioux hands will help tamp down any problems."

They rode silently through dry grassland, mostly treeless and flat with occasional slight undulations in the plain.

"Dillards?" said Josh.

"Yeah, Dillards. The Dillards are a badass family that lives a few miles east of my place. They have a big operation, bigger'n mine, and they think they own the country. I remind them that open range means—

"Speak of the devil." Four horsemen riding over the grassy flat ahead turned on the trail and rode toward Dan's outfit. The riders pulled up in front of them.

"Who we got here, Leiter? You addin' some human beans to your operation?" He had stared at Jenny since reining up.

"Always lookin' to improve the place," said Dan. "These are top-drawer cowboys."

"She ain't no cowboy." He still stared at Jenny.

"No, but she makes cowboys happy. She's my new cook. If you promise to mind your manners, maybe I'll invite you over someday for dinner."

"She could make me happy fer sure, and I don't mean her cooking."

Josh shook his head. "Dillard, I don't know you, and I don't think I want to know you, but I get damn tired of yahoos like you making that sort of comment about the woman that's going to be my wife."

The cowboy behind Dillard stiffened. "You cain't talk to the boss like that!" He reached for his pistol, but before he cleared the holster, Petey's six-shooter was leveled on him.

"Whoa, I'm impressed," said Dillard. "So you're hiring gunslingers, are you, Leiter? I wonder why. You got somethin' in mind I don't know about?"

"I hire good cowboys," said Dan. "If they can defend themselves and their friends, that's a plus. It ain't what I hire 'em for."

"We'll see," said Dillard. "C'mon, boys, we got business in town. Then we need to git home and talk." The horsemen kicked their mounts into a lope toward Cheyenne.

"Sorry if I spoke out of turn," said Josh. "I get so tired of having to deal with every lout that wants to hit on Jenny."

"No worry. You couldn't sour my relations with Dillard any more than it already is. At least, he will know that I have hands that can stand up to his thugs. I hope I haven't invited you into employment that you're going to find unpleasant."

"We'll manage." He looked up at Jenny. She shrugged.

Chapter Thirteen

DAN LED his four new hands on a walking introduction to the ranch. They saw a solid two-story ranch house, substantial barns, and corrals, a tack room attached to the side of a barn, a cookhouse, and dining room. He explained how he planned to improve the kitchen and dining area and described the wing that he planned to add for Jenny's and Josh's home.

Jenny was particularly delighted to meet Consuelo, Dan's wife. He met her on a cattle-buying visit to Mexico four years ago. At the end of his three-day visit, he persuaded her to come away with him. Her parents were aghast but agreed that the match was good for Consuelo. They married in San Antonio and now had two small children, Tony and Maria, both born on the ranch, assisted by the town doctor. Tony was the retired army doctor's first birth, coming but a month after arriving in Cheyenne three years ago.

Josh was equally pleased to meet Kohana and Matoskah, Dan's Sioux hands. They had been with him almost two years and had acquired English remarkably quickly. When Josh commented on this, they smiled.

"English easy for Indian," said Kohana. "Sioux language hard for white man."

Josh learned that the Sioux hands were happy with their transition from warrior to cowboy, though they kept in contact with their band and even visited infrequently. They said that their friends in the band were not pleased with their new cowboy status, called them red white men. This was not a compliment, they said. They said the Sioux were becoming more and more angry with the white encroachment on Indian lands. The Sioux cowboys were afraid there would be fighting, maybe a war.

JENNY MOVED her chuck wagon operation into the cookhouse. The first sit-down supper was a great success, as the near silence in the dining hall suggested. Occasional soft comment by someone with a full mouth suggested enthusiastic approval of their new cook.

The most extravagant compliments came from Chester, the cookie who had lost his job to Jenny. With his first mouthful of apple cobbler, he closed his eyes and waved his fork, able only to say "mm, *umm!*"

"Didn't I tell yuh?" said one of the hands who had brought the remuda to the ranch. This was received with nods and mumbling agreement.

After supper dishes were collected, washed, and put away, Jenny and Josh strolled toward the corral. They stopped and looked to the west where the sun had just touched the flat horizon. The lacy horizontal clouds were colored pink at the bottom, a light red at the top, a riot of pastel shades between. They walked on to the corral. Jenny put her arms on the top pole and rested her chin on her arm.

"What do you think?" said Josh. "Ready to put down roots?"

She turned to face him, her cheek on an arm. She reached over and put her arms around his neck, kissed him lightly. "I'm with you, cowboy. Looks like a good place and a good bunch. Got some complications, but a good place to put down roots. Not too deep, hear?"

If You Liked This, You Might Like Leaving Ah-wah-nee: A Historical Western Romance

BY HARLAN HAGUE

FROM AWARD WINNING AUTHOR HARLAN HAGUE COMES A HISTORICAL ROMANCE SET IN THE OLD WEST.

In desperation following a family tragedy, Jason takes ship in 1850 for California, the jumping off place of the world, prepared to relinquish responsibility or life.

There he is caught up in the forlorn attempt of an ancient people to live in peace in the land of their ancestors, opposing an invading force of Yankees who believe they have a higher use for the land. Jason takes the side of the Ahwahneechee people, finding new meaning in their struggle and in his love for Tah-nee-hay.

"The author spins a good yarn with all the right ingredients: loss, love, family, conflict, heroism, villainy, and endurance."

AVAILABLE NOW

About the Author

Harlan Hague, Ph.D., is a native Texan who has lived in Japan and England. His travels have taken him to about eighty countries and dependencies and a circumnavigation of the globe.

Hague is a prize-winning historian and award-winning novelist. History specialties are exploration and trails, California's Mexican era, American Indians, and the environment. His novels are mostly westerns with romance themes. Two are set largely in Japan. Some titles have been translated into Spanish, Italian, Portuguese, and German. In addition to history, biography and fiction, he once wrote travel articles that published in newspapers around the country, and he has written a bit of fantasy. His screenplays are making the rounds.

For more information about what he has done and what he is doing, visit his website at harlanhague.us. Hague lives in California's Great Central Valley.

Made in the USA
Middletown, DE
06 October 2022